The Second Honeymoon

ALSO BY McGARVEY BLACK

My Sister's Killer
The First Husband
Trust Only Me
The Woman Upstairs
Twice On Christmas
The Baby I Stole
The Girl Who Killed Her Mom
The Second Honeymoon

THE SECOND HONEYMOON

McGARVEY BLACK

Joffe Books

Joffe Books, London
www.joffebooks.com

First published in Great Britain in 2025

© McGarvey Black 2025

This book is a work of fiction. Names, characters, businesses, organizations, places and events are either the product of the author's imagination or are used fictitiously. Any resemblance to actual persons, living or dead, events or locales is entirely coincidental. The spelling used is American English except where fidelity to the author's rendering of accent or dialect supersedes this. The right of McGarvey Black to be identified as author of this work has been asserted in accordance with the Copyright, Designs and Patents Act 1988.

No part of this book may be used or reproduced in any manner for the purpose of training artificial intelligence technologies or systems. In accordance with Article 4(3) of the Digital Single Market Directive 2019/790, Joffe Books expressly reserves this work from the text and data mining exception.

Cover art by Nebojša Zorić

ISBN: 978-1-80573-160-3

CHAPTER ONE

Becca

I hate surprises almost as much as I dread being alone. Out for a walk near my house in Connecticut, I receive a text from my husband, Andre, and it freaks me out.

I'll be home early — we need to talk

A pit forms in my stomach. *Need to talk? What does that mean?*

My lifelong fear of abandonment, which directs so many of my decisions, starts to creep in. For a split second I'm paralyzed, as the phrase 'we need to talk' reverberates inside my head. Those were the same words I heard years ago on the worst day of my life.

I was a kid, and my dad worked from home as an insurance agent. One day he took a break and climbed on the roof of the house to clean out our gutters. Nobody knew for sure what happened. They say he slipped and fell, because my mom found him next to the house — dead. The doctor said my father broke his neck.

When I got off the school bus an hour later, my mother was waiting for me at the end of the driveway. Her eyes were red and swollen. There were two police cars in front of our house. Right away, I knew something terrible had happened.

All Mom said was, "Becca, we need to talk."

After that, everything was different. My life that had been full of rainbows and unicorns turned to black and white. Ever since then, I've lived in a constant state of low-grade anxiety, always afraid of being left alone again. I know my dad didn't leave on purpose, but he was gone, nonetheless. I was only eight, and it sucked.

After that, things were never the same. I was always "the girl with the dead father." It wasn't until I met Andre that I felt whole for the first time. I belonged to someone, and he lifted me up. That's why Andre's text today unnerves me so much.

Does he want to divorce me? Things have been weird between us lately.

My lifelong fear of being alone can pop up without a warning. It's always lurking underneath and I have to squash it down every single day.

I take a breath and respond to my husband's cryptic message asking *what exactly* he wants to talk about? His answer is obtuse and only rattles me more.

I'll tell you in person — tonight

Panicking as I head for home, I call my best friend, Stella.

"I'm spinning into a death spiral," I say, sweat forming on the back of my neck. I read Andre's texts to her. "What if he doesn't want to be married to me anymore?"

"Why do you always go to the worst possible place?" she says. "Maybe it's something good."

"He's been so distant lately."

"Has he really been distant, or has he been working long hours and is just tired? Remember, you and Andre have been on completely different schedules since you stopped working."

"If it was something good," I say, "why wouldn't he say that?"

"It could be a surprise."

"I hate surprises."

"Most people like them," says Stella.

"I guess it could be something good," I say, trying to reset my negative mindset. "Maybe he got that promotion at work."

Before Stella hangs up, she congratulates me on getting outside for a walk today. She's my go-to person for everything. More like a sister than a friend, she's always there for me and keeps me tethered when I become unmoored.

Andre's a good listener, too. Although once in a while, I've seen him roll his eyes when he thinks I'm not looking. I don't blame him. Hearing about my health problems over and over is boring. I don't know why, but I have this weird need to overexplain why I can or can't do something. Note to self: nobody cares. Shut up.

My health issues have become so chronic that I never know how I'm going to feel when I wake up. Leaving my teaching job broke my heart. Giving up my kindergarten class because of this stupid illness was the hardest decision of my life. I miss my students. My goal is to go back and teach one day soon. That idea is what keeps me going.

Managing my illness takes up so much space in my life — too much. Sometimes it feels like there are three of us in the marriage — Andre, me and fibromyalgia. I think that's why he's been pulling away from me. He's married to a thirty-five-year-old woman who can't do normal things because of my intermittent pain and exhaustion. I can tell Andre's tired of all my medical stuff. Some people think fibromyalgia is a bullshit illness, but it's not. The pain and numbness are very real. Some days, I can barely get out of bed.

I walk up my driveway rereading Andre's mysterious texts.

We need to talk

I'll tell you in person — tonight

If he leaves me, I'll be alone. Shit.

3

CHAPTER TWO

An hour later, the grinding sound of the garage door opening beneath the house startles me. I dash into the powder room, apply my favorite pink mauve lipstick and run a wide-toothed comb through my long curly red hair. I want to look as good as possible when Andre sees me in case it's something bad.

I push my dark-framed eyeglasses up the bridge of my nose and wait nervously in the kitchen. I hear Andre's familiar stomp coming up the basement stairs. The door into the kitchen opens slowly, hinges creaking. He doesn't see me standing there until he turns fully around.

"Oh, you're downstairs," he says, stepping back. "I thought you'd be up in the bedroom resting."

"Nope. I was feeling really good today. I went out for a long hike. How was work?"

"Annoying clients and impossible deadlines." He drops his black leather backpack on the kitchen counter. "The usual."

"I made dinner. I thought we'd have a nice quiet evening. Maybe watch a movie?"

"Sounds good. I'm glad to see you're up." He sniffs the air. "Whatever you're cooking, it smells fantastic."

I walk over to the stove and stir the simmering pot of chili. "Dinner should be ready in about thirty minutes," I say. "We could open a bottle of wine and hang out."

He nods and digs through his backpack.

I turn to my chili and stir the pot. "So . . . what's the big thing you wanted to talk about?"

As I wait for his answer, I hear his footsteps clomping up the stairs to the second floor. I guess he didn't hear me.

I busy myself with dinner prep until Andre comes back down, bouncing into the kitchen. He's changed out of his work clothes into jeans and an old sweatshirt from college. I love the way he looks in jeans. He looks bone-jumping good. He was dressed like that the night we met.

It was winter, and there was a fair amount of snow on the ground. Stella and I were at a dive bar with some girlfriends. We were all drinking beer and playing darts — badly.

"Hey, Red," Andre shouted to me as he walked across the room to our group, "you know how to play?" He was so boyish and cocky that I think I'd fallen in love with him before I lost the darts game. That was over eleven years ago, and we've been together ever since. Time flies when you're having fun. But are we? I'm never sure anymore.

Andre walks over to the pot on the stove, lifts the lid and breathes it in. "That smells incredible. Can't wait to eat it."

I hand him a glass of red wine and pour a half one for myself. He's smiling at me with a twinkle in his blue eyes like he's up to something. *Maybe it's not going to be something bad?* I feel a sudden rush of love for him. He's been so patient with me since I got sick. I got my fibromyalgia diagnosis after our second wedding anniversary. I know we both pledged "in sickness and in health" but that can be a tall order.

When I quit my job teaching kindergarten two years ago, Andre said he understood my decision. Still, now all our financial burden is on him. I want to go back to work soon. My old principal said I could come back whenever I was ready. I really hope I can make it happen.

I place the pot of chili on a trivet in the center of the kitchen table next to a bowl of homemade guacamole. I top off our wine glasses, and we sit. The chili is delicious. A little pinch of cinnamon is my secret ingredient. But not too much or your chili will taste like raisin bread.

Andre reaches for the ladle to take more. Meanwhile, I'm trying to be patient while I'm literally dying inside.

"So, what did you want to talk about?" I say, dipping a corn chip into the guacamole as if I was only marginally interested in his answer.

He smiles. "I was planning to wait until we finished dinner before we discussed it."

"C'mon, Andre, just tell me," I say.

He smiles, and his eyes twinkle again.

It can't be that bad. He seems relatively cheerful.

"You look great tonight, by the way," he says. "You must be feeling okay. That makes what I'm about to say more poignant."

At this point, my heart's beating like a drum in a jazz band. A high-pitched ringing is in my ears.

"What is it?" I say with a big, forced smile.

CHAPTER THREE

Andre gets up from the table, walks over to the counter where he left his backpack and opens it. My eyes follow his every move like a dog eyeing a lamb chop. My husband takes his seat at the table again, grinning at me like an idiot. I'm all nerves.

"Becs," he says, pulling a large envelope out of his bag, "there's something I want to show you."

He's milking whatever this is, and I don't know what to think.

I decide to play along. "You're being very mysterious tonight, Mr. Gifford. What's this all about?"

Slowly, he opens the envelope and pulls out a packet of papers. He looks me in the eye and grins as I hold my breath.

"Becca, you look like you're going to pass out." He sits back and flashes that big Andre Gifford smile again. He's got beautiful teeth. I'll give him that. Never had braces. I had them for years, but now they're slightly crooked again. I should have worn my retainer.

"Becs, we've been married for almost ten years," he says, now holding up a shopping bag that I hadn't noticed before. Andre's like a magician tonight.

"Our tenth wedding anniversary is next month," he continues.

I smile.

"In honor of ten wonderful years of marriage," he says, "I've booked us on a six-night, seven-day Beacon Star Cruise leaving from Port Canaveral, Florida."

"What? A cruise? Are you serious?"

"We'll fly into Orlando, spend two days at Disney or Universal Studios and then board the ship in Port Canaveral. From there, we sail to Fort Lauderdale, Puerto Rico, the U.S. Virgin Islands and finish up in Miami. How does that sound?"

I jump up from the table and hug him. He kisses me.

"And here's the best part," he says. "We leave this weekend."

"This weekend?" I say, my mind overwhelmed. "Oh, my God, I have to pack."

"But wait, there's more," he says with another laugh. "I've also booked a cabin for us with a balcony and a few extra amenities, including unlimited champagne. How does that sound?"

"I'm totally blown away. We're going on a cruise. Can we afford all this?"

"It's all under control. Only the best for you. Dig out your sunscreen, Becs. What do you think of my little surprise now? Worth the wait?"

I sputter. "I'm blown away. How long have you been planning this?"

"A while. There were a lot of details, and I had to get the time off from work," he says. "It's a busy season at the agency, but when I told them it was our tenth anniversary, they signed off on it."

"I can't believe it," I say, my smile stretching from ear to ear.

"I told my boss I wanted to take my beautiful bride on a magical anniversary cruise." He leans over and gives me another kiss.

Andre places a thick cruise brochure in the center of the table. It has pictures of the Beacon Star ship as well as some of the destinations we'll be stopping at. Together we flip through the pages looking at the photos of food, cocktails and beaches. All my worries have disappeared. I'm genuinely excited.

"Look at this," says my husband as he places his hand over mine. "They give tango lessons on the ship every afternoon. We should sign up for that. You've always wanted us to learn to dance together. Now we can."

I smile. This is an incredibly sweet gesture on his part. I've been asking Andre to take dancing lessons with me since we got engaged. He always found an excuse not to, claiming he had two left feet. I usually don't like surprises, but this one was worth the angst. I want to do a tango right now.

Bursting with the cruise news, I reach for my phone and take a picture of the brochure. I want to text Stella to tell her about the amazing surprise. As I punch in her number, I hear Andre sigh.

"What?" I look up at him.

"Do you have to pull out your phone right now? Can't we just enjoy this moment together?"

"It will only take a second. I just want to tell Stella about the cruise." I send a quick text. As soon as it goes, I place my phone across the table and out of reach.

"All done," I say. "You have my undivided attention."

"Good," he says, his smile returning. "Because there's also . . ."

"What am I going to wear?" I say, doing an inventory of my clothes closet in my head.

"There's a part B to this surprise," he says.

I sit up straight and fold my hands in front of me.

"Bring on part B."

CHAPTER FOUR

Still acting the showman, Andre picks up the big brown shopping bag and places it on the kitchen table in front of me.

"Since we're going on the cruise, I figured you might need some new things to wear," he says. "Last month when we were out shopping, I noticed you were looking at a dress in a particular store window. Do you remember?"

"The Gretchen Scott dress?" I say, squealing ever so slightly.

He reaches into the bag and pulls out the hot-pink-and-orange summer dress with a belt that I've been drooling over for months. I loved it, but it was expensive and I had no place to wear it. I couldn't justify buying it.

"Oh, my God. I love this dress." I reach for my new favorite outfit. The fabric feels rich and silky. "It was so sweet of you to remember."

He laughs. "And guess what, there's even more," he says loudly, enjoying his role as he digs into the bag again. This time, he retrieves an adorable straw hat with a medium brim and hot-pink ribbon. "The woman at the store said this hat is completely packable. You can fold it into a ball and it will take its shape back immediately."

I reach for the hat, walk over to the mirror in the hallway and try it on. I feel giddy.

"I love this hat," I say, still looking at my reflection.

"I'm not done yet," says my husband gleefully.

Sometimes, Andre can be so serious, but I love it when he gets silly. He was like that when we met.

Once again, Andre's hand goes into the magic brown bag. This time he pulls out a pair of dark-framed oversized Gucci sunglasses.

My mouth drops. "Gucci? Andre, they're so expensive."

"It's our anniversary. I even had your prescription put into the lenses. Don't worry about the money. I should be getting that promotion and a good raise at work pretty soon. It's our tenth, so let me spoil you a little."

With the sunglasses in my hand, I walk over to the mirror a second time. Taking off my eyeglasses, I try on my new, very cool shades. I place the straw hat back on my head and spin around.

"You look like a movie star," says Andre, winking at me. "May I have your autograph, Mrs. Gifford? You should wear this outfit when we board the ship. You'll look very chic."

After the sunglasses, Andre presents me with a pair of creamy beige-colored sandals and a matching bag to go with the outfit. I go upstairs to our bedroom, put the whole ensemble on and run back down to model it.

"Seriously, you look like a cover girl," he says as I prance around in front of him, both of us giggling.

I grab my phone to take a selfie. "Just a quick pic to show Stell."

Andre makes a face, so I take one shot quickly and get back to talking about the cruise.

"It says in the brochure that we can go kayaking, sailing and snorkeling," I say, looking through the book.

"Will you paddle this time?" He raises his eyebrows. "The last time we went kayaking, I did all the paddling."

"My arms got tired," I say, giggling while walking over to the hall mirror to take another look at my dress.

Suddenly, something occurs to me and I spin around. "We may have a problem," I say. "I don't have a current passport."

He smiles, gets up from the table and takes my hands.

"Everything's under control," he says. "You won't need a passport for this cruise. We're not technically leaving the country. The islands we're going to are all possessions of the United States. We're doing a full-on American trip from start to finish. All you need is your driver's license."

"Really?"

"Start packing."

***

Later that night, after making love for the first time in a while, I lie in bed making mental notes of all the things I need to do before we leave. It's going to be tight. The surprise part turned out great, but I'll have to scramble to get everything pulled together in time.

Andre's clearly not worried as he's asleep and snoring softly beside me. I turn over and reach for my phone on the nightstand. Quietly, I slip out of bed and into the bathroom to text Stella. It's 12:30 a.m. She's a night owl. She'll be up, bingeing some TV series on Netflix or Apple TV.

Sitting on the closed toilet, I send a bunch of pics that I took earlier of me wearing my new designer outfit. Within seconds, she texts me back.

You rock that dress. Who knew Andre had such good taste?

Truthfully, neither did I. As long as I've known him, he's never taken much interest in my clothes. Although, he did pick out a really nice black leather bag for my birthday last year. It was so sweet of him to remember I liked that pink dress.

I text Stella again.

Btw, Andre practically carried me up the stairs to the bedroom tonight. I'll leave the rest to your imagination.

I creep back into bed and continue dreaming about our upcoming anniversary cruise. Before I fall asleep, it occurs to me that I should buy a really good waterproof phone case. If we're going to be on boats, on beaches and in pools, I need something to protect my phone.

As I doze off, my imagination conjures up an image of me wearing the pink-and-orange dress and Gucci sunglasses on the deck of a big white ship.

CHAPTER FIVE

After a frenetic few days getting ready, the day of the trip finally arrives. Our Uber picks us up right on time. I check Google Maps, which shows no traffic whatsoever. Once I see it will be smooth sailing all the way to Kennedy Airport, I sit back and relax.

As the car moves down the Hutchinson River Parkway, Andre is in another zone responding to work emails. I'm feeling a bit tired because we were up at 5 a.m. I close my eyes, hoping to catch a few winks before we get to the airport.

Last night, I barely slept thinking about the fun we're going to have on this cruise. We haven't been on a proper vacation in five years. I think we really need this to reconnect. It will be good for us to get away and just have fun for a change.

I make sure I set my phone to vibrate so I don't disturb Andre with dings from texts that come in. They're mainly from Stella. She and I probably text fifty times a day, sometimes more if she's going through a romance crisis and needs moral support, which is often.

The Uber is about halfway to New York City when Andre puts his phone away and begins chatting with the driver

— Manny. He looks like he's in his fifties and proudly tells us he's done over seven hundred trips.

"Seven hundred?" says Andre. "That's impressive."

"Going away on a vacation?" says Manny.

"We are. My wife and I are going on a cruise to celebrate our tenth wedding anniversary."

"I went on a Royal Caribbean cruise once. Lots of food. Where are you going?"

"Tell him about our trip, babe," says Andre.

I lean forward. "We're flying into Orlando and spending a day at Universal Studios. Then, we're picking up a shuttle van that will take us over to the east coast of Florida. We board our ship in Port Canaveral."

"That's near where they shoot off the spaceships, right?" says Manny.

"That's right," says Andre. "Our ship's port is not too far from the NASA space center."

"We'll be stopping in Fort Lauderdale and then going on to a few Caribbean islands," I say. "We finish up in Miami and fly home from there."

"Sounds nice," says Manny. "We've had a cold spring. You're lucky to be down in the warm weather right now."

"Tell Manny about all the rest," says Andre with a wink.

Confused, I look at my husband. *The rest? What's he talking about?*

"Tell him about your dress, the sunglasses, shoes and hat."

I smile and squeeze my husband's hand as I tell the driver about the new outfit I'm wearing.

". . . and in addition to the dress and shoes, my very thoughtful husband bought me these sunglasses to go with the whole outfit," I say as I put on my new shades.

Manny looks at me in his rearview mirror and nods. "You look like an actress in those glasses, Miss," he says.

"That's what I told her," Andre says, bumping his shoulder to mine.

I giggle like a schoolgirl from all the positive attention. I've been shut in my house for so long that I forgot what it feels like to get dressed up and go somewhere special.

"I'm Andre, by the way, and this is my beautiful bride, Becca," says Andre. "Where are you from, Manny?"

Within seconds, the two men are talking all about sports, so I zone out into my own thoughts. Closing my eyes again, I fantasize about all the activities and meals on the ship. I can't wait to do the tango lessons with Andre. I'm imagining the two of us moving around a dance floor looking very chic when our car slows down, and I'm catapulted back to reality.

"Here we are," says our driver as he pulls up in front of the American Airlines sign. From inside the car, I see that the terminal is mobbed. Half of New York City must be taking a flight somewhere.

"Nice talking to you, Manny," says Andre. "Do you have a card? I take the occasional business trip. Be nice to call you next time I need a ride."

"Let's hope the Mets play better this year than last, Andre." Manny hands my husband his card, then helps us get our luggage out of the trunk.

Both waving as the Uber pulls away, I wrap my gray wool shawl around my shoulders to take the chill out of my bones. There's no doubt in my mind. This anniversary cruise is just what the doctor ordered.

Like the airport terminal, our plane is also filled to capacity with New York vacationers. You can tell they're not business travelers because they're ordering alcoholic drinks on a morning flight.

Three hours later, we arrive in Orlando. An hour after that, we check into our hotel on the Universal Studios grounds. Andre booked us a room at the Cabana Bay Beach Resort. Its theme: 1960s on steroids. As soon as we've changed our clothes, we head out to the parks.

For the next day and a half, the two of us go to every ride or exhibit in Universal Studios. Our favorites are Spider-Man and the Harry Potter pavilions, where it actually snows inside the building. I'm having so much fun that I barely notice my aching joints. I feel surprisingly good — there's only a little pain. Maybe the sunshine and warm weather help?

"My knees hardly hurt at all today," I say as we climb onto a scary-looking rollercoaster.

"That's great, babe," he says as our car, attached to a dozen others, starts its ascent.

At noon the next day, we catch our transfer van to the ship. I put on my new cruising outfit, complete with sunglasses. When our shuttle bus stops in Port Canaveral, I peer out the window at the massive ship in the harbor — the Beacon Star. It's much bigger than I'd imagined. *How does something that big and heavy actually float?*

We grab our luggage and get in line behind a stream of passengers also boarding the ship. Soon, we're greeted by several cheerful attendants. After handing over our tickets, our luggage is taken from us and sent to our cabin.

The next stop is for ship IDs. Having never been on a cruise before, this is all new to me. Our photos are taken, and we're told our pictures are connected electronically to our Beacon Star key cards. I ask them why they take our pictures.

"So we know who is getting on and off the ship," says the young woman taking our photos. "We want to make sure everyone on the ship is supposed to be here."

"You mean you're looking for stowaways?" I say.

"That's one reason," she says. "But it also enables us to keep track of where passengers are. For example, when we pull into a port, if someone isn't onboard when we leave the port, we'll know. It means they haven't checked back in."

"Does that ever happen?" I ask, a perennially late person myself. "Do you leave people behind?"

"It happens. We have a specific time that our ship must leave the port. When that time comes, we go," she says as we move along the line and place our new IDs on the scanner. It beeps as we each put ours through. We can now board the Beacon Star.

Andre takes my hand. "You ready, babe?"

I nod. "Yes, and thank you for this, Andre." I reach my arm around his waist and pull him into me. "It means more to me than you could know."

"It makes me happy to make you smile," he says. "Now, let's go find our room and have a glass of that champagne."

CHAPTER SIX

Hunting for cabin #4006, Andre and I take the elevator up to the fourth floor. Several other confused people appear to be doing the same thing.

According to Andre, the ship is only two years old. The hallways look newly decorated in blue and gray finishes complemented by light wood accents. Everything seems so clean and polished, like you could eat off the floor.

We get to the door of our room and Andre unlocks it with his key card. Before we go in, he insists on carrying me over the threshold. I protest, telling him it's silly and that he'll hurt himself. My real worry, because of my fibromyalgia, I've put on a little weight. While I'm rather pleased that he *wants* to carry me, because it's romantic, I'm not sure he'll be able to lift me. That would be embarrassing. He won't take no for an answer, so I give in. A moment later, he sweeps me off my feet.

He grunts and gets red in the face as he takes me in his arms. Carrying a full-grown woman is apparently more than he bargained for. It's only about eight or nine feet to the bed, but he struggles, and when we get there, he drops me on the duvet like a sack of potatoes.

After that quasi-romantic moment that looked nothing remotely like what you see in the movies, we lie on the bed.

The room is lovely, bigger than I'd imagined. The blues and grays out in the hallway are continued inside the cabin. I kick off my new sandals and go check out the bathroom.

While opening every cabinet in the bathroom, I notice warmth on the soles of my feet. Heated floors. Nice. On the counter, I find lots of fabulous little toiletries. *Free souvenirs.* Immediately, I scoop up all the free stuff and place them inside my luggage. I've never been on a cruise before, but Stella has. She told me that if we "use up" the toiletries, they replace them with new ones every single day. That's my game plan — seven days, seven shampoos, seven conditioners.

"Trust me. You'll have a nice collection of soaps and lotions to bring home with you, and you won't have to pay a penny for them," she instructed me before we left. "Take some extras for me."

When I walk out of the bathroom, Andre is already outside on our balcony checking out the action in the port.

"So, what do you think?" He gazes out at the light blue-green water. "Pretty sweet, isn't it? Happy anniversary, babe."

I follow his gaze. "I can't believe we're really here," I say. "We're going to have the best time on this cruise. This is like a second honeymoon."

"I was thinking the same thing."

As Andre waves at two small passing boats, there's a knock on our cabin door. He goes back into the room to answer it. I stay on the balcony enjoying the Florida sun on my face. A minute later, Andre returns with a bottle of champagne on ice and two glasses.

"A little bon voyage surprise. Now it's really like a second honeymoon." He pours us each a glass. "To my beautiful and most amazing wife. Thank you for ten unforgettable years."

We clink glasses and I take my first sip. The little bubbles tickle as they slide down my throat. The champagne tastes delicious and soon my glass is empty. Playing host, Andre pours me a little more. As we sip our champagne, enjoying the great weather, it's my turn to make a toast.

"I know it hasn't been the easiest with me the last few years," I say. "But I'm feeling so much better now, more like my old self. I've even been thinking about going back to work."

"This cruise is all about new beginnings," he says, holding up his glass. "Let's not dwell on the past. Let's just think about the future and all the good times and surprises that lie ahead."

I smile and nod. I don't really like surprises, but he's right. No point in revisiting old times that were tough. From here on in, we move forward.

"Hey, I think the ship's moving," says Andre, excitement in his voice as he stands on his tippy-toes and leans over the railing.

"Be careful," I say, reaching out and pulling him back to safety. I give him a kiss. "I don't want to lose you now. We haven't even arrived at the first port."

As our ship sails out of the harbor, we unpack our bags. Once our things are stowed away, we take a walk around the ship to find out where everything is located. I want to get a sense of where all the restaurants are and locate the gym and spa. After thirty minutes of wandering, we go back to the room to get ready for dinner. I start to take my belt off, but Andre stops me.

"Are you changing out of your dress?" he says.

"I thought I'd put on something else."

"You look so pretty in that dress. The orange in the dress compliments your hair. Wear it tonight. Why not?"

Who am I to mess with perfection? I love the dress. If my husband thinks I look great the way I am, then I won't disagree. I retie my belt, apply some lipstick, clean the lenses on my glasses and we head off for dinner.

The Beacon Star has a few buffet options, as well as several specialty restaurants, but those require reservations. There is one restaurant with waiter service that doesn't require a reservation, Portsmouth Alley. Since we want our first dinner to be really special, we pass on the buffet and opt for Portsmouth Alley.

We looked up the restaurant on Tripadvisor, and it has good ratings. One post says it serves an American cuisine that includes a French fries sampler platter with four dips that they give to you the minute you sit down. French fries are my number-one "stranded on a desert island" food item, so I'm excited.

We enter a very large restaurant that has a spectacular white-and-blue Chihuly-esque glass chandelier hanging in the center of the room. The hostess seats us along a wall at a square table sandwiched between people on either side. The tables are very close together, which means conversations can be easily overheard. I slide into the banquette seat against the wall while nodding hello to the people next to us.

The couple to my right appears to be finishing their dessert. They inform us that this is their eleventh Beacon Lines cruise.

"Wow, eleven," I say. "This is our first, but hopefully the first of many."

As they leave the dining room, they assure us we'll have a wonderful time and that one day we'll be on our eleventh cruise. *That would be nice.*

To my left, next to Andre, an older woman sits alone, quietly eating a crab cake appetizer. I'd put her somewhere north of eighty-five. Even though she's seated, I can tell she's tiny. Her elfin face is surrounded by a short brown bob with bangs. She's wearing very large, thick eyeglasses with bright-blue frames. The glasses match her outfit — a colorful blue kaftan with gold accents.

As soon as the "eleven cruises couple" leaves, blue kaftan introduces herself.

"I heard you mention this is your first cruise," she says loudly before she puts a forkful of crab into her mouth. "You're going to love it. I'm Olive Walker, by the way. I'm Beacon Cruise Lines' number-one fan."

CHAPTER SEVEN

"Forgive me for eavesdropping," says Olive in a clear voice laced with a strong lilting southern accent. "It's very tight quarters in these restaurants. Hard not to hear what everyone else is saying."

"We've got nothing to hide. We're celebrating our tenth wedding anniversary." I smile at Andre. "My husband surprised me with this trip. Isn't that sweet?"

"Congratulations," she says. "Aren't you two just the cutest?"

"How about you?" I say. "Sounds like you've been on cruises before."

"Who, me? I've been on dozens of cruises," she says as she snaps a picture of her crab cake with her phone. "I just love taking pictures of pretty food. I post them all on my Insta page. My handle is HotToddie123, if you want to follow me. I'll follow you back. I've got 3,489 followers. I post pictures of all my cruises."

Her comment surprises me. This woman is very old. I doubt there are many people her age posting on Instagram.

"Is Beacon Cruise Lines your favorite?" I say.

"Absolutely," she says, still taking pictures of her half-eaten appetizer. "They always treat me so nicely when I'm on one of their ships. I have elite status, you know. They give me all sorts of extras. That's probably why I chose this particular ship for my final cruise."

Andre, who until now has been silently absorbed in the menu, turns his head. "Had enough of the old Beacon Star, have you?"

"Oh no. I love this ship and the crew. I'm always happiest when I'm cruising. But I'm ninety-one now, and my doctors have informed me that . . . well, there's no other way to say it. Simply put, I'm dying. I was given two months to live."

"Oh, I'm so sorry to hear that," I say, fumbling for the right words, knowing there are none.

"It is what it is," says Olive, throwing up her hands. "When they told me I only had a little time left, I cashed in my savings and bought the most luxurious suite on the Star. I don't expect to make it to the port in Miami, I'm afraid. You'll love Miami, though. It's so . . . international."

Andre and I look at each other. *How the hell do you respond to someone who tells you they came to die on a cruise ship?*

"Are you here with any friends or family?" I ask, taking note that she's eating dinner by herself.

"No, it's just me. You come into the world alone and you go out the same way," says Olive, snapping another picture of the small flower arrangement at the center of her table. "Besides, the lovely people who work on this ship are like my family. Everyone makes me feel so at home here. They always take such good care of me. They all leave me little treats like extra shampoo or chocolates, too."

Unsure of the appropriate response after hearing the *dying on the ship* speech, we're luckily saved by our waiter bearing our French fries platter. After he takes our dinner order, Andre and I dig into the fries.

"These are so good," I say. I pop one dipped in truffle sauce into my mouth.

"Aren't they delicious?" says Olive, cutting into an enormous steak that has just been placed in front of her. "I'm not supposed to eat red meat, but I guess when you're dying, you can eat whatever the hell you want."

"Excuse me if this is too personal," I say, "but isn't there anyone at home you'd like to be with during this time?"

I feel Andre gently kick me under the table. I look at his face and he gives me the "zip it" look. But seriously, how does a person "zip it" after a ninety-one-year-old woman tells you she's going to kick the bucket all alone at any moment? I'm not wired to ignore something like that.

Olive looks at me and smiles. "There's really no one back home who I'm particularly close to. But here on the Star, I always make all sorts of new friends." She puts a piece of steak into her mouth and chews with vigor.

"Take us, for example," she says. "We didn't know each other before, but here we are having dinner together. I don't believe I caught your names."

Andre clears his throat. "I'm Andre, and this is my wife, Becca."

I'm dying to ask Olive more questions about her pre-planned death at sea, but Andre is having none of it and abruptly changes the subject.

"Olive, tell us about some of the ports we'll be visiting since you're such an old hand at cruising," he says.

For the next thirty minutes, Olive regales us with descriptions of far-flung places and the hidden secrets of each port we're stopping in. She's funny, quick and very entertaining. I find myself wondering why such a delightful person would have no friends or people who care about her. I won't ask her again because Andre would undoubtedly give my other shin a kick. He's a lot more private than I am. He doesn't like interacting with strangers. I love it. You never know what you're going to learn.

We continue chatting away with our unexpected dinner companion as our meal comes and our wine is refreshed. Olive happily takes pictures of the waiter, the dining room and the busboy as the evening progresses. I wonder why she's taking all these pictures if she's dying? Presumably, one takes photos to remember an event or a moment. According to her, she'll be stone-dead at any moment. In light of that, photography seems like a waste of time, but who am I to judge?

By the time our dessert arrives, there aren't many people left in the restaurant. Olive has already finished her dinner and only remained at her table because we were chatting.

"I taught kindergarten for ten years," I say to Olive.

"That must be so rewarding," she replies. "All those little minds curious about the world. You must love it."

I look over at Andre. He's on his phone and completely disengaged from the conversation.

"I've taken a leave of absence from my school," I say. "I've been ill and was missing a lot of days. It didn't seem fair to the kids."

"You seem fit as a fiddle to me," says Olive. "If you loved it, you should go back."

I nod. "I'm planning to. I'm hoping for the next school year."

Olive smiles and yawns as she slowly pushes her chair back.

"I think it's time for me to go to bed," she says, adjusting her blue glasses on the bridge of her small but rather bulbous nose. "A girl needs to get her beauty sleep, especially at my age."

She extends a wrinkled and somewhat arthritic-looking hand to me. I shake it. Her hand is cold, and I wonder if the angel of death is already hovering.

"See you tomorrow," she says, picking up a green cane with a faux-diamond handle. I watch her methodically lean on it as she walks away. Once she's gone, Andre and I attack the blueberry pie the waiter has just brought. I've just put a forkful of pie into my mouth when a woman's voice calls out.

"Smile."

Andre and I look up as Olive snaps a picture of us. "I always take pictures of all my new friends on cruises. Let's meet for a drink tomorrow afternoon. My treat."

"Sounds good," I say as the old woman shuffles off. "That was one of the most bizarre conversations I've ever had in my life." I look at Andre. He's scowling.

"What's wrong?" I say, taking another bite of my pie.

"Why did she take that picture of us?" he says, clearly annoyed. "She didn't ask permission. Who knows what she's going to do with it."

"Babe, she's ninety-one and according to her, dying. She's not going to do anything with the photo. If it makes her happy, let her have it. Forget about it. Trust me, that sweet old woman is harmless."

CHAPTER EIGHT

After our delicious dinner, Andre takes my hand and leads me down to the casino. When we enter, DJ Vanta is spinning house music at the far end of the room. The shipboard club is crowded, and everyone is drinking, dancing and having a good time. Andre and I aren't gamblers but when in Rome . . . We decide to give blackjack a try. For a couple of hours, we sip champagne and play a little blackjack and roulette. Eventually, we hear "last call" and that the place is closing in ten minutes.

"Where did the time go?" I say as Andre and I leave the bar area. Feeling full and pretty buzzed, we head to our cabin. When we get into our room, it's after midnight. I take off my dress thinking there might be a little romantic interlude. As I'm about to go into the bathroom to get ready for bed, my husband gets a second wind.

"I have an idea. Let's put on something warmer and go take a walk around the deck before we go to bed," he says. "The sea air will make us sleep like babies. Besides, I need to walk off those French fries."

These days, I'm trying to be open to everything. Even though I'd rather go to bed, I slip on a pair of leggings and put a light windbreaker jacket over my long-sleeved cotton top. Andre also puts on a light jacket, and we head out for an evening stroll on the deck.

When we open the heavy door to the outside deck, we're greeted by the silvery glow of a bright half-moon nestled among a million twinkling stars. After stopping to admire the magnificent sparkly vision in the sky, we slowly walk arm-in-arm to the front of the ship. It's late, and it feels like we're the only ones still up.

When we get to the bow, we lean against the railing and gaze out at the black sea as the Beacon Star cuts through the water. Andre puts his arm around my shoulders. Slightly chilled from the wind, I nuzzle into my husband's warmth. I'm feeling very tipsy but also extremely content. I feel good.

Andre steps up on a bench at the center point of the bow and reaches his hand out to me. "Come on."

I take it and giggle as he pulls me up in front of him and places his arms around my waist. As I lean my head back on his shoulder, he grabs my hands and pulls them out to the sides.

Tears fill my eyes when I realize he's reenacting the scene from one of our favorite movies, *Titanic*. We watched it together when we first started dating and still watch it every holiday season. With the wind in our hair and our arms outstretched, we soar like Jack and Rose on the bow of that ship. It's an amazing moment, and I'm filled with pure bliss.

After a few minutes of stargazing, we climb down and continue our slow walk along the deck still holding hands. After tonight, I know things are going to be better between us. We needed to find us again. I think maybe we have.

It's nearly 1 a.m. when we reach the stern. With not a soul in sight, we have the whole ship to ourselves and it's kind of magical. I lie down on an empty chaise lounge chair and make a contented groan.

"This has got to be what heaven is like," I say looking up at the sparkly sky. "Thank you for planning this trip. I'm so happy. Are you?"

"Of course," says my husband with a wicked smile as he stands up. "Wait here. I'll be right back. No peeking."

As he races off to who knows where, I put my hands behind my head and try to identify constellations. Minutes later, Andre is back holding two full champagne glasses and has a blanket slung over his shoulder.

"I thought you might be a little cold." He hands me a glass and then places the blanket over my legs.

"Where did you get the champagne? I thought everything was closed," I say, lying back on the chair.

"I have my ways. There's one bar that stays open until one thirty."

He sits at the end of my chair by my feet. I'm so relaxed I could melt. We clink glasses and I take my first sip. Nothing's better than good champagne.

"This is nice," he says.

"Are we the only ones out here?" I look around at the empty corridor and deck.

"Most people are probably asleep. They don't know what they're missing out here late at night. It's beautiful, isn't it?"

I take another sip. "Who needs sleep? It's so peaceful."

"Guess what? It's after midnight," he says, looking at his watch. "You know what that means? It's officially our anniversary right now."

I hold up my left hand and wiggle my ring finger. "Ten years ago today, you put this gold ring on my finger. Remember?"

"Like it was yesterday." He leans over and kisses me. His soft lips brush against mine and I gently part them. I don't know if it's the salt air, the wine or the kiss, but I'm feeling really relaxed.

Holding hands, we sip our champagne and talk about all the things we're going to do in port the next day.

"What do you think of our anniversary cruise so far?" he asks.

I smile. "Perfection. It's been like a dream. This is the beginning of a new chapter for us. Things are going to get better and better."

He takes my hand again. "I couldn't agree more. That's why I booked it, to start a new chapter."

We stay outside for quite a while drinking and talking. Eventually, I look at my watch. It's nearly two and I'm pretty drunk and very tired.

"Maybe we should go to bed," I say, slurring my words. "We have a full day tomorrow."

"I need to use the men's room first," he says. "There's one right around the corner. Wait here, and when I get back, we'll go to the cabin."

When Andre leaves, I take a few minutes of alone time to do a quick video to send to Stella. But I'll have to be fast. Still seated, I unzip my jacket pocket and take out my phone. My glasses keep slipping down my nose, so I take them off, stick them in my jacket pocket and zip it up.

Standing, I start taking a video of the back deck, so Stella can see what I see.

"Stell, this ship is so amazing. Everything has been perfect, including Andre. Look at the moon." I turn my camera up to the sky. "Andre's been so romantic. He's thought of everything. I think I'm falling in love with my husband all over again. He's been so sweet and . . ."

A door slams in the distance and I quickly jam my phone into the pocket of my jacket, zip it and sit down. I don't want Andre to know I was taking videos to send to Stella. He'll get annoyed, which would ruin our perfect night.

"Come on, old girl," Andre says as he walks up and extends his hand. "Time to call it a night. Tomorrow's a big day."

He pulls me up to a standing position and that's when everything gets really loopy and my head starts to spin — fast.

"Whoa," I say, grabbing for his arms and laughing. "I can't feel my feet, Andre. I think I need to sit down again."

"Don't worry, babe. I've got you." He puts a firm arm around my shoulder to hold me up. His warm touch is comforting. "Let's get you over to the railing so you can breathe in some air and get your bearings before we try to go to the cabin."

I try to nod, but my head feels so heavy. My legs are like jelly as he walks me across the back of the ship. When we reach the railing, I throw my arms around Andre's neck for balance.

"Do you love me?" I whisper into his ear as I heavily lean on him for support.

"How can you ask me that question? This whole trip is all about commemorating our ten years together. Here's to you, Mrs. Gifford."

As I close my eyes and kiss him on the neck, everything starts spinning again. I feel like I'm going to throw up.

"Andre, I don't think I can stand by myself," I whisper. "I think I had too much to drink tonight. I feel really weird."

My husband scoops me in his arms, a pirate capturing his bride after raiding a ship. He grunts as he lifts me and holds me close.

"Don't worry, Becs. I've got you," he says. "You're safe with me."

The strong sea breeze makes me shiver. I wrap my arms around my husband's neck and bury my head into his shoulder. I feel his heart beating against my chest as he half-carries me across the deck.

In his arms, I tilt my head back to look up and extend my arms. Suddenly, Andre and I are dancing and twirling around on the deck.

"Look at all the stars, Andre," I shout. "It's like I'm flying."

CHAPTER NINE

Andre

Becca was a lot heavier than I thought she'd be.

Even after months using weights at the gym preparing for this trip, lifting my wife took every ounce of strength I had. I lean back against the ship's railing and look up at the large half-moon while I try to catch my breath.

Once I got her up on my shoulder, I wasn't sure I'd be able to get her over that damn railing. It was a lot higher than I anticipated. I'm still sweating like a pig from carrying all her dead weight. I nearly fell in myself when I hoisted her over the side. She packed on a few pounds during the months she spent in bed eating and watching reality TV. I warned her about that. Once you let yourself go, there's no turning back.

When we arrived at our cabin today, I tried to gauge her weight by insisting I carry her over the threshold. She thought it was so romantic, but I was simply trying to get a sense as to what kind of tonnage I was in for tonight. She didn't feel that heavy this afternoon.

But tonight it felt like I was carting around a baby elephant. It probably had something to do with the drugs I put in her drinks. Lifting a limp, practically unconscious person over one's shoulders is not easy. All those workouts at LA Fitness didn't prepare me for that. I used all my strength for that one last heave I gave her. Then she flipped over the railing like a giant tuna and down she went.

As I watched her body fall into the black water below, I noticed she hardly made a splash. It was so quiet, and she disappeared surprisingly fast. I didn't even have time to say goodbye.

Right after she went under, it occurred to me that she might get tangled up in the propellers, which would screw up everything. Visions of her body setting off the ship's alarm bells and the engines screeching to a halt flashed through my mind. I froze for a second and waited, but nothing happened. Once she went under, she never came back up, and the Beacon Star never slowed down.

I'd done my homework for months and picked the perfect place on the ship for Becca's big send-off. It had to be a location with minimal exposure to cameras and people. I did a lot of research and learned that the stern on this particular ship was the optimal location. And it looks like that was correct. I'm here standing on the deck of the ship, and my wife is at the bottom of the deep blue sea, or inside a fish. I can hear the engines still humming, and the ship is still moving. There will be no cavalry coming to the rescue.

Right before I pushed Becca over the railing, I took one last look around — the coast was clear. All my fellow passengers are asleep and not a single crew member is in this part of the ship. I look around again to make sure no one is watching. The entire deck is completely deserted.

I walk over to the table where my late wife left her champagne glass and toss it over the side of the ship. Don't want any evidence lying around. I reach for my glass and drain what's left to give my wife a proper final farewell.

"Goodbye, Becca," I whisper. "I'm afraid our marriage just wasn't working for me. I'll never have to hear the word *fibromyalgia* again. That fact alone is worth it."

After downing my glass in one gulp, I toss it over the railing. My heart is still racing as I look at my watch. It's nearly two thirty. Time to head back to my room before anyone sees me out here. I've got a few more things to do and then I need to get some sleep. Killing one's wife is rather exhausting.

Thankfully, I make it to my cabin without passing another soul. Once inside, I dial room service and order another bottle of champagne. Why not? I paid for the unlimited beverage package. I put on my robe, turn on the shower in the bathroom, place my phone on the bathroom counter and turn up the music. With the stage perfectly set, I throw one of my wife's dresses carelessly onto the bed, making it appear as if she had just tossed it there.

Soon, there's a knock on the door. While the dark-haired steward sets up two champagne glasses and an ice bucket, I engage him in some important and hopefully memorable small talk.

"My wife and I are on this cruise celebrating our tenth wedding anniversary," I say.

He gives me a crooked disinterested smile as he uncorks the bottle.

"Ten years? Congratulations," he says, obviously not the least bit interested but trained to pretend he is.

"My wife's taking a shower right now," I whisper as if I don't want her to hear what I'm saying. "She doesn't know I ordered champagne. It's supposed to be a surprise. Listen to her singing in there. She's such a happy girl."

The steward nods and puts his fingers to his lips. "This champagne will make her even happier. Have a good night," he whispers before he turns and leaves the room.

The power of suggestion is an amazing thing.

Obviously, my wife isn't really in the bathroom singing. My iPhone is playing music with a female singer. But I'll bet that steward would swear he heard my wife singing in the bathroom if he were ever asked in a court of law. With that little sleight of hand, I now have a witness who would most likely swear Mrs. Gifford was singing in the shower when he came to our room. Of course, it was actually Taylor Swift, but he didn't know that. All that matters is that he bought the whole thing. Honestly, so far, this entire plan is going much better than I expected. It makes you wonder why more people don't dump their wives over the sides of ships. It's not that hard, extremely effective and you get to take a vacation, too.

I go out on the balcony with my celebratory glass of champagne to contemplate my new life without my old wife. What's the line in the song? How can it be wrong if it feels so right? Let me tell you, this feels so right.

After I finish my champagne, I go straight to bed. Tomorrow is a critical and pivotal day. There can be no mistakes. Everything has to be done perfectly, or I'll end up in jail. In many ways, tomorrow will be even more difficult to pull off than today.

CHAPTER TEN

My alarm rings at 7:45 a.m. I want to be up before the waiter arrives with our preordered room service breakfast for two. Once again, I employ the same "wife singing in the shower" routine. Like the steward from the night before, the breakfast man also extends his hearty congratulations for our anniversary and comments that my wife has a lovely singing voice.

After he leaves, I take my coffee and croissant out onto the balcony and watch the harbor as the ship is secured in the port. It's warmer here. The South Florida sun is shining and there's not a single cloud in the sky. I note that the weather accurately reflects my current disposition. With each sip of my coffee, I consider what my new life will look like. I'm a free man now. I'm no longer shackled to a complaining woman living in her pajamas who wore makeup only for special occasions.

Last night, I didn't drink anywhere near the amount of champagne that Becca guzzled down. I kept refilling her glass, but I barely touched mine — I still had a lot of work to do. After she'd finished that drugged glass of champagne, she melted into a limp rag doll. Perfect.

Sadly, Becca left me no choice. I couldn't stand living with her, but her damn illness, which is apparently a legitimate medical condition, locked me in. I was trapped. Two years ago, I consulted with a divorce lawyer, using a fake name, of course. He wasn't very encouraging. Because of Becca's fibromyalgia and her inability to work consistently, the lawyer told me I'd likely be responsible for supporting her. He said I'd get screwed financially if we split up. I'd be stuck paying her alimony until my dying day. I make decent money, but not enough to support two households. In essence, I was shackled to her. That didn't sit well with me. In fact, it tore me up.

After meeting with the lawyer, it became abundantly clear that Becca was going to suck me dry for the rest of my life. I came up with a million ideas to address my problem, but none of them solved it. I was still on the hook for her. It took me a while before I got to murder. But eventually, it became clear that tossing my wife over the side of a ship would be a lot quicker and cheaper than a drawn-out divorce. Frankly, after I'd thought about it for a while, it just made good sense.

An announcement blares over the ship's loudspeakers. Apparently, "we've arrived in Fort Lauderdale and disembarkation begins in fifteen minutes." I brush my teeth, tidy up the room and grab my bag for my first day ashore.

As I carefully planned, it's imperative that I be in the middle of a crowd when I disembark from the Beacon Star. Throwing my wife overboard last night had its own set of challenges, but getting off the ship this morning is the far more critical part of the plan. If I screw this up, even a little, everything falls apart. There's a good chance I'll end up in handcuffs. Today must go perfectly. No mistakes.

I wander with purpose down to the area where people line up to leave the ship. There are over three thousand passengers on the Beacon Star, and when I arrive in the disembarkation hallway, it looks like two thousand of them are already waiting there. I quietly insinuate myself into the middle of a large crowd and make small talk with several people around me. After nearly fifteen minutes, the line begins to move, and I find myself approaching the security area.

Without my wife's knowledge, I took a test run on a two-night cruise a few months back. I wanted to practice the little sleight of hand at security that I'll be doing today. It worked extremely well on the other ship, so it should work here, too. It has to.

As the line lurches forward, I clutch my security tag and Becca's tag in my right hand. Everyone in the crowd is excited about getting off the ship. Three thousand passengers will spill off this ship in the next thirty minutes like ants going to a picnic. And no one in this crowd is more anxious to get off than me.

What I learned on my trial-run cruise was that the security crew is far more interested in checking faces when people are getting *on* the ship versus when they're getting *off*. When the passengers are leaving, security doesn't really examine each person. They mainly listen for a beep. Because so many people are streaming by so fast, it's impossible to match the faces. If they did that, it would take forever. But it's a whole different ball game when passengers are getting on the ship. When people are returning, security is much more likely to match tags to the ID photos in their system to prevent stowaways or your run-of-the-mill bad guys from boarding.

As the line moves faster, I sidle up to the scanner along with hundreds of other passengers and hold my breath. When it's my turn, I deftly slide my tag and my wife's over the scanner seconds apart. I keep moving as I hear two beeps, one after the other. I don't look back, and no one stops me as I move out of the security bay. From here, I stroll down the gangplank with all the other excited tourists looking forward to their first day in sunny Fort Lauderdale.

I walk with ease down the ramp, making sure to remain in the middle of the crowd. Until I'm far away from the ship, I'm still waiting for that accusatory hand to tap me on the shoulder and escort me to the ship's brig. My heart is still racing when my feet finally hit solid ground. I walk briskly away from the pier.

I made it.

CHAPTER ELEVEN

Several blocks from the ship, there's a line of taxis, and I get into the first one.

"Lauderdale-by-the-Sea," I say assuredly to the driver while checking my watch. I'm right on time and even have a few minutes to spare before my appointment.

As my car glides along, I look out at the beautiful palm trees and the blue-green ocean peeking out between the hotels. I breathe in the fresh air and smile. So taken by my surroundings, I forget for a moment what's transpired over the last twenty-four hours. The car stops several blocks from the ocean in a laid-back but heavily touristed area that has lots of shops and restaurants. It's the perfect place to get lost in a crowd.

After paying for the taxi in cash, I get out of the car and head down the street toward the ocean along with dozens of other vacationers. I'm supposed to meet near a bunch of oversized multicolored Adirondack chairs. I was told they'd be right off the beach near a restaurant named Aruba.

As I get closer to the water, I spot the big chairs in front of me and scan the surrounding crowd for one particular face. It takes a moment, but then I see her. Actually, the first thing

I see is the pink-and-orange Gretchen Scott dress, cream-colored shoes and floppy straw hat with a pink ribbon.

She turns around, and the first thing I notice are the dark-framed glasses. For a second, she takes my breath away. It's like seeing a ghost. The long coppery wig she's wearing looks exactly like Becca's hair. From where I'm standing, I would swear I'm looking at my wife. Of course, that's impossible. My guess is that Becca's become lunch for some large fish or a plaything for an eight-limbed mollusk somewhere off the coast of the Sunshine State.

The woman I'm meeting looks a little panicky and doesn't see me as I approach.

"Becca," I say as I walk up behind her and give her a kiss on the neck.

We embrace and she whispers into my ear.

"Oh, my God, Andre," she says, swallowing. "I was so worried. You were supposed to be here fifteen minutes ago. I can't see anything in these stupid glasses."

She steps back from me and smiles. But it's not a smile of joy — it's one of relief.

"I told you I'd be here at ten thirty," I say, rubbing Lily's shoulder.

"I know," she says. "I haven't slept in days. I've been a wreck thinking about this afternoon. You said it yourself. The first time you got off the ship alone and the first time we *both* get back *on* the ship together are the most dangerous parts. When you were a little late, I didn't know if something happened to you. I wasn't sure you even went through with it last night."

I smile. "Relax. Everything went beautifully." I take her hand. "We're good to go."

From there, Lily and I stroll around the beach area, stopping in shops and buying a few souvenirs. It's important we look as normal as possible and do the things that tourists do. We stop in a pet store and look at some puppies. We stop for a drink, even though it's morning, because that's what tourists do. While we each have a beer to calm our nerves, I quietly walk her through all the events that transpired the previous night and this morning.

"You're sure no one noticed anything? What if someone finds her body?" says Lily, chewing on one of her pink nails, painted with the same color polish that Becca used.

"Don't bite your nails. Becca never did," I whisper. "They won't find her body. I always do my homework and left nothing to chance. I had it all timed. The exact spot where I dumped her overboard happens to be a massive shark zone, one of the biggest. If Becca wasn't ground up by the ship's propellers last night, she's surely been eaten by now. And last night when we were out on deck, the ship was completely dead. Not a soul was around. No one saw anything. And if they had, I would have been arrested before I left the ship."

Lily presses her lips together and nods. "That's true."

"And this morning, there were thousands of people getting off the ship at the same time. The crew and security people had no idea who was who. Passing Becca's and my ID through the security scanner together was easier than I'd imagined. Nobody noticed and here I am."

We head out of the restaurant and casually wander into a few more shops. Lily picks up a woven tote bag from a sale table and examines it.

"We're not out of the woods yet. When we try to get on the ship this afternoon, things could still go wrong," she says, taking off her eyeglasses and replacing them with a pair of Gucci sunglasses identical to ones I bought for Becca.

She looks at me and holds up the eyeglasses. "Why the hell did you get these eyeglasses for me with a prescription in them? You know I don't wear glasses. When I have them on, I can't see anything. I nearly killed myself wearing them today."

"I wanted to make sure I got the exact same pair Becca had. I ordered them from the optometrist in town, so they automatically put her prescription in it. There wasn't time to change the lenses. Just wear the glasses for now. When we're getting on and off the ship, you hold on to my arm and I'll guide you. I'm afraid you'll have to wear them when we're in the ship's public areas, too."

Lily pouts. "The lenses make me nauseous, Andre."

"You'll be all right. Do everything exactly the way I've told you and it will be fine."

She nods and reaches for another tote bag.

"Buy it," I say. "It's important we look like typical tourists who've spent the day shopping and buying things we'll never use or look at again."

Wandering around Lauderdale-by-the-Sea browsing for trinkets for over half an hour, Lily buys a few scarves and some candy. Now she actually *needs* to buy a woven basket to carry everything. I give her Becca's credit card, so she can create a second paper trail for Rebecca Gifford.

When our shopping is complete, we take an Uber over to Las Olas, the main designer shopping street in downtown Fort Lauderdale. On the ride over, I strike up a lively conversation with our driver, who mentions that he's planning to take a trip up north sometime soon. I give him my business card and tell him to look me up if he ever gets up to New York City or Connecticut. It's an empty gesture. He won't look me up. But if ever asked in a court of law, he'll likely remember Andre Gifford and my red-headed wife.

When we arrive at Las Olas, the strip is hopping. After stopping for lunch at a hamburger joint, we take a riverboat cruise along the intracoastal. The weather remains warm and sunny. On the riverboat we learn about how South Florida was settled. The history we learn on the boat ride takes my mind off the critical last leg of our journey today — the ever-so-tricky return to the ship — boarding, where they do watch.

As the riverboat trip draws to an end, I make sure we introduce ourselves as Andre and Becca Gifford from Connecticut to anyone who'll listen. If it ever comes down to it, the more witnesses who saw Mrs. Gifford alive in Fort Lauderdale, the better.

After traipsing around Las Olas a while longer, it's time to return to the Beacon Star. She sets sail tonight at seven, and we've been told to be back onboard by five.

Lily and I look around for our Uber to go back to the pier. She's become extremely quiet, something she never is.

"What's wrong?" I say. "Everything's going to be fine."

"What if they notice I'm not Becca when we're trying to board? We could get caught."

"We won't. Nobody blinked an eye this morning when I got off the ship. Besides, you look exactly like Becca in that outfit. I'd swear on a stack of bibles that you were my wife. No one will know you're not. I promise."

"But what if . . ."

"Don't you trust me, Lily?"

She nods. "I'm just nervous," she says as she puts her hand in mine. "Feel it? I'm shaking, and my heart is beating as fast as a rabbit."

I squeeze her hand and pull her over to a nearby bench to sit.

"Let's breathe," I say. "Take a few slow deep breaths." She follows my direction. "That's it. Breathe. You're going to be fine."

She nods and forces a smile.

"You can do this, Lily," I say. "*We* can do this. And my angel, once we're on that ship, it's game over. Nothing but smooth sailing is ahead for us."

CHAPTER TWELVE

When Lily and I arrive at the port, hundreds of our fellow passengers are already there standing in lines five deep waiting to board the ship. I take Lily's hand again. It's cold and clammy, so I give it a squeeze. Lily removes the sunglasses and replaces them with a copy of Becca's eyeglasses. I look at her face. There's sweat above her upper lip and her pupils are dilated.

"You gonna be all right?" I say. "Are you going to choke? It's showtime, Lily. You've got to pull yourself together. Put on a happy face. Remember, you're on a cruise vacation."

"I'm trying, but I'm so scared. What if they see I'm not her? What do I say?"

"I've told you. You look exactly like Becca. They'll only notice something's wrong if you look like you're going to pass out. That's what's going to screw us up."

Lily lets out a defeated sigh. "I can't help it. I feel sick."

I take both of her hands in mine and look into her eyes. "Listen to me. We've been planning this for a long time. The hard part is done. Becca's gone. I took care of that. We're right at the finish line now. In five more minutes, we'll be in the clear. All you have to do is walk up with me and put your pass on that scanner. You don't stop. You keep moving. Got it?"

We get in line, and while we wait for our turn to board, we make small talk with other passengers. We laugh and share details about the sights we saw in Fort Lauderdale. We show each other all the useless junk we bought.

The boarding process is exactly as I expected. The crew is trying to move people onto the ship as quickly as possible so they can depart. The Beacon Star must exit the port in ninety minutes. As long as those security people hear a beep, they let the passengers go right through.

As we near the security area, I can already hear the rapid beeps coming from key cards as they register one after the other on the ship's system. People are moving through so fast, their pictures are coming up several seconds after the passenger has already walked by and onto the ship. With ten people in front of us, I lean over and whisper into Lily's ear.

"Remember, act like everyone else. Slide the pass on the scanner and don't stop. Keep walking. I'll be right behind you."

She nods and I see her swallow when it's her turn to put her card on the sensor. I confess, my heart is thumping watching her. As she reaches out with the key card, I deliberately start a lively and inquisitive conversation with the security team.

"Don't you just love Fort Lauderdale? Did you guys get a chance to go into town today?" I say, hoping to distract them. "My wife and I did some real damage shopping."

"Nah," says one of the security guards, looking up from his scanner. "I get my leave in San Juan. I like Puerto Rico better, good food."

By the time he answers me, Lily has already made it through. I run my key card across the sensor and follow her. Once on the other side, I grab her hand and lead her to the elevator.

We've done it. We're both on the ship and no one has a clue. As far as anyone knows, Andre and Becca Gifford left the Beacon Star this morning and have just reboarded the ship. There is now a complete digital record of Becca Gifford boarding the ship in Port Canaveral, disembarking in Fort Lauderdale and then returning to the ship in Fort Lauderdale.

After today, Lily and I can come and go as we please. Nobody's looking for Becca Gifford because she's not missing. She's taking a wonderful surprise anniversary cruise with her husband.

I bring Lily up to the cabin. She gasps when she sees the amazing balconied suite we have and flops down on the king-size bed. I pour her a glass of champagne from a bottle I had delivered to the room earlier in the afternoon. After we finish the champagne, Lily touches up her hair and puts on one of Becca's dresses, so we can go out and explore the ship. Before we leave, I hand her Becca's bag.

"Take this. All of Becca's IDs and other personal items are in this bag. Use her lipstick, that's in there, too. She was using this bag early last night, before she went for her 'evening swim.'"

Lily grimaces and I wonder if she has the stomach to see this whole thing through. She dabs on a little of Becca's lipstick. Since it's still light out, I tell her to put on the Gucci sunglasses I bought for her. She'll have to switch to the prescription glasses later, but for now, she can wear the sunglasses. She puts on the glasses and faces me.

"Becca's own mother would think you were her daughter," I say.

She smiles and, hand in hand, we head to one of the outside bars on the seventh floor to enjoy the warm sunny evening. The cocktail hour has started, and the bar is in full swing. We get the last two empty barstools at one end and sit. Reaching into a bowl of warm cashews on the shiny mahogany bar, I let out a satisfied sigh.

"Our job is to be slightly memorable. Everyone we encounter on the ship should take away some tiny memory of us being here," I say softly, so no one else can hear. "If the police were ever to ask a crew member or passenger about Becca . . ."

"Why would they do that?" she says. "You told me no one would ever connect her being missing to this cruise."

I rub the top of her thigh under the bar. "And no one will," I whisper. "It's just a precaution."

Clearly, when under stress, Lily's not as tough as I thought. I'll have to do a lot of hand-holding to keep her from falling apart on this cruise.

"I want us to be careful on the off chance that the police might look at the cruise at some point in the future," I say. "As long as we make a consistent presence for Becca throughout the week on the ship, there will be people to verify that my wife was absolutely on the ship for the entire week. Okay?"

"Yes," says Lily softly, her breath quick and shallow.

"But we can't hit people over the head with it. We have to be subtle while letting people know we're here."

Lily nods.

"And keep those sunglasses on," I say as she starts to take them off. "You're a dead ringer with the glasses on, not so much with them off."

She takes a deep breath and pushes the glasses snugly into her face.

"I think we can start to enjoy ourselves now." I raise my glass. "To us."

As we take a sip of our drinks, the Beacon Star's loud horn sounds throughout the ship. "Looks like we've set sail," I say. "We're officially on our way to Puerto Rico."

Lily gives me a weak smile. Damn, I thought she was made of tougher stuff. She talks a good game, but she's not the cool, detached femme fatale she makes herself out to be.

I've always been good at compartmentalizing things. When I was a kid growing up in northern Connecticut, I threw a rock at a squirrel in my backyard. I thought I would just scare it, but my aim must have been better than I thought because I had a direct hit, and then it didn't move. I went over to the squirrel and saw blood seeping out of its head. I got a bit of a rush. No one saw me do it. I picked it up with a stick and hurled it into the wooded area behind our house. I never thought about it again. It's just like now. I'm already able to put Becca and her plunge to the bottom of the sea completely out of my mind. I wish Lily would do the same. It would make things so much easier.

Ten minutes later, there's music playing and I'm starting to enjoy myself. I'm chatting with some other passengers at the bar about sports teams when a familiar female voice with a southern drawl rings out behind me.

"I had a feeling I'd run into you two," says the husky female voice. I spin around on my stool. It's that nosey old dying woman from the previous night, Olive Walker. Guess she hasn't croaked yet. She comes over and gets so close to me that she's practically sitting on my lap.

"How did you like Fort Lauderdale, Becca? Did you find that saltwater taffy I was telling you about? I'd love a piece if you have any left you can spare."

Thankfully, Lily still has her sunglasses on when Olive walks up. I have no doubt that underneath the glasses, my girlfriend has a look of terror in her eyes. Lily has no idea who Olive Walker is or why the woman knows Becca's name. That's my fault. Knowing that Becca had contact with Olive, I should have told Lily about it to prepare her for something like this. Hopefully, Lily can think on her feet. Olive Walker is old, but she's not stupid or blind. She got a good long look at Becca during dinner last night. I jump in to rescue Lily, who I can tell is starting to sputter.

"We did get that taffy," I say. "Excellent recommendation, Mrs. Walker. We bought a small package at a market, but I'm afraid it was so good, we devoured it all."

"Please, call me Olive. Like I told you last night at dinner, there's nothing better than a little taffy." She looks down at her watch. "Now, I've really got to run. I have a massage in the spa in fifteen minutes. After a good deep-tissue massage I feel like a teenager again. Let's meet in the Lighthouse Lounge after dinner for a drink. My treat."

As the old woman walks off, I look at Lily. She's hyperventilating, and I take her hands.

"Relax," I whisper. "Everything's fine."

"You didn't tell me that you made some friends. What if she notices I look different?"

I had no idea Lily could be so easily rattled. Her persona has always been one of a tough, no-nonsense woman of the world, a girl who can handle anything.

"Don't worry about that old hag. She's practically senile," I say. "Becca and I met her briefly at dinner last night. I know her type. She's a pest who gloms on to anyone who'll talk to her."

"What if she . . ."

"She won't. According to Mrs. Walker, she doesn't expect to make it to the end of this cruise. She told us and half the crew that she's terminally ill and has just days to live. Her big swan song plan is to die on this cruise and go out with a bang. So you see, there's nothing to worry about. Dead women tell no tales."

"She looks pretty healthy to me," says Lily, shaking her head and taking a sip of her wine.

"Forget about Olive Walker. We need to stay focused on our plan. Tonight, it's important that we communicate with a few people. We need to send texts from Becca to some of her friends and family. We especially have to send one to her best friend, Stella. They text each other every day, all day. Dig Becca's phone out of her bag now and we'll text Stella and send a couple of pictures from the bar."

Lily digs through Becca's oversized black bag for the phone. After a full minute of searching, she begins to remove everything and place the contents on the shiny wooden bar.

"There's no phone in the bag," she finally says as she looks up at me. "Andre, Becca's phone isn't here."

I take the bag from her and rummage through the various zippered compartments inside. Lily's right. Becca's phone isn't in there. I excuse myself and run back to our cabin to find my wife's phone. Twenty minutes later, after tearing our room apart, I return to the bar.

"That stupid bitch," I hiss into Lily's ear as I take my seat. "She must have had her phone on her when she went into the water."

CHAPTER THIRTEEN

Maybe it's the wine or the balmy sea breeze, because Lily finally relaxes during our buffet dinner, which includes every international cuisine imaginable. When we discovered Becca's phone was missing, Lily started to lose it. She went far out on the proverbial ledge, and I had to talk her down and reinforce our path forward.

"We'll tell people that Becca lost her phone," I said to Lily, "and that's why she's using my phone to text and send pictures. It's not a big deal. Believe me, Becca's lost her phone before."

As soon as Lily calms down, I change the subject. Waxing poetic, I list all the great future adventures she and I will have without that thirty-five-year-old red-headed anchor dragging us down. Soon, Lily is enjoying herself and forgetting her angst.

After dinner, we get up from the table and take a walk out onto the deck. The moon is a bit larger and brighter than last night. Good thing it wasn't this way when I dumped Becca into the sea, or someone could have seen something.

Sitting in two lounge chairs with our feet up, Lily and I compose a text to Stella, and then another to her mother, Martha.

Becca's mother only needs one text and one picture to make her think everything is normal. But Stella is another story entirely. Stella and Becca are attached at the hip, something that's always annoyed me. I never understood why my wife needed to talk to her friend so often when she had me. They would call each other and text constantly. Stella will definitely expect daily updates from her best friend. If she doesn't get them, she'll think something's wrong. Stella has always gotten on my nerves.

Now that I think about it, there's a residual bonus with Becca being gone. I won't have to see or hear from Stella anymore. Sometimes, it felt like there were three of us in the marriage — Becca, me and Stella. I should have put a stop to that friendship a long time ago.

While we were in Orlando, I took an inordinate number of photos of Becca, so I'd have plenty of different shots to use. I also took a lot of pictures of her during our first day on the ship. I've got a wide assortment of photos to pull from when needed.

First I get the easy one out of the way. I send a quick text to Becca's mother with a selfie of Becca and me that we took on our first day at Universal Studios. We were standing in front of Hogwarts.

Hi Mom. Phone died so using Andre's. Having a great time. Universal was awesome. Last night on the ship we had lobster and champagne for dinner. Living the good life! xx

After the message goes out to Martha, Lily and I carefully put one together for Stella. The wording is critical. Stella will notice if Becca doesn't sound like herself. I take the first pass, but then Lily softens it to make it sound more like a woman talking to another woman.

Hey Stell, having a blast. Universal was fun. On ship now, it's so beautiful. Food great, weather fantastic. Spent today in

Ft Lauderdale. Andre is being crazy romantic. I'm attaching a pic of us boarding the ship and another from Hogwarts. Miss you. Btw, internet is spotty so I'll text when I can. XOX

"What do you think?" says Lily when she finishes doctoring the text. I read it five times and nod.

"It sounds like Becca. Let's wait for Stella's response, which I guarantee will be within minutes, maybe seconds. That's how those two are."

We send the text and pictures to Stella and wait. We don't have to wait long, because within five minutes, a text comes back from my wife's best friend.

Looks so damn cool. I'm up for a girl's weekend to Ft Lauderdale anytime, just say when. Also, you look so glam. Keep the pictures coming. XOX

That was our first test and Stella bought it. One text per day should be enough to keep Stella McCrystal in check.

Over the next five days, Lily and I are like two carefree kids as the Beacon Star stops in Puerto Rico and the U.S. Virgin Islands. I've put Becca completely out of my mind and focus only on Lily. Our days and nights are filled with local Caribbean culture, fancy tropical meals and excellent wine and beer. We make sure to do several text exchanges with Stella and occasionally include one of the photos I took from the first two days. Good thing I took a lot of pictures.

Consistent contact with Stella comes with its problems, though. The more I give her, the more she wants. It's never enough. Just when I think my text ends our conversation, Stella comes back with another question or comment. But we've got to do it, or she might suspect something's not right.

As our week draws to an end, we spend our second-to-last night at one of the Beacon Star's specialty Italian restaurants, Vibo Marina. It's one of the larger dining places on the ship, and they make an amazing red clam sauce.

We've finished dinner and have just started our desserts, sorbet for me and tiramisu for Lily, when I hear a vaguely familiar voice over my shoulder.

"Well, if it isn't my two friends from our first night at sea."

Lily has just put her spoon into her mouth as I spin around. It's that old woman again, Olive Walker. *Why isn't she dead yet?* Lily and I made a point of avoiding her and hadn't seen her all week. A few times, I actually wondered if she had croaked like she had predicted.

I force a smile as I look at her.

"Olive, good to see you again," I say with as much enthusiasm as I can muster, which isn't a lot.

"I've been keeping my eyes out for you two," she says as she takes the empty seat next to me. "Hard to believe we haven't run into each other on this ship, isn't it? Have you two been hiding from me?"

"It's a big ship," I say, trying to keep her eyes focused on me and off Lily. "How has your week been going?"

"A little of this, a little of that," she says. "Frankly, I'm amazed I'm still here."

I pepper her with inane questions, the answers to which I'm not the least bit interested. I'm trying to keep Olive from engaging with Lily, who isn't wearing the sunglasses to hide her face. The light in the restaurant is dim, but it's not dark. Despite Olive's advanced age and deteriorating medical condition, she seems surprisingly alert and spry for someone who's about to keel over at any moment.

I look across the table at Lily. She's got a giant question mark on her face. Through her glasses, I see fear in her eyes. She's starting to freak out. Lily's not cut out for this cloak-and-dagger stuff. I'm not sure how she'll handle it if Olive starts grilling her.

I do everything I can to keep the old woman's attention on me — short of doing a tap dance. But when the waiter comes over to ask me if we'd like anything else, Olive turns to Lily and inundates her with questions about how we liked each port of call.

Lily keeps her head down, literally, and does her best to give short, cheerful answers. I commend her for holding it together. She tells Olive about our visit to the big fort in San Juan and our relaxing afternoon at a relatively deserted beach thirty minutes from the old town. Olive seems satisfied that we've seen the appropriate sights.

"I'm so glad you've enjoyed your time on the Beacon Star," says Olive. "I wouldn't consider taking any other ship. As I told you both before, I'm planning to pass to the great beyond from this very ship."

After that last comment, Lily's eyes get really round, and she looks at me.

"Now, Olive, let's not be morbid," I say. "You seem quite healthy to me. I'm sure you'll be around for a long while."

"Time will tell," says the old woman with a wave of her hand. "I could go at any time. It could be tonight for all I know."

I do the only thing I can — change the subject.

"Are you going ashore in St. Thomas tomorrow, Olive?" I say.

"No," she says, now peering at Lily. "I'm not leaving the ship for a few days. I need to rest. When we get to Miami, I'll probably stay onboard for the next leg of the cruise into the Gulf. The Beacon Star keeps going after Miami, you know."

Lily is sinking down in her chair and looking extremely uncomfortable as Olive continues to examine her.

"Going to the Gulf sounds like fun," I say, trying desperately to redirect Olive's attention away from Lily. "We're planning to do a biking trip in St. Thomas tomorrow, aren't we, Becca?"

"Yes," Lily squeaks out. "Should be really fun."

Olive looks down at her phone. For an old woman, she's amazingly tech savvy. She appears to be searching for something but then stops and locks her eyes on Lily again.

"St. Thomas has an interesting history," I say, still trying to divert Olive's attention. "The island was at one time a colony of Denmark. I hear there are great examples of Danish architecture there."

Olive ignores me and leans in to get a better look at Lily.

"You look different," says Olive.

"Do I?" says Lily, looking over at me for a lifeline. "I don't look different, do I, Andre?"

"You look the same to me," I say with a chuckle. "Maybe you got a little sun?"

"You look different from before," says Olive, holding up her phone so we can see it. "See? Here's the selfie I took of you and me from the first night of the cruise. That was the night we met."

I stare in horror at the picture of Becca and Olive on Olive's phone.

When did she take that photo?

"The week has really flown, hasn't it?" says Olive, looking at the picture again. "You really do look so different."

CHAPTER FOURTEEN

Olive leans over and shows Lily the image on her phone.

When did that old cow take that goddamn picture?

"It's so strange," Olive says, shaking her head. "On the one hand, the photo does look like you, but at the same time, it doesn't. Your eyes are different. Right now, they look further apart than they do in the photo and seem to have a slightly rounder shape."

There's a long pause where no one speaks. Finally, Lily springs to life.

"It was probably my eye makeup combined with the allergic reaction I had from my new contact lenses. My eyes were a bit swollen that first day or two. I had gone for a makeover at a cosmetics counter. My eyes blew up, and I had to take my contacts out. That's probably what it was."

I'm impressed by Lily's ability to think on her feet. I lean over and look at the original photo of Becca on Olive's phone.

"She looks the same to me," I say. "Lighting always makes people look different."

Olive glances at the photo again and then studies Lily's face.

"I suppose so," says the old woman. "It's not only the shape of your eyes, though, but their proximity to your nose.

Don't you see it? I thought you told me you don't wear contacts."

I need to stop this conversation. Now.

"You know, Becca and I are really exhausted. I think we're going to call it a night."

"What? No drink in the lounge?" says Olive, looking surprised and sad at the same time.

"I'm afraid we'll have to pass," I say. "Maybe tomorrow."

"I may not be here tomorrow," she says, getting up from the table, holding her green cane with the fake-diamond head. "They say I could go at any time."

"I'm sure you'll still be here tomorrow," I reply as I look at Lily and signal that we should get going. And I'll be damned, it happened so fast. Just as that menacing old busybody is about to walk away from us, she spins around and takes a picture of Lily and me.

"See you manana," she says with a wave of her hand as she shuffles out of the restaurant.

As soon as Olive is out of earshot, Lily leans over to me.

"What the hell are we going to do?" she whispers loudly, her pupils now pinpoints. "That old lady knows something's off."

I let out a groan and shake my head. The last thing I need right now is Lily going to pieces again.

"Olive Walker doesn't know anything," I say. "She's a gossip and she's fishing for information about anything. She sticks her nose where she shouldn't, but I don't think she really suspects anything. She likes to be the center of attention and hear herself talk. That's all."

"Andre, she's got Becca's picture," whispers Lily, "and mine. If she really compares the two photos, she'll see we're not the same person. How could you let her take a picture of Becca?"

"I don't know when she took that selfie with Becca. I was there the whole time."

"Well, apparently not."

Then it hits me. When I was ordering the wine, the steward asked me to accompany him across the room to select a bottle from their wine rack. I wasn't gone for more than sixty seconds. Olive must have taken the picture then. *Shit.*

"Everything will be fine," I say.

After all my preparation and planning, those two photos the old woman has could be our undoing. I reach for Lily's hand, and we walk back to our cabin whispering about what to do next.

As soon as we're inside, Lily starts pacing.

"Can you stop that?" I say. "Getting yourself worked up doesn't help the situation."

"That old bitch is going to land us in jail. She's got those freakin' pictures. That's hard evidence, Andre. People have been incarcerated for far less than that. You've got to do something."

Lily breaks into the minibar and pulls out a small bottle of vodka. As she tosses it back, I sit on the bed to think. Keeping a cool head and remaining focused on the problem is critical.

"Well?" Lily says a few minutes later while opening another bottle.

I stand, take the bottle from her hand and take a sip.

"I've looked at this a dozen different ways. We don't have much of a choice," I say.

"So, what do we do?"

"We'll have to kill her."

Lily's eyes bug out of their sockets and her mouth forms a large O.

"Are you serious?" she says. "Kill her? As in dead?"

"Yeah, as in dead, Lily. You got a better suggestion?"

"You can't keep killing people, Andre. That would make you a serial killer. There's got to be another way. She's an old woman. She's nice. She reminds me of my grandmother."

I look at her, wondering what exactly it was that I initially found so appealing. Certainly not her intellect.

"We don't have another choice," I say. "You said it yourself, she's got those pictures. Those photos could send us to prison for life — or worse. Florida, where I think Becca was technically killed, has the death penalty."

"Can't we just steal her phone?" says Lily, reaching for another vodka.

I shake my head. "No. Olive knows. She hasn't figured it out yet, but she will. If the police ever question her, she'd have a lot to tell them."

"But couldn't we just . . . do we have to . . ."

"The old lady is dying anyway. She told us she wasn't planning on ever getting off this ship. We're just expediting things. Worst-case scenario, she loses a couple of extra days. When you're ninety-one, what's a couple of days?"

Lily continues to advocate for stealing Olive's phone until I remind her what life is like in a maximum-security prison. Finally, Lily gets onboard. We're offing the old lady — tonight.

I know exactly how to handle the nosey Mrs. Walker. The old woman is fond of a cocktail, and I still have plenty of extra "medication" left over from what I brought to use on Becca.

"I'll dose her the same way I did with Becca," I say, "only I'll give her a lot more, enough to kill her."

Lily grabs my arm. "What if they do an autopsy?"

"They won't. The woman's dying. Half the crew and the cruise director know that Olive Walker came on the ship to croak. It's what she wanted anyway, to die on the Beacon Star. In a way, we're helping her fulfill her dream."

While Lily downs another small bottle, I uncork some champagne from our fridge and prepare it for Olive. I pour a little champagne into a small glass and mix the drug into it. Once it dissolves, I pour the liquid back into the bottle and gently mix it in.

"There," I say, placing the spiked bottle on the dresser while I comb my hair. "Olive Walker won't know what hit her. Wish me luck."

Out in the hallway, I get into the elevator and go up three flights to Olive's floor. She's on seven, and her suite is at the other end of the ship. It takes me a while to get there. As I near her cabin, I see a number of crew milling around in the hallway outside her door. I wasn't counting on a crowd being around when I bumped off the old woman.

Getting closer, I can see the door to Olive's room is wide open.

"What's going on?" I ask one of the crew members who's standing in the corridor holding a walkie talkie of some kind. The young man has an accent. I think it's Portuguese.

"The old lady in this room," he says in somewhat broken English, "I think maybe she die."

"What?" I say, my eyes widening. "Are you talking about Olive Walker, the older woman with the cane?"

The young man nods. "I think that's the lady's name. She order room service, and when they bring the food, they find her. She not moving."

"Dead?"

"I think so. They took her away," he says. "Maybe to the morgue."

I shake my head in disbelief, but at the same time, I'm filled with enormous gratitude. I was going to knock off the old lady and I've been spared. Despite what Lily insinuated earlier, I don't *like* killing people. I only kill if someone gets in my way. Becca was in my way and so was Olive Walker.

"That's very sad," I say to the young man. "She was a lovely woman."

I go outside on the deck to walk back to my end of the ship. I need to breathe in the sea air to calm myself down. My adrenaline is amped up. As I near the bow, I lean over the side and empty the bottle of tainted champagne into the sea and throw the bottle into the water as far out from the ship as I can. Then, I head back to my cabin to tell Lily the good news.

Olive's dead, and we're safe. Nothing but smooth sailing from here on out.

CHAPTER FIFTEEN

The next morning, the Beacon Star arrives in the port of Miami. We're in the land of sunshine and scantily clad women, where life is one big endless party. The comedian Lenny Bruce once said, "Miami is where neon goes to die." As Lily and I wander around South Beach, I'm thinking Bruce got it right. It's Vegas without the casinos and lots and lots of palm trees. Our ship will stay in port for two days before continuing around the tip of Florida to the Gulf and then on to New Orleans. Lily and I will disembark here in Miami tomorrow and fly home.

We're only doing the first leg of a longer cruise. Olive Walker, on the other hand, presumably to have enough time to die, booked herself all the way through to Louisiana for an additional ten days.

As I look back over the last week and all I've accomplished, I'm rather proud of how well it all went. Other than that one little glitch with the old lady and the photos, everything else has gone remarkably well. That's why careful planning is so important. You've got to prepare for the unexpected, stay nimble and be innovative when things take a different turn. It's all about how one *responds* to things in life that matters.

So far, Lily has successfully used Becca's ID without anyone suspecting a thing. In fact, the crew has been calling her Becca all week. I've reminded her to keep her eyeglasses or sunglasses on at all times and to always tip well.

"People remember good tippers, Lily," I told her. "We want them to remember that Becca Gifford was a big tipper the entire cruise, just in case anyone ever asks."

We've got one more day and night in Miami, and I plan to make the most of it. When we get home, the shit will hit the fan. Until then, I plan to enjoy myself. Right after breakfast, Lily and I grab a couple of towels from the room and head out early to the white sands of South Beach.

The seashore is hopping and filled with beautiful people. Practically naked, young sinewy bodies are everywhere. Lily fits right in wearing her red G-string bikini. She looks amazing in it. Becca could never have pulled off a G-string. Especially not after her last year lounging around the house drinking tea.

"Do I *have* to wear the wig at the beach?" Lily leans back on her towel while picking at the corners of her hairpiece. "It's so freakin' hot with this thing on my head. Can't I just wear the straw hat?"

"We've talked about this," I say firmly. "We can't take a chance of running into someone from the ship. There could be members of the crew here on their day off or other passengers. What if someone noticed your short blonde hair? We can't risk it. We've come too far."

With my eyes closed, I lie back on my towel, taking in the sun and listening to the sounds around me. Barely twenty minutes pass before Lily complains about the wig again. Now I'm wondering if I've swapped one anchor for another.

"I can't take this wig anymore, Andre," she whispers. "I'm going to have a heatstroke."

I can't take her *complaining* anymore, so I suggest we leave the beach and get some lunch. We take a cab to Wynwood, a section of Miami that's been revitalized as an art center. The outsides of all the old buildings have been covered with frescos. At one time, Wynwood was a blighted area. Now, it's a mecca for tourists and a location people put on their itineraries as a must-see in Miami.

We walk around to the various art installations, enjoying the freedom of being back on land and away from prying eyes on the ship. Suddenly, Lily's sharp nails dig forcefully into my upper arm.

"Look, over there," she whispers loudly. "Those people, they're from the ship. They're looking at us."

"Keep your sunglasses on and act naturally," I say, my heart starting to race. "We're so close to the finish line. Don't screw us up. Stay calm."

"They're coming toward us," hisses Lily, her nails digging deeper into my flesh. "What should we do?"

"They're probably coming over to say hello," I whisper. "Relax and let go of my arm. You're going to draw blood. Pull the brim of your hat down over your hair and push up your glasses."

While on the ship, Lily and I made a point of keeping our conversations with other passengers to a minimum. A short exchange at a bar or a quick greeting in a restaurant was the extent of our interactions. I want people to remember both of us being on the ship, but I don't want to give anyone enough time to study us or get to know us.

Planting a smile on my face as the couple gets closer, I turn and look at the fifty-something duo as they walk toward us.

"Hey there. You're from the Beacon Star, right?" says the heavyset man wearing an orange-and-blue Hawaiian shirt. *He looks like a giant beach ball.*

I'm about to respond to his question when, out of nowhere, Lily begins an Oscar-worthy performance.

"Hello, and yes, we're from the Beacon Star." She puts out her hand and shakes both of theirs. "We've seen you on the ship. We're the Giffords. I'm Becca, and this is my husband, Andre. We're celebrating our tenth wedding anniversary."

"How nice," says the woman, who has short dark hair and is wearing a dress version of her husband's Hawaiian shirt. Clearly, this couple is made for each other. "Congratulations. We're from Iowa. How do you like Miami? Pretty wild, isn't it?"

"It's beautiful. But it's pretty crazy here," I say, looking around at the busy scene.

"And on the ship, too," says the woman. "Did you hear that one of the passengers died last night?"

"Really?" says Lily, cool as a cucumber.

"Yes, it's so sad. We *think* we know who it was. We actually had a drink with the poor woman just a few days ago. You may have seen her around the ship. She was a lovely older lady named Olive something, from Nashville, I believe. She had a green cane with a faux-diamond handle."

"How did she die?" I say, curious myself.

"Not sure," says the woman. "We overheard people talking about it this morning at breakfast. Someone said they found her in her cabin unresponsive. She was very old. It must have been her time."

I nod and look at my watch, thinking it's *my time* to end this conversation. We've been conversing with them for far too long and I don't like it. Lily and I agreed five minutes is the maximum we should spend with anyone. It's time for us to move on.

"Well, we'd better get going," I say, looking around for an escape route.

"We were just about to go for a bite to eat," says the woman. "Would you like to join us?"

Definitely not.

"What a nice invitation," I say as I take Lily by the elbow, "but we're supposed to meet up with some old friends who are here in Miami. We need to get a cab right now, or we'll be late."

As we hurry away, I hear the woman's voice calling out from behind us.

"Maybe we can grab a drink later on the ship." I turn around while still walking, smile and wave my arm as if meeting for drinks might be an option. *It won't*. They've had their five minutes with us, and that's all they get. Walking briskly, Lily and I scurry across the busy street into a crowd and turn the corner.

"Why are we walking so fast?" she says with a tinge of a whine in her voice.

"I wanted to get away from them."

"I'm hot and tired," she says, "and these sandals are giving me blisters."

I push her gently up against a wall and look into her eyes.

"You did just fine back there," I say softly. "But we can't afford to get sloppy now. You've only got one more day of playing Becca. Don't fuck it up."

That night, our last on the ship, we dine at a specialty Asian restaurant and share a bottle of champagne. While we eat, I'm aware that I'm somewhat anxious. I shake it off by telling myself it's normal given what's happened and what's coming.

After tomorrow, Lily's off the hook for a while. She doesn't have to do anything. It will be all me moving this story forward. I reach across the table for Lily's hand.

"You okay?" I say, looking deeply into her sultry brown eyes.

She nods. "I'll be glad when we get home and we can just be a normal couple."

I tilt my head and squint at her. "You know we won't be together for a while."

"I know."

"We can have no contact whatsoever. We agreed."

"I know, Andre. I'm not stupid. I'll wait until I hear from you."

"Because if you did contact me and anyone found out . . ."

"I won't."

CHAPTER SIXTEEN

On our last night on the ship, Lily and I were in bed by eleven. This morning, we're up bright and early. We're supposed to be off the ship by 10 a.m. That's when all the cleaning crews get into the vacant rooms. They need to prepare them for the new passengers boarding in Miami for the New Orleans portion of the trip.

As poor old Olive Walker had predicted, she sadly won't be making it to the Big Easy. Thankfully, I didn't have to kill her. That snoopy shrew expired on her own without requiring any help from me.

Our last test on the ship will be our final disembarkation. The steward took our bags late last night, so now all we've got left with us are our small carry-ons. We head down to the lower level, line up with the crowd and wait for our turn to leave the ship. As the crowd starts to move, many of the crew, now dressed in their fancy whites, stand at attention to say goodbye. Lily and I smile and nod as we quickly scan our cards one last time before racing down the gangplank.

When we get onto the shore, there's a charter bus waiting to take us to the airport. Arriving at the American Airlines terminal, I hand Becca's driver's license to Lily. She looks at the picture and replicates Becca's smile from the photo.

We get our boarding passes from the machine and go to check our luggage. I'm still a bundle of nerves. It's only after we board the plane and sit in our seats that I finally relax. In a few hours, we'll be landing at Kennedy Airport. Then, Phase Two begins.

As the plane takes off, I close my eyes and review all the things I'll need to do over the coming weeks. Phase One went extremely well. In my opinion, I'd give myself a B+. It would have been an A had it not been for those unfortunate pictures the old woman took. I also took away points for losing Becca's phone. But in the end, we made lemonade out of lemons, which is all that counts.

While on the ship, I had two things to accomplish. I had to dispose of Becca and then make my former wife's presence known on the ship throughout the remainder of the cruise. I achieved both of those things.

But starting tomorrow, everything changes. Phase Two will require a different type of performance. My role will be that of the anguished husband, so in love with his beautiful wife and so distraught that she's gone missing.

Our plane lands in Queens, and once we get our luggage, I summon an Uber. As I'd done before, I deliberately make small talk with the driver. The Uber takes us to my house in Connecticut. As far as Uber is concerned, they've just delivered Mr. and Mrs. Gifford to their home.

After the Uber drops us off, we get into my car, and I drive Lily to another town where she's left her old gray Subaru parked on the street. Before she gets out of my car, she climbs into the back seat and opens up her small overnight bag.

While I check my phone for messages, Lily removes the red wig, releasing her short platinum blonde bob. Then she changes into her street clothes, which are vastly different from the outfit she's been wearing.

Becca and Lily dress nothing alike. Lily's clothes are sexy and hug every curve of her extremely well-toned body. Becca, on the other hand, tended to wear more traditional clothing, boxier and sexless. Frankly, I'm very happy to see Lily back in her own clothes. I never liked Becca's "prim farm girl" style. Whoever told her that was sexy?

Lily holds up a hand mirror and flicks her hair into place using a little of her own spit. She leans over the back of the seat and kisses me on the neck. I'm amped up from everything that's happened and want to climb over the seat and take her right here, but I don't. There's too much at risk, and there's no time to waste.

"Come on," I say, pulling away from her. "We have to stay on schedule."

"You don't want one for the road?" she says with a wicked smile.

"Oh, I do. Believe me. But we can't. We've got to move."

I kiss her goodbye and remind her one last time that she should do and say nothing until I contact her.

"How many times are you going to tell me?" she says, boredom in her voice. "I got it."

"Remember, no calls, texts or anything through normal channels." I reach over to the glove compartment and open it. I fish out two cheap flip phones and give her one.

"My number is programmed into yours and yours is in mine," I say. "But you must wait until I reach out to you. That's when it will be safe. Clear?"

She makes an irritated sigh.

"We don't want to fuck this up after everything we've been through," I say, handing her Becca's handbag. "Take the bag and dump all the contents into different public garbage cans, then toss the empty bag into a dumpster."

Lily nods, but I see trepidation in her eyes. Things have suddenly become very real for her. I reach for her hand.

"It will all be okay. We're almost there, Lily. You've got to trust me."

She nods again, kisses me and gets out of the car. From here, she'll drive to her apartment in Astoria, Queens, that she shares with another girl. Her roommate thinks she went to visit her parents in Chicago.

Before she shuts the passenger-side car door, she leans inside the vehicle.

"I love you," she says.

"And I love you."

I watch her walk over and get into her car, waiting until she pulls out of the parking lot before I leave. I give her five minutes to put some distance between us, and then I go.

During the ten-minute trip back to my house, my mind is all over the place. There are so many tiny details that I have to remember. Forgetting even one could be disastrous for both Lily and me.

When I pull into my driveway, I remember that the last time I entered my garage, Becca was beside me, yammering about the cruise we were going on. I have a momentary pang of something and try to identify the feeling. It's regret. I've felt that before.

When I was a senior in college, I was in a fraternity. The freshman pledges were so whiny and willing to do anything I said just to get into the fraternity. I loved it. On the last night, we took them out in the woods, made them take off all their clothes and drink a bottle of vodka. We brought switches with us, made of thin smooth branches. The pledges were told to walk in single file between us as we whipped them with the switches. I had the same feeling of regret that night when it was over. I regretted not bringing a branch with sharp knots or thorns on it. That would have been so much more entertaining. It's the same way with Becca now. I wasted so many years married to a woman who was nothing but a burden. I should have gotten rid of her a long time ago. That's my regret.

After pulling into my garage, I close the door and lug both Becca's and my suitcases up two flights of stairs to our bedroom. Working fast, I take everything out of our bags, put all our clothes into the washing machine and turn it on. I don't want any of Lily's DNA popping up on Becca's things.

For a little added ambiance, I leave Becca's toiletry kit open on the bathroom vanity. On the bathroom counter, I place all the Beacon Star shampoos and soaps that Becca swiped that first day on the ship. Now it looks like she went on a cruise and came home.

As I take the now-empty bags to the hall closet, my stomach rumbles. I go down into the kitchen, heat up a frozen pizza, crack open one of my favorite craft beers and watch the news. At eleven, it's time to call it a night. If everything goes as planned, tomorrow will be an incredibly long day.

CHAPTER SEVENTEEN

In the morning, my alarm rings at 6 a.m. I groan and turn over, forgetting for a moment that Becca isn't here. It's only when my hand hits her empty pillow that the events of the past week flood back at me.

I open my eyes and stare at the empty place in our bed. Two strands of Becca's long red hair remain on her pillow. I'll leave them there so that the police will find them and use them as DNA samples. The day we were leaving for the cruise, Becca suggested we change the sheets to come home to fresh ones, but I pushed back. It was important that her DNA remain on them. It would be a critical component to proving that Becca had been in the house the night we came back from the cruise, that she had returned to Connecticut. In order to distract her, I did the only thing I could think of — I seduced her. After making love, there would even be more of her DNA on the sheets for the police to collect. More is better.

I turn off the alarm, get out of bed and head for the bathroom to shower and shave. Today has to look like a totally normal morning. I've got to be sharp and act like nothing's wrong when I get to the office. If anyone gets a whiff of something not being right, it could ruin everything.

I put on a pair of gray pants, a white t-shirt and a navy pullover sweater. Before heading down the stairs, I put one of Becca's lipsticks in my pocket. When I get into the kitchen, the automatic coffee pot has already brewed, and I pour myself a cup. I carefully take out Becca's favorite mug, which I had previously stashed in the back of a cabinet inside a plastic bag.

Before we left on our trip, I hid her mug right after she used it. Making sure not to touch the handle with her prints on it, I pour fresh coffee into that same mug. Next, I place a tissue over my lips and coat my tissue covered lips with Becca's pink lipstick. When I get it on good and thick, I place my mouth on the edge of Becca's mug to leave a light pink lip mark on the inside and outside of the rim. It looks perfect.

I toss the tissue into the toilet and flush before checking Becca's calendar, the one she has hanging inside the kitchen cabinet. I'm double-checking myself today. I don't want to make a careless mistake. There's too much riding on this. Measure twice, cut once, as they say. As I scan through her calendar, it's exactly as I remembered. Becca is supposed to do volunteer work at the local soup kitchen this morning. Obviously, she won't make it.

I leave to catch my regular train, the 7:49 train to New York City. It pulls into Grand Central Terminal. My office is on Madison Avenue about four blocks south of the train station. It's an easy walk.

I wave to the security guard in the lobby as I slide my ID through the scanner. The gates open and I cross the open marbled space and step onto the elevator. While waiting for the doors to close, Dave from Accounting gets on.

"Looking very tan, Andre," he says. "Been away?"

"Took my wife on a little tenth-anniversary cruise."

"Nice. Where'd you go?" he says, looking down at his phone. He's obviously not interested and just making small talk to be polite.

"We went to Orlando for a few days, then on the cruise, which ended in Miami."

"Sounds great," says Dave, his eyes still on his phone. "We had a long winter and a cold spring."

I nod as I get off the elevator and walk toward the far end of the floor. I share an office with another creative executive at the agency. Walking through my department, several of my colleagues wave and call out to me.

"How was the cruise, Andre?" shouts one.

"Great," I say. "We had a fantastic time. You should do it."

"Have a good vacay?" says another.

"It was amazing. My wife fell in love with Puerto Rico. She says she wants to learn Spanish now."

"Glad to have you back, Andre," says my assistant as she drops a large folder on my desk. "Artie's been all over me about this new business pitch next week. Sorry to do this to you since you just got back, but he wants the outline for the presentation by tomorrow."

I let out a sigh of exasperation, but it's *only* for effect. I already did the new business pitch outline before I took Becca on the cruise. I knew things would get crazy when I got back. It's how one responds to things during a crisis that counts. That's what separates winners from losers.

For the next hour, I get caught up on what went on in the office while I was away. Throughout the day, a stream of coworkers stop by my desk inquiring about my trip. They feign jealousy over Becca and I having ten days in warm weather. I tell various preplanned stories about our Caribbean adventures and show everyone pictures of Becca and me as well as other shots of Lily dressed as Becca. Nobody notices the dual women playing my wife.

Throughout the trip, I made sure all the photos were carefully shot from advantageous angles. All pictures of Lily were taken from the back or the side. I also made sure to always include prominent landmarks or a section of the ship in the background. As far as the people in my office can tell, Becca and I had an incredible trip.

By late afternoon, I feel really tired. It must be the stress getting to me. It's going to be a long night, so I run to the break room for a cup of coffee to keep me alert. Later, back at my desk, I clean up a few presentation issues and run some new ideas by my office mate.

While I'm trapped in an inane conversation with someone from the research department, the burner phone inside my jacket pocket rings. The research guy notices my iPhone lying silently on my desk and the shrill ringing coming from somewhere else. I smile weakly as I reach for the flip phone in my breast pocket, wondering who the hell is calling on this number.

It's Lily. What happened to our no-contact rule? She didn't even make it twenty-four hours.

I turn off the phone and mumble something about a robocall while casually mentioning that my iPhone isn't working.

"Damn thing keeps shutting off," I say. "I bought this cheap flip phone to use until I have time to get over to the Apple store."

The research guy nods, clearly not interested in my tech problems. At least now he's not wondering why I have a second phone — that could seem sketchy. The bigger question is, what do I do about Lily? She's not following the rules.

At five o'clock, I print out the pitch deck that Artie wants and hand it to my assistant. When the shit hits the fan tomorrow, and it will, I don't want Artie wondering if I can still do my job in the midst of my family crisis. As long as he has this deck, he'll be happy for a few weeks. By then, things with Becca should die down a little.

Before I leave to go home, I call my wife and leave her a message.

"Becs, it's me," I say, in the center of a crowd waiting for the elevator. "I'll be on the 5:30 train to New Haven. Hope you had a great day and got some rest. I'm still thinking about our cruise. See you soon, babe."

As I walk to Grand Central Terminal, I'm aware I have a new spring in my step. I stop in a shop to pick up a beer for the train ride home. I sip it slowly as the train leaves the station.

At seven, I pull my car into our driveway and walk in through the front door. Closing it behind me, I call out to my wife.

"Becs, I'm home. What's for dinner?"

CHAPTER EIGHTEEN

Locking the front door behind me, I'm aware my wife will not answer my query regarding the dinner menu. But if I'm going to pull this thing off, everything has to feel real to me. I'll go through all the motions as if it were really happening. I guess you'd call me a method actor.

"Becs," I shout again. "Are you here?"

I shrug when I hear no answer and go upstairs to change out of my work clothes. I tell myself Becca must be out shopping, with Stella or one of her other friends. By the time I come downstairs, it's nearly seven thirty. That's late for Becca to not be here without telling me she'd be out.

It's time for my first *concerned* outreach.

I text Becca several times, call her once and leave a message. I wait fifteen minutes, not expecting a response. In fact, if I got one, that would be alarming. The way I see it, if I believe it, the cops will believe it.

At 7:46, I text Stella.

Is Becs with you? Got home from work and she's not here. I texted her but they weren't delivered. My calls go straight to her voicemail??

Stella gets back to me right away.

I haven't talked to her today, figured she'd be tired. I left her a couple of messages. There's a 6:45 yoga class at the Y she sometimes takes. She's probably there. I'll text her.

I immediately respond to maintain control of the narrative I've crafted.

Becca's phone died on the cruise. She was using my phone to text you, remember? She was supposed to go get it fixed today or buy a new one. Don't know if she did.

That was the perfect opportunity to reinforce Becca's missing phone, in case anyone asks down the road. I text Stella again.

If it says the text wasn't delivered, does that mean her phone still isn't working?

Stella tells me she's not sure. She says she's going to send out a group text to a bunch of their mutual friends to see if anyone knows where Becca is. In the meantime, I get myself some cheese and crackers from the fridge and turn on the TV while I wait for the next phase to begin.

At 8:15, with no response from Becca, I call the YMCA looking for her and ask about the yoga class. The receptionist confirms that there *was* a class, but it ended at 8:00. Sounding a little frantic, I give her my name and number, beginning a neat little paper trail for later on.

I put myself into the mindset of a worried husband by pretending that my wife really *is* missing.

It's possible if Becca took a class that got out at eight, she could have stopped at the store on her way home. Maybe she's at the store?

I give it a little more time and text and call my wife again. This time the voice on my messages sounds more concerned.

When the cops eventually listen to all my messages, and they will, they'll hear my panic escalating.

At 9 p.m., I dig out Becca's Christmas card address book from her desk and call a couple of her other friends in town. No one has talked to her, but they all say they will put out the word.

At 9:20, Stella calls me.

"Is she home yet?" she says, clearly worried.

"No. I'm starting to get really freaked out, Stell. Where the hell could she be?" I sprinkle tones of anguish into my voice.

"I called the Y," says Stella, "and asked them to look on the class sign-up sheet to see if Becca had been there."

"And?"

"Andre, she wasn't in that class or any other class today."

"Shit," I say, now voicing real concern. "Where could she be? She's never done this before. Not in ten years."

"There's more," says Stella, now sounding very somber. "You know that Becca does a shift at the Community Pantry on Monday afternoons, unless she's not feeling well. I called the woman who runs the Pantry. Becca didn't show up today."

"What? Where is she, then? What's going on?" I force my voice to crack.

"Did you check the whole house carefully?" she says. "Maybe she fell somewhere. You know with her fibromyalgia sometimes her legs give out. You need to check the whole house again. Look in the basement and the attic. Maybe she was putting something away from the trip and had an attack or lost her balance."

"Stay on the phone with me, okay?" I say as I get up.

"Of course."

With Stella on the phone, I race down to the basement and move and turn over boxes, sticking my head into corners.

"She's not here, she's not in the basement," I report into the phone as I race up the stairs to the first floor.

"She's not in the office, the living room or kitchen. I'm going upstairs now," I shout as I slam a few doors.

Running up the stairs two at a time, I open every closet in all three bedrooms. I even look under the beds. Like I said, if I believe it, the cops will believe it.

"She's not up here, Stell," I say, out of breath.

"Check the attic."

As much as I like to give an authentic performance, I'm totally winded. I look at the steep attic steps and decide to skip this part of the charade.

Standing on the bottom step, I pretend to walk up the stairs by stamping my feet in place. I wait a beat.

"She's not in the attic, Stell," I say, still breathing hard.

"You need to check outside the house," says Stella.

"Right. I'll get a flashlight."

I turn on the outside lights, which illuminate a good portion of our property. Throwing on a jacket, I flip on the flashlight and walk out into my backyard. Combing around the base of the house, I shine the light into all the bushes, giving Stella a blow-by-blow as I go. Once I come full circle on the house, I move toward the outer portions of the yard, shining my light into every nook and cranny.

"She's not out here," I say to Stella. "Something's happened to her. I can feel it. Something's very wrong."

"Don't panic," says Stella. "Maybe her car broke down, and without her phone, she had no way to contact you."

"Her car. Oh, my God. I didn't check the garage," I say as I run toward the garage door.

"Was her car in the garage when you came home?" says Stella.

"I don't know. I didn't come in through the garage. I parked out front," I say while punching in the code to open the garage door. As it slowly goes up, I see the back of Becca's blue Honda inside.

"Stell," I whisper for effect as I put my hand on the hood. "Her car is here and it's cold. What does this mean?"

"Her car is in the garage? Oh, my God. We should call the police."

Now Stella's freaking out, which is ideal. I keep pace with her mood and match her hysteria to play my part properly. Hers is genuine. Mine isn't.

"There's no place she could walk to from your house," she says, getting more upset. "It's dark out now. What if she went for a walk and fell and couldn't get up? She could be lying in the woods somewhere."

"Becca never goes for walks because of her joints," I say.

"Sometimes she does. She's been feeling better lately. She told me she went for a walk a few days before you left on your trip. How did she seem on the cruise?"

"She was great," I say. "None of this makes any sense."

"I know the walking loop she sometimes takes," says Stella. "I'll be at your house in ten minutes and we can go look for her together. Maybe she went for a walk and got too tired and then couldn't make it back."

CHAPTER NINETEEN

Waiting for Stella to arrive, I pull out a few more flashlights and load them with fresh batteries. As soon as Stella pulls into the driveway, I run outside and jump into her car. I hand her a flashlight, and the two of us drive to the loop that Becca likes to walk.

It's a three-mile circle. We drive very slowly so we don't miss anything. It takes us thirty minutes to cover the whole loop. Not surprisingly, we don't find her. When we pull back into my driveway, it's after ten.

"I'm calling the police," I say, my voice catching as we get out of the car. Blinking several times as if I'm trying to hold back tears, I sniffle. Stella notices and rubs my back.

"Don't worry. We'll find her," she says.

As soon as we get inside, I call the Woodmere Police Department and explain to the officer that my wife is missing. Ten minutes later, a patrol car with lights flashing pulls into the circular driveway in front of my house.

A young male cop is about to knock on my front door when I pull it open. I take him into the kitchen where Stella's waiting.

"Becca and I had coffee together this morning. Our mugs are still here on the counter." I point to the one with her lipstick and prints on it. "Then I left for work and we didn't talk all day."

"Do you normally communicate with your wife during the workday, Mr. Gifford?" says the officer.

"Only if there's a reason. We were on vacation last week for our tenth anniversary. We got home last night. This was my first day back at work and I was swamped. Becca wasn't expecting to hear from me."

The cop nods and makes a note. "When did you first realize something was wrong?"

"I got home tonight at seven, my normal time, and my wife wasn't here."

"And she's usually here when you get home?"

"Always," I say. "I tried calling and texting her, but her phone died while we were on the cruise. She was supposed to go have it fixed today. I don't know if she did or if her phone is even working."

The cop looks at Stella. "And you are?"

"Becca's best friend, Stella McCrystal. Andre called me when he couldn't find her. I contacted a bunch of our friends. No one's seen or heard from her. She didn't show up for her volunteer shift at the Community Pantry today. She always goes unless she's not feeling well."

The cop nods as he bites his bottom lip.

"Something's happened to her, officer," I say, trying to emote extreme distress. "We've got to find her. She could be hurt. Something else you should know, Becca isn't well. She's got fibromyalgia and can become very weak, and her balance can be off."

"Mr. Gifford, from what you've told me, your wife has technically been missing for a few hours. Could she have skipped her volunteer work to get her phone fixed? The Apple store in the mall is open until nine o'clock and that place can take hours to get anything done."

"Tell him about the car," says Stella, chewing on her thumb.

"Right," I say. "My wife's car is still in the garage, so she couldn't be at the mall."

"I see," says the officer, trying to maintain calm, but I can read him. He knows something's wrong. "Do you have any reason to believe that your wife might hurt herself?"

Interesting. I never considered suicide as a possible storyline when I was planning this. But I like the idea. Maybe Becca hurt herself. It would certainly take the onus off me. Thank you, Officer Krupke, for the creative suggestion.

"Becca would never hurt herself," says Stella emphatically. "We've been best friends since we were freshmen in college. She's got some physical pain she deals with, but her head is on totally straight."

The cop looks over at me for validation.

"She's right," I say. "Becca is a very grounded person."

"To be honest, we don't normally look for an adult who's only been missing for a few hours," says the officer. "You can imagine if we did, that's all we'd be doing. People go off to do benign things and forget to tell anyone all the time. But I do understand your concern given your wife's other health issues. I'll call it in."

The cop talks to his commander. After they finish, he explains that they can't officially start looking for a mentally competent adult until they've been gone for at least twenty-four hours. I cover my face with my hands.

"Where could she be?" I say through my fingers.

The officer asks for a picture. I pull a framed photo of Becca from a shelf in the kitchen and hand it to him.

"We'll do everything we can to help find her," says the officer, looking at the photo. "We'll alert our patrols so they can keep an eye out for a woman fitting your wife's description. More often than not, the people turn up. Try not to worry."

After the policeman leaves, Stella makes a few more calls. No one has seen or heard from Becca, nor will they. She's lying at the bottom of the Atlantic Ocean or inside the belly of one very happy fish.

CHAPTER TWENTY

Stella leaves to go home to walk her dog. She and I text back and forth until nearly two in the morning. We try to come up with ideas of where Becca might be. At one point, I ask her if Becca has a boyfriend.

"No. Of course not," she says emphatically. "Becs loves you, Andre. Believe me, if she had a boyfriend, I'd know about it."

"There are so many terrifying thoughts running through my mind right now. If there was another man, at least then I'd know she's safe."

It's nearly 3 a.m. when Stella tells me she needs to get a few hours of sleep, which finally lets me off the hook. Using my burner phone, I call Lily to let her know that everything has begun according to plan. I also remind her that there can be no more communication between us for some time.

"Why did you call me at the office today?" I ask her.

"I wanted to see if the phone worked and to find out how everything was going."

"We agreed, no calls. I'll reach out to you when it's safe."

We talk for a few more minutes. After I hang up, I lean back in my spacious king-size bed and take a sip of bourbon from a Waterford crystal glass we received as a wedding gift. The irony hasn't escaped me.

I like having this room to myself. I can spread out without Becca's legs dangling every which way. She used to sleep with orthopedic pillows and other apparatuses. It made the bed awfully crowded. Also, I'll sleep better tonight without constantly being disturbed by her getting up and going to the bathroom all night.

It's nearly 3:20 a.m., and I need some sleep if I'm going to play the desperate husband tomorrow. From here on, I'll be under a microscope. There can be no mistakes.

The next morning I'm awakened by a 7 a.m. call from Stella. She wants to know if I've heard anything from the police or Becca.

When I tell her no, she starts to cry. I tell her I'm about to call the police again and that I'll keep her in the loop. Making good on my promise, I log in a call to the Woodmere PD at 7:15 a.m. No one besides the operator is available to speak to me. I'm assured that someone will get back to me shortly. Fine with me, gives me time to make some eggs and have a cup of coffee.

After I text Stella to let her know I've called, I head downstairs and make myself a pot of coffee. I pull out all the stops today and grind the beans, something I don't often take the time to do. But today feels kind of special, and I'm craving a really tasty cup of joe.

While the coffee's brewing, I scramble up a couple of eggs with some buttered toast. Sitting down at the kitchen table to enjoy my breakfast, I call my assistant at the office. She won't be in yet as it's only 8:20. I leave a message.

"Hey, it's Andre," I say in a really flat, sad voice that makes me sound like I'm on the brink. "I've got a family emergency, and I won't be in today. I don't know when I'll be in, actually. I'll try and call you tomorrow. Please let everyone know. Say a prayer for us."

I disconnect the call feeling rather proud about that last call for prayers. It just came to me suddenly. I thought it set the tone nicely while also being a little provocative. I can only imagine the massive tongue-wagging that will be going on in my office today. My assistant is a nice woman, but she's a gossip. She won't keep my little soundbite about prayers to herself, that's for sure. The wild speculation in my office over the next eight hours regarding my "family emergency" will be nothing short of epic.

I finish my eggs and toast and top up my coffee before calling the police again. They said they'd call me back, but I think a really frantic husband with a missing wife would be calling them nonstop. So, I play the part.

I put my dishes in the dishwasher and water the plants by the kitchen window. It's 9:01 a.m. when I call the police again. I'm informed that a detective is on the way to my house. I run upstairs and throw on a pair of jeans and a tee shirt. Other than flossing and brushing my teeth, I do no other grooming. That would seem wrong given the situation, though I do like to take care of my gums. But the other stuff, I don't think one combs one's hair or shaves when one's wife has disappeared.

I'm spitting out my toothpaste into the bathroom sink when the doorbell rings downstairs. I rub my eyes hard to make them look red, like I've been crying, before I race down the steps. Slightly out of breath, I fling open the front door.

A fifty-something man with a full head of salt-and-pepper hair, wearing a light blue button-down shirt and a navy suit jacket stands in front of me.

"Mr. Gifford?" says the man. "I'm Detective Bill Contessa with the Woodmere PD. May I come in?"

I whip a tissue from my pocket and blow my nose before letting him in. Walking into the kitchen, I ask if he's heard anything about Becca. We sit down at the kitchen table.

Contessa sits across from me, leans forward and looks me in the eyes. For some reason, he reminds me of a lion about to devour a small animal. I feel myself squirming inside but maintain my composure outside. I can tell already that this cop is going to be a thorn in my side. He's obviously been around the block a few times and doesn't suffer fools. Woodmere is a small town, and most of the police here are small-town cops. They mainly trade in petty thefts and domestic disputes. But I detect a strong New York City accent from Contessa. I suspect he started out with the NYPD and then moved up here for a quieter lifestyle. I make a mental note to be careful around him.

"I'm afraid we've received no reports of your wife at this time," says Contessa. "You do understand that it's department policy not to deploy resources when an adult is missing for less than twenty-four hours."

"I've been told," I say, tears in my eyes. "But this is different. My wife doesn't work, Detective. She's not well. Becca has fibromyalgia and sometimes she can't even get out of bed. On good days, she might go to the market or get her hair cut or maybe take a yoga class. But she never goes far and wouldn't take off without letting me know. This is totally out of character for her. Something's happened."

Contessa leans in closer, and I feel myself sitting back to create some distance between us.

"What exactly do you think could have happened to your wife, Mr. Gifford?" he says, peering at me.

"Please, call me Andre," I say, hoping to get on more familiar ground with this man. "I only know that Becca wouldn't have gone anywhere on her own without her car. It's not who she is. You've got to help me find her. If she's hurt, every minute we wait might put her life in jeopardy."

"I can understand your concern. Let's start with some details and get a basic timeline," says the detective. "Tell me about her movements over the last few days."

I walk him very briefly through our cruise itinerary, not wanting to draw too much attention to the trip. I do make sure to mention that Becca was happy and feeling pretty good.

"And you both got home two nights ago, correct?" says the detective.

"Correct," I say, my voice cracking again. "We were exhausted from traveling and went to bed as soon as we got home. Yesterday morning, we got up, had coffee together. Then I kissed her goodbye and went into the city for work."

I explain that Becca's phone wasn't working and that she was supposed to go to the Apple store, I think, and get it fixed yesterday.

"So as far as you know, she doesn't have a working phone at the moment?" says Contessa. "I think we start there. Has anyone contacted the store to see if she turned up?"

I shake my head as Contessa makes a note on his phone.

"I presume you've contacted all of her friends?" he says.

I nod.

"Was she upset about anything?" he says.

"No," I say. "We had just returned from this amazing trip. We were both so happy."

"You mind if I take a look around the house?" he says.

"Please," I say, wringing my hands. "Whatever you need to do. I just want to find her."

"Does your wife have a handbag or purse that she uses?"

"She's got a big black leather bag," I say. "I've looked for it, but it's not here."

I lead the detective upstairs to our bedroom.

"What about her luggage?" he says, sticking his head inside our closet.

"I didn't think to check that." I paint my face with self-recrimination as I lead him to the hall closet where we keep our bags.

The detective's question has given me an idea, so I go off-script. My original plan was that Becca was missing due to a possible abduction or an accident. It never occurred to me to position it as either a suicide or that she left of her own accord, hence the missing purse and luggage. If Becca intentionally left, it would take the emphasis off a violent crime and diminish intense police scrutiny. *I'm feeling it.*

I open the hall closet with Contessa right behind me and show him our luggage. My black wheelie bag and Becca's blue one stand side by side. At least they'll be mates for life.

I point to them. "Both of our bags are still here."

I'm about to close the closet door when I make a sudden plot change decision and pretend to have an epiphany. "Wait a second. Becca also has a brown canvas weekend bag. It's not here. It was definitely in here when I put the luggage away after we got home."

My wife has never owned a brown weekend bag. But not even Stella would know if that was true or not, so I run with it.

Detective Contessa's steely eyes immediately lock onto mine.

"Have you and your wife had any problems recently, Andre?"

CHAPTER TWENTY-ONE

As the detective stares me down in the upstairs hallway, he peppers me with questions about the state of my marriage. Do I tell him that I married a vivacious, outgoing woman who got some mysterious hokey illness, quit her job and took to her bed for years? And that she expected me to take care of her forever, not to mention losing her entire salary and benefits?

Once Becca curled into a ball, I had to find relationships outside of my marriage to survive. Divorce was out of the question — financial suicide. I had to come up with an alternative plan.

Contessa clears his throat, waiting for my reply.

"You're asking if Becca and I have problems?" I say to the detective standing over me like a wolverine over a T-bone. "We have no significant problems. Like all couples, we have the occasional disagreement. But everyone has those, don't they?"

"There's been nothing of note recently that might have upset her?"

I shake my head.

"What was your wife's state of mind for the last few weeks?" he says.

I hold my right index finger in the air as I reach for the phone in my pocket with my left hand.

"A picture is worth a thousand words," I say as I scroll through photos on my phone. I show him a few selfies that Becca and I took on the deck of the ship and several others of the two of us kissing or embracing.

"These were taken a few days ago during our cruise," I say, pointing at picture after picture of my smiling, and seemingly happy, wife. "Does she look like she's upset or depressed? We were having the time of our lives. Please, you've got to find her. A long time ago, she had a seizure. It was only once but . . . I don't know if she has any of her medication with her."

"We'll distribute the information you provided to all the police departments countywide," says the detective.

Contessa spends another half-hour poking around my house, garage and yard before he finally leaves. His parting words: "If she's not back by tonight, give us a call."

Minutes later, I hear the gravel rustle on the driveway in front of the house. Stella's red SUV is pulling in. She jumps out of the driver's side holding a paper bag over her head to protect herself from the light rain that just started.

I open the front door, and she runs in and shakes herself off.

"Have you heard anything?" she says, brushing the water droplets off her sleeves.

Her eyes are red, and I wonder if she's sick and contagious. Getting the flu is the last thing I need right now. I'm about to ask her if she's not feeling well when I realize Stella's not sick. She's been crying. Her best friend disappeared. Duh.

"No," I say as we move into the kitchen, "I haven't heard anything more." I put the kettle on, thinking I should offer her some tea. "A detective was just here. They keep saying they can't do anything until Becca's been missing for twenty-four hours."

"That's bullshit," says Stella as she sits on a counter stool. "You and I know Becca better than anyone. She'd never take off like that on her own. If she was going to do something crazy, she would have run it by me first. That's how we roll."

"Agreed," I say, about to pour her some tea, which she refuses. "The detective had a few different theories."

"Like what?"

"When I was taking him through the house, we noticed that in addition to Becca's handbag being gone, her overnight bag was also missing. The detective insinuated that she may have left on her own accord." I grab a tissue and blow my nose. "But here's the thing. How would she have traveled to another location? Her car is still in the garage."

"She could have gone out for a walk or met someone on the street when she went to get the mail?"

"Becca wouldn't take her overnight bag to get the mail," I say.

Stella sighs, buries her head in her hands and groans.

"You sure her overnight bag isn't somewhere else in the house?" she says.

I shake my head as I continue to weave my fabricated tale. "Becca kept the bag in the same closet where we keep all the luggage. It's not there now."

Stella gets up and moves around the kitchen as I pour milk into my tea. I go to the cabinet to get some cookies but stop myself. A distraught husband with a missing — possibly dead — wife wouldn't be able to eat. Reluctantly, I close the cabinet.

Stella turns and faces me.

"Last month, Becs told me that she was cleaning out the house. She said she took a bunch of stuff down to the Goodwill store in town. Maybe she donated the overnight bag?"

She smiles triumphantly as if she's solved an incredible riddle.

"I guess it's possible, but if that's the case," I say, "that means she *didn't* go off on her own. It would mean that someone took her. Either way, it's not good news."

The victorious smile fades from Stella's lips. "You're right," she says, her voice catching.

We kick around a few other possibilities, but nothing adds up. Finally, Stella volunteers to drive down to the Goodwill shop and find out if the overnight bag I invented had been donated. I stay at home to make more phone calls and to "be here, in case Becca comes home."

Thirty minutes later, Stella calls me. There's no record of an overnight bag in the Goodwill donations ledger book from the items Becca had donated. It's a dead end, as I knew it would be.

Hours later, after calling half the stores in town asking about my missing wife, I notice it's already 6 p.m. Becca's now officially been missing for about twenty-four hours. I leave a message for Detective Contessa alerting him to that fact. I follow that call with another to Becca's mother, Martha, in Philadelphia. Her mom needs to be made aware that her daughter's missing. It's only fair.

Becca's mother and I have never totally gelled. We're cordial but have little in common. While I explain what's happened, she starts to cry. I attempt to calm her fears. She says she and her husband Ed, Becca's stepfather, will drive up to Connecticut tonight.

That's the last thing I need.

"It's late already, Martha, and Becca may still turn up tonight," I say. "Why don't you come in the morning if she's still not home."

After a little back and forth and promises from me that I'll call if anything happens, no matter how late, Martha agrees to wait until tomorrow.

While I was on the cruise, I sent Martha several "happy couple" photos of Becs and me. Before Becca went for her final evening swim, I had her pose with her hat and sunglasses both on and off. I took her picture with her shawl over her shoulders and a couple more in the cabin wearing a Beacon Star white spa bathrobe.

I even had Becca change outfits and go out and pose on the balcony a few times. She thought it was all silly and fun, like she was some kind of a supermodel on a yacht. I put on a faux Italian accent and pretended I was an international fashion photographer and she was my muse. I got enough pictures to make it look like they were taken over the course of a week. Mission accomplished.

I also texted Martha a number of times during the cruise pretending to be Becca. I even sent her a message from Becca on the night we supposedly returned home to Connecticut saying we had a great trip.

Becca's mother has no reason to suspect me of anything. As far as she knows, I just took her baby on an amazing tenth-anniversary cruise. Ironically, after such a nice gesture on my part, it now looks like her daughter may have run off and left me.

CHAPTER TWENTY-TWO

Another day passes. Becca is officially missing for forty-eight hours. Now the cops have finally taken things seriously and have sprung into action. Detective Contessa comes back to the house with four patrolmen and they scour both inside and outside the property for clues. They even move Becca's car out of the garage and give it a forensic once-over.

Look all you want. Nothing's going to turn up in Connecticut, and nothing ever will. My wife is at least a thousand miles south of here.

At this point, I'm feeling pretty good about the whole thing. The cops are looking in all the wrong places and not paying too much attention to me. I may have actually figured out how to commit the perfect murder. It's a shame I can't brag about it.

The police put out an APB to all of Fairfield County, and they assure me that they're doing everything possible to find my wife. Periodically, I put my acting skills to the test by launching mini-breakdowns, which often include sobbing uncontrollably. Sometimes I flip the switch and get pissed off, ranting about not enough being done to find her. I like to mix it up for a little variety.

Today is day three of the Rebecca Gifford missing-person show. Stella's here and has been camping out in my house since the first day, leaving only occasionally to go home to walk and feed her dog and sleep. Becca's mother, Martha, and her insufferable know-it-all husband Ed arrived here from Philly this afternoon.

Ed and Martha are my wife's only living relatives. Due to the police presence at my house, and the fact that Ed and I can barely be in the same room with each other, they're thankfully staying at a nearby Holiday Inn.

Naturally, I protested when they told me they had checked into a hotel. I was assured they were very comfortable there and that it was better they stayed out of the way. That's true. The last thing I need is the two of them hanging around here weeping and carrying on.

"I don't understand how someone can vanish into thin air," I say to my mother-in-law and Ed while sitting in our living room. I force tears into my eyes. "Becca and I had such an amazing trip and were both so happy. We made so many plans for the future. The last thing I did for her was pour her coffee that morning before I left."

I look over at Martha to see if she's buying what I'm selling. My mind wanders, and it strikes me that for an older woman, Martha's fairly attractive. Her short, white, closely cropped spiky hair makes her look younger. And her twinkly blue eyes light up when she smiles. I've seen pictures of my mother-in-law from when she was young. I would have done her.

Martha walks over and sits on the couch next to me. She's not smiling today, and there are tears in her blue eyes when I look up at her.

"Becca told me how you always put out her coffee cup in the morning," says Martha, dabbing her eyes. "She loved that you did that. Made her feel special."

"She *is* special," I say, biting my lower lip. "Let's not use the past tense. We're going to find her. We have to."

Martha gets flustered. "Of course. I just wanted you to know how grateful I am for the way you cared for her, especially when she had her flare-ups."

"That last morning before I went to work, I called up the stairs and told her that her coffee was ready and that I loved her."

Martha nods as a tiny tear trickles down her cheek.

"You know what the last thing she said to me was?" I conjure up more of my own tears. "She shouted from upstairs and said—" I pause here and swallow for dramatic effect "—'I love you, babe, even more today than the day we got married.'"

As expected, Martha loses it and starts sobbing. To keep up with her, I begin bawling — tears, snot, dribble — the works. When I lose it, my mother-in-law puts her arm around my shoulders to comfort me.

Ed, on the other hand, sitting across the room in an armchair, stares at me. After my riveting performance, I think I deserve a little more than that. *How about offering me a little sympathy, Ed? My wife of ten years is missing and might be dead, you asshole.*

As Martha rubs my back, I try to compose myself.

"That conversation on the stairs was the last time I heard Becca's voice. And you know what really gets me, Martha?" I say, deliberately pausing and turning on the waterworks again. "When I got home that night, her coffee cup was still on the counter and her lipstick was on the rim. It was like she left me a kiss as her last message to me."

At this point, I go into a full-fledged crying jag. We're talking an Oscar-level performance here.

"Pull yourself together, Andre," says Ed. "This is no time to fall to pieces. We all have to stay strong and focused if we're going to help find Becca."

I wipe my eyes with the palms of my hands and nod.

"You're right," I say as I stand. "I'm sorry. The whole thing is so profoundly painful. It's like someone cut my heart out of my chest."

Martha touches my arm. "I understand," she says. "It's awful for us, too. I cried the entire drive up here from Philadelphia. Becca's my only baby. But Ed's right. We need to stay calm and mobilize. I promise you we're going to find my daughter. There's no time for tears now. We need to act."

Ed leans forward in his chair, puts his hands on his thighs and looks at me.

"Refresh me on everything that's happened so far," he says. "Did the police find any evidence of a break-in or anything tampered with here at the house?"

"Nothing," I say, shaking my head. "All the windows and doors were intact. I think they even dusted for prints on the outsides of the windows, just to be sure."

Ed gets up and starts walking the floor, reciting the particulars of the case and the possible places Becca could be. I'm only half-listening as he makes ludicrous suppositions and draws idiotic conclusions not based on reality. From the way he's carrying on, you'd think he's a master detective like Poirot or Sherlock Holmes. He thinks because he watches cop shows all the time that he's a criminal justice savant.

"The way I see it, there are a limited number of scenarios we should examine," says Ed, his back to us as he stands in front of the living room window. "The first one is that Becca left the house of her own free will. Since her car was still in the garage, that would mean she would have been on foot or got a ride."

Thank you for that, Captain Obvious.

"If she was walking, where could she have been going from here? Did she go out for exercise with no specific destination, or was she going to someplace in particular?"

I decide to play along because I'm bored, and it could be amusing.

"There are a lot of thick wooded sections in this part of town," I say, shifting into a mild panic mode for this part of the story. "She could have gone for a walk in the woods and had a seizure. What if she fell and is lying somewhere outside, deep in the woods, hurt."

"We should organize a community group to scour all the nearby wooded areas," says Martha. "We can't leave her out there alone."

"I think the police are searching the woods right now," says Stella, walking in through the back door. "One of the cops told me they were going to do that today. But we could certainly get some neighbors to help. Let me make some phone calls."

The last thing in the world I feel like doing on this cold, damp spring day is tramping around in the muddy woods.

"Wouldn't we get in the way of the police?" I say.

"I'll call Contessa and see what he thinks," says Stella, walking out of the room and into the kitchen.

"Now, scenario number two," says Ed, clearly wanting his spotlight back, "is that Becca willingly left with someone. One of the officers said they were looking into the possibility that someone picked her up in their car."

"But who?" I say with a touch of anger in my voice. "We've been in communication with all of Becca's friends. She would have told me if she was doing something unusual that day. Besides, she was supposed to work at the Community Pantry, remember? She never showed up."

The doorbell rings. Stella walks into the room with Detective Contessa behind her. As soon as I see him, I start the waterworks up.

"Have you found anything?" I stand, my face full of hope as I wipe my nose with my sleeve.

Contessa grimly shakes his head. "Mr. Gifford, we'd like you to come down to the police station so we can properly interview you."

"Why can't you do it here?" I say. "I'm with my family."

"It would be better if you come down to the station," he says firmly. "We'll have the whole team sitting in there."

I look squarely at him. "If you think it will help find my wife, I'll do whatever it takes to bring her home."

As I get my things together to go to the police station, I overhear Stella talking to the detective.

"All I know is Becca wouldn't go out for the whole day without a phone," she says. "Getting her phone replaced would have been her first priority. I think somebody took her against her will."

CHAPTER TWENTY-THREE

It's been three weeks since my wife disappeared, and there are still no new leads. I've been interrogated by the police six times and given them my DNA. I've also hired a lawyer, mainly to help with the media but also to protect myself. My attorney has advised me not to take a polygraph test.

"Polygraphs aren't admissible in court," says Seth Shapiro, Esq. "Still, it's not worth having it come back to bite you or give the police any extra ammo to use against you. Only give them your DNA and we'll be done with it."

Almost a month into the search, I'm feeling very good about the lack of any developments or any meaningful leads coming to light. It means the cops have nothing. If they were able to poke holes in my story, it would have already happened.

I gave the police several pictures of Becca, which they've plastered all over the local Connecticut news. Stella, Martha and a bunch of people from Woodmere have stapled plastic-covered pictures of my wife to telephone poles all over the county. The police tell me they've received a lot of tips. Supposedly, there have been numerous Rebecca Gifford sightings, which is obviously impossible. The cops told us they followed up on all the calls, but nothing checked out.

Contessa comes back to talk to me again today. He wants to know more about my wife's health. I walk him through Becca's fibromyalgia issues, all of which I'm painfully familiar with.

"She does get depressed from time to time," I say, "but she's not suicidal, if that's what you're driving at."

"You said sometimes she can't get out of bed for days," says Contessa. "Did you ever consider hospitalizing her?"

"No. I don't think she would have hurt herself," I say, adding an ever-so-slight amount of doubt into my voice. I try to throw just enough in to make the cop wonder.

The suicide angle keeps popping up. I can't believe I never thought of that when I was manifesting on ways to get rid of her. My rationale on why Becca disappeared was much more limited in scope. All these other possibilities that have been introduced — like Becca running off with a boyfriend or taking her own life — only makes the case murkier. This unexpected suicide development is a win-win, as it leads the cops further away from me and the truth.

I can tell the police are frustrated. They've searched everywhere. They have a thirty-five-year-old missing woman and absolutely no clues to follow up on. They're literally grasping at straws. The best part is, they aren't even talking about the cruise or looking for her in any other part of the country. Like I said, it's the perfect murder.

To be fair, Contessa did contact the cruise ship. But according to him, everything checked out. The Beacon Star reported that their logs showed that a Rebecca Gifford boarded in Port Canaveral, Florida, and got on and off the ship every day during the cruise. The records also established that we dined together in the restaurants on the ship and that Becca even got a massage twice. That was actually Lily, but they don't know that.

According to Detective Contessa, who shared all this with me, American Airlines confirmed that Andre and Rebecca Gifford flew home to Kennedy Airport from Miami.

Apparently, Kennedy Airport security supplied video of Becca and I leaving the terminal in Queens when we got our Uber. And the Uber driver confirms that both of us were in his vehicle when he dropped us at home.

As far as the police are concerned, my wife's disappearance happened the day after she returned to Connecticut.

* * *

We've hit the four-week mark since Becca went missing. Since the beginning, my role is of the grieving and desperate husband. My lawyer, Shapiro, has helped me and my in-laws get access to local media. Martha, Ed, Stella and I have all been on the local news shows, talking to reporters and pleading for Becca to come back. We're also putting together a reward for any information leading to my wife's safe return. Despite all our efforts, not a single thing has emerged pointing to her whereabouts.

Friends and neighbors here in Woodmere have been dropping off enough food to feed a stadium full of people. We end up throwing most of it away. There's only so much the three of us — four, if you count Stella — can eat.

As the days go on, interest in our story wanes. I make my obligatory phone call to the police every day, begging them for answers. They never have any, and they never will. After a while, the local news outlets get bored with the story because there's nothing new to report. Even the public seems to be losing interest.

* * *

Five weeks after Becca's "sudden departure" Ed announces that he has to go back to Philly. "At least for a while," he says.

"My plumbing business is going down the tubes," says Ed as he explains to me why he's abandoning his missing stepdaughter. "Also, Martha's a mess. She has some heart issues, as you know. She needs to get home and rest for a while. This has been very stressful for her."

I plaster a sad, hopeless expression on my face and walk over to this man I loathe and put my hand on his shoulder.

"Ed, you and Martha have been my rocks," I say with so much heart that I almost believe it myself. "I couldn't have made it through these weeks without you two. I completely understand."

He nods. We're having a moment. At least, he is.

"We can be back up here in three hours if anything happens," he says. "You going to be all right? Maybe someone in your family can come stay with you?"

Yeah, that's not going to happen, Ed.

My father and I haven't spoken in ten years. The last time I saw him was at my and Becca's wedding. As usual, he got loaded. It wasn't because he was extremely drunk at our wedding that ended it between us. Lots of people drink at weddings. The tipping point for me was while our guests were doing the Hokey Pokey, my father pulled his pants down on the dance floor, undershorts included. That was a bridge too far even for me.

And my only sister? She's cut from the same cloth as Dad, only her drug of choice is rampant, aggressive narcissism. I can't be in the same room with her for more than five minutes. So no, I will not be enlisting the support of my family.

CHAPTER TWENTY-FOUR

Standing in front of my house as Martha and Ed pull out of my driveway, I can see Martha weeping as she gives me one last anemic wave. Now that they're gone, all I want to do is kick back, have a vodka martini and watch a ball game. For five weeks, everything has been about Becca. I haven't had a minute to myself. Like Martha, I need a little "me" time.

After I came back into the house, I shut the front door and head straight for the liquor cabinet. Yeah, it's only midafternoon, but if anyone deserves a drink right now, it's me. I stick a martini glass in the freezer to get it nice and cold, then pull a jar of olives out of the fridge. I'm about to reach for the cocktail shaker when I hear my back door open and close.

"Andre?"

Shit. I forgot about Stella. I shove the shaker back into the cabinet, let out a sigh and put on a beleaguered face.

"Was that Ed and Martha I saw leaving just now?" she says. "I thought I saw Ed's car pass me. Will they be back for dinner?"

I explain the situation with my in-laws and Stella nods.

"So, what's our next move?" she says. "I was thinking maybe we should hire a private investigator."

Oh, for fuck's sake. Is she ever going to let this go? We've already invested five weeks in this futile project.

I make my face serious and sad while preparing my tear ducts for action if needed.

"Our next move is that we keep looking for Becca. We never stop, no matter what. But I also think we need a little normalcy in our lives," I say. "We can't go at this pace indefinitely. That's what happened to Martha and Ed. They were emotionally exhausted."

"But Becca's still out there somewhere," says Stella. "She could be hurt."

"And we're going to bring her home. You've been so amazing, Stell. But I've been out of work for five weeks, and they're only going to pay me for so long. There's been so many expenses, too. I feel like a loose balloon in the wind. I need some structure. I'm not sleeping. I'll be honest. I'm starting to lose it, Stell."

My wife's best friend rushes over, wraps her arms around me and holds me for a long time. For a second, I wonder if she has romantic intentions. Stella's not unattractive. I don't move, but as she hugs me, I feel my nether regions come to life. I pull away immediately and cross to the other side of the room with my back to her, so I can recover.

"What if the theory that Becca took off on her own is the right one?" I say. "What if she left me?"

"I don't believe it. She wouldn't do that."

"I'm still going to keep looking for her, but," I say as I begin to weep, "I'm falling apart, Stell."

As soon as she hears my voice crack, she softens and goes into comforting mode again.

"Of course you are, you poor thing," she says, taking my arm and moving us both over to the couch. "Maybe you should go back to work, Andre. We can still keep things moving along with the police. It doesn't help Becs for you to sit around the house all day suffering."

A week and a half later on a Monday, seven weeks after my wife disappeared, I walk into my office on Madison Avenue.

I get off the elevator onto our floor and notice the looks from my coworkers. Pity vibes are bouncing off the walls like a meteor shower as people flash encouraging smiles in my direction. I press my lips together and nod at various well-wishers as I make my way to my office. There's a note of support on my desk from the guy who shares my office. He's going to be out all week on a business trip. That's welcome news. Sitting at my desk, I swivel my chair around to look out the window at the New York City skyline.

Moments later, my assistant enters my office.

"How are you doing, Andre?" she says softly.

Before I spin around, I glance up at the window to check my reflection. I want to be sure my face looks appropriately sad before I turn.

"I'm okay," I say as I swivel around, a tear landing on my right cheek.

She's holding a cup of steaming coffee.

"I thought you could use this," she says as she hands it to me. "Anything you need, you call me. Okay?"

Throughout the day, my colleagues drop by my office to give me their sympathy and support. In the later part of the afternoon, one of the senior partners stops by and closes my office door.

"Glad to have you back, Andre. It's a helluva thing you've been through. We've missed you and your creative talents," he says. "Are you sure you're ready to be back at work? You've had a tough time."

"I can't sit at home any longer. It doesn't bring Becca back, and I'm losing my mind. I need to keep busy. Work is the best thing for me right now. It will take my mind off everything. The police are still actively investigating."

"If you're sure," he says. The next thing he tells me is a surprise. The agency is assigning me the new Chick'n Lick'n fast food restaurant account. It's the one I helped them win. Everyone in creative wanted to work on that one because it's now the agency's biggest account. I'm speechless.

"Really?" I say.

"You've earned it," the partner says before he leaves my office. "And remember, the entire agency is here for you. Anything you need, you let us know."

Hopefully, now my life will get back to normal. Tonight, I'm going to call Lily and let her know we're moving to Phase Three.

CHAPTER TWENTY-FIVE

Sirena

I can hear a man and woman talking softly. Their voices aren't familiar, and they're not speaking English. I think it's Spanish. I can't open my eyes. My lids are too heavy. I don't even want to try.

"Javi, creo se está despertando," says the woman's voice. "Javi! She's waking up. Come in here. Now."

I hear rustling and then a man speaking.

"She's awake? Seguro?" he says.

"No," says the woman, "I'm not sure at all, but she's moving for the first time."

Someone holds my hand. It must be the man because it feels big and warm.

"Come on, Sirena, abre los ojos," says the man softly. "Open your eyes."

My lids feel like they're made of lead. I try to open them a crack, but the light in the room makes me snap them shut. It's too bright.

"You can do it, Sirena," the man gently says as he squeezes my hand. "Open your eyes for me."

Slowly, I lift my lids a tiny bit. At first, everything is blurry and in black and white. Soon, the images in front of me start to come into focus. Two faces I've never seen are standing over me. They're hovering. I don't know them. What do they want?

"Finally. There you are," says the man with a thick Spanish accent. He's got dark hair and dimples and he's smiling at me. Somehow, I know he's kind.

"Puedes oírme?" says the woman, shining a flashlight in my eyes, which makes me close them again. She has a thick accent, similar to his. "Can you hear me?"

Why wouldn't I be able to hear you?

I try to speak, but I can't. I swallow, but my throat is so dry that it hurts. I move my lips, but no sound comes out. The woman, who looks about forty, puts a cup to my mouth and carefully lifts my head.

"Here, drink slowly," she says. "Es agua, water."

I swallow a few drops. First one sip, then two, then three. I'm so thirsty. I could drink a barrel of water.

"No tan rapido, Sirena, slow down," says the man as the woman pulls the cup away and gently places my head back on the pillow.

"We'll give you more water in a little while," she says. "You need to pace yourself, or you'll make yourself sick."

I look at the two of them with their dark wavy hair and dark eyes. Who are they?

"Where am I?" I whisper.

"She's speaking English. I was wrong. She's not a Cubano," says the woman, shaking her head.

"I told you," says the man.

"We have redheads in Cuba," says the woman. "She could have been Cuban."

The man grins.

"Who are you?" I say, feeling so weak and groggy.

"So many questions from a person who's been asleep for so long," he says. "For now, all you need to know is that you're safe. I'm Javier, and this wonderful woman is Ines. She's been taking very good care of you."

Why is she taking care of me? Am I sick?

"Where am I?" I repeat.

The man sits on the bed next to me. "You are on the beautiful island of Puerto Rico. Paradise on earth."

How did I get here?

My eyes get heavy again and everything goes dark.

* * *

I'm not sure how much time has passed, but it must have been a while, because the next time I open my eyes, the light in the room has changed a lot. The sun is going down.

"Javi, she's awake again," shouts Ines. She jumps up from a chair in the corner of the room and goes to the door. "Javi, ven aqui."

Seconds later, Javi steps into the room. He smiles at me, and I can see now, he's very handsome, tall and fit. At least, I think so from where I am. He's got wavy black hair, large dark brown eyes and two very prominent dimples when he smiles. I don't know why, but I like him.

He sits on the edge of my bed. "Back to the land of living? How do you feel now?"

"Tired," I whisper.

"I'm not surprised," says Ines. "For a while, we didn't think you were going to make it."

"What do you mean?" I say, clearing my throat and starting to find my voice. Ines brings a cup of water to my lips and I gratefully drink.

"Are you hungry?" she says.

I didn't realize I was until she said it.

"Yes," I reply.

"Rest for a minute," she says as she leaves the room. Javi stays and holds my hand. I pull it away.

"Don't be afraid. Ines tells me you're going to be all right. She's an amazing nurse."

Holding a coffee cup with a spoon in it, Ines sits in the chair next to the bed.

"It's a scrambled egg," she says as she puts a spoon with a tiny bit of egg to my lips. "You need to eat this very slowly, okay?"

I nod and greedily swallow the spoonful of egg. When I finish the entire thing, they both seem delighted, like two parents whose one-year-old has finally eaten their dinner.

"Good job," says Ines as she gets up. "Javi will give you something more later."

They talk to each other in Spanish. After a back-and-forth that I don't understand, Ines leaves the room and I'm alone with Javi.

"Do you remember anything about what happened to you?"

"What happened?" I say, confused.

He smiles and his dimples engage. "Let's start with something easier. What's your name?"

I try to say my name when I realize I don't know it. Why can't I remember my name? They both called me Sirena. That must be it.

"Sirena?" I say with very little conviction.

His gentle smile turns into a chuckle as he shakes his head. "No, I'm afraid that is not your name."

"But you called me that. I heard you."

"That has been my name for you ever since I pulled you out of the water. Sirena. It means mermaid in Spanish. You're the little mermaid I fished out of the sea."

I look at him, trying to decide whether he's crazy, menacing or just playful.

"I don't understand. Fished out of the sea?"

He sits in the chair next to the bed. "Do you really not remember anything?"

"I don't know . . ." I say.

"Try to tell me your name," he says.

I look into his dark velvety eyes wanting desperately to answer his question, but nothing comes. I don't know my name. That's crazy.

"Do you know where you live?" he asks softly.

"I live in . . . I live in . . . I-I-I don't know. Why don't I know where I live?" Hot tears prick at my eyes.

He puts his hand on my arm.

"It's okay. Everything will be all right. You've obviously got some kind of memory loss. You had a big bump on your head when I found you. Ines said that can happen sometimes."

"How can I not know who I am?" I say. "I don't remember anything."

"Do you remember your mother or father or brothers or sisters? Your childhood, perhaps?"

I shake my head.

"A boyfriend or a husband?"

I shake my head again. "I don't know. What's wrong with me?"

"You've been very sick."

"Explain," I say, trying to sit up but failing. "Where did you find me?"

Javi tells me he was on a fishing trip up north. He had taken his boat to the Bahamas and was cruising along the Florida coast heading back to Puerto Rico.

"This one morning, it was very early," he says. "The sun had just come up, and I was drinking my coffee on the back deck. As I looked out on the horizon, I saw something bobbing in the water out in the distance. At first I thought it was garbage of some kind or a seagull. When I looked through my binoculars, it was a woman — you."

"What?" I say, as if he'd just told me I have seven heads.

"You don't have any memory of being anywhere near the ocean?"

"No."

"I dove into the water and pulled you to my boat. Ines was with me that day. You were very lucky. She used to be an emergency room nurse back in Havana before she left. We got you onboard and she knew exactly what to do. Since then, she's nursed you day and night."

"Is anyone looking for me?"

"That I wouldn't know."

"Did you call the police?"

Javi shakes his head.

"Why not? Why didn't you call them, or bring me to a hospital? Maybe people are trying to find me?"

"That was my decision," says Ines, standing in the doorway. "Javi wanted to take you to the hospital in San Juan, but I wouldn't let him."

"Why?" I suddenly feel so tired.

"I'm from Cuba. The people there live in terrible conditions. Every year thousands risk their lives trying to get to the shores of America so they can have a better life."

"What's that got to do with me?" I say, not following her logic.

"Ines thought you might be a Cuban refugee trying to get to America," says Javi. "You had no ID. We didn't know if you were American or Cuban or where you were from. Ines begged me not to tell anyone until you woke up and we knew for sure. She *was* one of those people who escaped Cuba by boat and nearly died. She didn't want to ruin your chances and risk you being sent back."

I look at her with a grateful smile. "You were trying to protect me. I understand. Thank you for taking good care of me."

"De nada," she says, nodding as she walks over to me before handing me a pair of glasses. "These must be yours. We found them in the zippered pocket of your jacket. We also found—"

"I think that's enough for today," says Javi.

"You're right," she says. "Besides, I have to go home now. Javi, call me if you have any problems."

As Ines leaves the room, Javi helps me put the glasses on. Suddenly, the entire room comes into focus.

"Better?" he says.

I flash a weak smile. He's even more handsome in focus. "I can see you clearly now."

"That's good. You need to rest," he says as he stands. "Your body has been through a lot."

"But you didn't tell me who you are."

He smiles ruefully. "That's a long story for another day."

"But I . . ."

"Based on your accent, I presume you are an American. Tomorrow, we'll try to find out who you are."

"But what if . . ."

"You've been unconscious for a while. Give yourself some time to heal. Ines thinks your memory will come back as you get stronger."

"And if it doesn't?"

"Then we'll figure it out together."

CHAPTER TWENTY-SIX

Three more days pass before I'm strong enough to stand and go outside. Javi helps me down the three steps in front of his cottage to a chair several yards away. He seats me under a massive palm tree in front of his small bright-blue beach house. It has a small front porch, and there's a yellow surfboard and a gray paddleboard leaning up against the side.

While I get settled in my chair, Javi goes back inside to get some fresh juice for me. Looking out on the serene blue-green ocean, I spot Ines walking up from the beach. She's holding hands with a woman who she introduces as her partner, Gloria. An unexpected wave of relief washes over me, but I don't know why. I'm introduced as "Javi's houseguest," which sounds odd given my circumstances. A houseguest is the last way I'd describe myself.

"I see you've met Sirena," says Javi as he comes out of the house and hands me freshly squeezed orange juice.

"That's a beautiful name," says Gloria.

I don't know up from down or who I am, so I just smile and nod. After a few minutes of light conversation, the two women head off down the beach from the direction they came.

"I'm confused," I say when they're out of earshot. "I thought you said my name wasn't Sirena."

"Since we don't know your real name, we have to call you something. Sirena is as good as any, don't you think?"

I nod.

He sits on the ground next to my chair and digs mindlessly in the sand with a stick. We chat about the weather, the local fish and the beach. We talk about nothing in particular, avoiding the obvious — who I am and how I ended up in the middle of the ocean.

"How long do you think I was out there in the water?" I say.

"It's hard to know. But I don't think too long. You weren't terribly sunburned," he says. "You were very lucky. The sea was calm that day, almost like glass. Somehow you managed to flip onto your back and keep breathing. I don't think you could have lasted out there for too long."

"Can a person just stay afloat like that when they're unconscious?"

"You're here, so I guess they can. Everything was on your side that day. Well, not everything. You had calm seas, lots of clouds blocking the sun and of course, your jacket."

My eyes narrow as I look at him. "My jacket?"

He smiles. "The jacket you were wearing was a windbreaker with elastic sleeves and waistband, and it was zipped up. It's only a guess, but I think, maybe, when you went into the water, you somehow created an air pocket inside the jacket that was just enough to keep your head up."

Javi stops digging and jams his stick into the sand. His explanation as to why I'm still alive kind of blows my mind.

"Since you're feeling better today," he says, "maybe we should start trying to find out who you are."

"Okay," I say.

"There are some questions we need to answer before we alert too many people."

"What do you mean?"

He smiles kindly. "I found you fully dressed floating in the middle of the ocean nowhere near land. It's a miracle you weren't dead and even more of a miracle that I happened to see you."

"But why wouldn't we just call the police? Since we know I'm not Cuban . . ."

"Sirena, let me tell you a little about myself. My full name is Javier Manuel Guzman. I was born in Venezuela. My father was a very successful and wealthy industrialist in Caracas. We had a privileged life. I lived in a beautiful home, had my own horse and went to the most elite school in Caracas. I started learning English when I was five. When the government started taking over private enterprise and seizing money and property from citizens, my father made arrangements for our family to get out of Caracas. It was very dangerous. I was seventeen when they smuggled our family out of the country in the middle of the night."

"That sounds scary."

"It was, but we made it to Argentina. I finished school and graduated from the University of Buenos Aires. My father also had managed to get most of his own money out of Venezuela. Unfortunately, there were people who didn't like that. Five years after we settled in our new home in Buenos Aires, my dear father was gunned down in the streets of Recoleta, a normally safe and expensive part of the city."

I stare at him, my mouth partly open. "I'm so sorry. That must have been terrible."

Javi nods. "What's done is done," he says, rubbing his eyes.

"Why are you telling me all this?"

He picks up the stick again and resumes digging. "Because someone left you for dead. And until we know why you were in the middle of the ocean, you need to be very careful."

"I don't understand."

"There are many reasons why you might have been in the water. Excuse me for being indelicate, but I think we need to get to this quickly."

I press my lips together and nod. I trust him. I have to.

"Like I said, when I found you, you were fully dressed. I had to ask myself, 'Why were you in the water?' Was it a suicide attempt?"

"No, I would never . . ."

"But you said you have no memory. How do you know it wasn't that?"

I look out at the water trying to fathom what he's suggesting.

"Even if that were true, and I don't think it is," I say, "why wouldn't we call the police and get help?"

"Because that's not the only possibility. If you didn't put yourself in the water, did someone else put you there? Were you in the water by accident, or was it intentional and, if so, why? It's possible that someone tried to kill you. But maybe you were escaping from someone? Or running from something, perhaps? As you can see, the possibilities are endless."

I start to sputter. "All your scenarios are so negative and dark. What if I was the mother of two children and had a sailing accident?"

Javi purses his lips and shakes his head. "You only woke up a short time ago, but you've been here with me for many weeks. From the moment I brought you to my home, I've been scanning police bulletins and radios from North Carolina down to Florida and half the Caribbean. There's not been a single report of a boating accident or a missing woman who fits your description."

I run my fingers through my knotty hair. "No one is looking for me?"

"I don't know for sure. But until we *do* know why you were in the water, I think it's best that you keep a low profile. It's for your own safety."

I look out at the horizon and the beautiful aqua water, trying to unpack what he's just suggested. After evaluating his rationale, I have to agree. What other choice do I have?

"Okay," I say.

"Then it's settled," he says. "You'll take your time convalescing here with me. While you get stronger, we'll start digging around to see if we can find out who you are and how you ended up in the sea."

Over the next few days, my appetite increases. I'm suddenly ravenous and eat enough for two people. Javi seems delighted every time I ask for more food. In between bites, I promise to repay him for all his kindness, once I learn who I am. Each day, my legs feel stronger. By the end of the week, I'm able to walk for a full fifteen minutes along the beach without getting winded. I'm making progress physically, but my memory is still a blank.

* * *

It's now been nearly a month since I "woke up," and I'm feeling pretty good. My strength continues to improve. Javi has promised that, when I'm ready, he'll teach me how to use his paddleboard and maybe even how to surf.

Each day, he and I spend time online scanning news stories about missing persons in the southeastern part of the United States and the Caribbean. Occasionally, we find something that looks promising, only to be disappointed when the picture of the missing person isn't me.

Meanwhile, I've tried to embrace my new life here. The problem is, I'm living in Javi's shadow as his guest. I can't stay here forever. I need to find my own life again. I have to know who I really am, but part of me is afraid to find out. What if I was a bad person?

Today, the surf is calm, so Javi and I take a double kayak out on the water. One thing Javi doesn't lack is water sports toys. It's a beautiful day as we glide along with me upfront and Javi in the back. After half an hour of paddling, we stop for a rest and some water.

"What if I did something terrible in my past?" I say. "Maybe I killed someone? I might have been a horrible person."

"That's not possible," he says, handing me a water bottle. "I've been with you every day and I only see goodness in you."

I twist my neck around slightly to look at him. "But how can you be so sure that *I'm* not the negative entity in the story? I could have committed crimes and someone dropped me in the ocean as payback. Or what if I . . ."

Before I finish my sentence, Javi leans forward and kisses me. That's when I realize I've wanted him to do that from the minute I opened my eyes.

CHAPTER TWENTY-SEVEN

Convalescing in Javi's little blue beach house by the sea has been like a weird dream. Each day figments and splatters of images trickle across my mind in no particular order. I still can't make sense of anything, which is so frustrating. I see only random pictures of places and faces but with no underlying explanation. I don't recognize anything. As far as I know, my life began when I woke up here with Javi.

Since I didn't come here with any luggage, Ines went shopping and bought me some clothes. I don't know what I did in my previous life to deserve Javi and Ines. They take care of me like I'm one of their own. I'm treated only with kindness.

Until my real memories start to come through, if they ever do, I've agreed to stay in the shadows for my own protection. Things could be worse. I'm living in paradise with a very handsome and loving man who does everything in his power to make me feel special. I don't know what kind of life I left, but it's hard to imagine that it was better than this.

Sometimes I tell myself that I don't need to know about my past. But that feeling passes. I don't even know how old I am. I presume I have family and friends somewhere out there. Maybe I have a child and a husband. They would be searching for me, wouldn't they? Unless they thought I was dead. Still, it's hard for me to get emotionally attached to my past when I can't remember any of it. In the meantime, I spend my days fishing on Javi's boat and trying to be as helpful a houseguest as possible.

This week, Javi's been teaching me how to surf. Surfing looks so easy when you see other people standing on their boards traversing the waves. I've tried to get up on that damn board over thirty times, but I can't seem to do it.

"One thing we now know for sure," Javi says with a laugh after I slip off my board again, "you definitely weren't a surfer in your previous life."

I try to scowl, but I can't suppress the laugh. He's right. I am a terrible surfer.

"You must keep trying," he says. "You'll get it. I promise."

Javi's patience and thoughtfulness lifts me up each day. As time passes, I become less interested in finding out who I am because that would mean giving up this new life I've come to love. I'm positive there's no way my previous life could ever be as idyllic as the one I'm living now.

When I first woke up after being in the water, my bones and muscles ached. There was pain throughout my body, but not anymore. It must be the good care I'm getting. Javi feeds me mainly vegetables, fruit and fish. With a healthy diet, tons of exercise and lots of sunshine, I feel pretty fantastic right now. I still don't know anything about myself, but who cares? I'm so happy.

After my disastrous morning surfing lesson, Javi suggests we take his boat out and catch something for dinner. The first time we went fishing, I was a little squeamish about the fishhook and bait. But now I'm like a seasoned angler. I prepare my hook and am ready to cast my line in less than thirty seconds.

We catch two blackfin tuna before we head back to shore.

"We've got a lot of fish here," says Javi as he steers the boat. "Are you very hungry?"

I look down at our catch and bite my bottom lip.

"Let's invite Ines and Gloria for dinner," I say. "I can practice my Spanish. We can stop at the farm stand and pick up some vegetables and bread."

Javi smiles. "We'll still have more fish than we can eat. Maybe I'll ask my mate, Reno, to come."

"Reno? I haven't heard you mention him before."

He laughs. "He's Australian, I think. At least that's what he told everyone. He's a character. You'll like him. Eccentric but brilliant."

I feel my eyebrows knit together. Though Javi and I have only known each other a short time, it feels like he can read my mind.

"Don't worry," he says looking at my face. "Reno's all right."

"But you said I should keep my head down. Not talk to anyone until we . . ."

"And you should, but trust me, Reno's okay," he says as he drops the anchor into the lagoon in front of the beach house. "Aside from enjoying his company, I also thought he might be able to help us."

"How?" I say as I climb down the ladder of the boat into the water.

"You'll see," says Javi.

He lowers the two wrapped fish by rope to me. I grab our future dinner and start pulling it to shore as Javi jumps into the warm light blue water behind me.

That night before our guests arrive, Javi and I are treated to a gorgeous pink-and-orange Caribbean sunset. As we watch the sun drift downward, he puts his arm around my shoulders, and we silently watch nature's miracle. Reveling in the moment, we're interrupted by a man's voice.

"Hey mate, whatcha got cookin'? Smells good. Got a beer?"

Javi and I spin around as a stocky barefoot man in his late forties approaches us. His blond hair has more than a few strands of gray, and he's wearing an oversized red-and-gold dashiki top over a pair of tattered blue shorts. A pair of aviator wire-framed sunglasses sit halfway down the bridge of his generous nose. Gold hoop earrings hang from both of his earlobes.

"Reno," shouts Javi as he walks toward our visitor with his hand extended. The two shake and then shift to a hearty embrace. "Glad to see you, my friend."

"Qué pasa?" says Reno, narrowing his eyes as he looks over at me.

Javi smiles. "Mi amigo, I'd like you to meet the woman I told you about. She's very special to me. Reno, this is Sirena."

Reno clips his bare heels together and bows to me from the waist. "An honor, my lady," he says.

I try to stifle a laugh. Reno's corny but charming and I like him instantly. He's got a contagious charisma about him. For the next few minutes, the three of us chat about nothing important — the weather, the fish and the surfing conditions.

Soon Reno and Javi are arguing about the nuances of the perfect surfing wave. I'm trying to keep up with them when Ines and Gloria arrive carrying a large bowl of fruit and two bottles of wine.

"They say you can never have too much wine," says Ines, examining me like a doctor. "How are you feeling, Sirena? You look very well. The beach is obviously good for you."

I smile and glance over at Javi. "Yes, the beach is very good for me."

The whole evening is wonderful. The freshly caught tuna is grilled to perfection by Javi on the barbecue. We've got salads and cheese and all sorts of breads. The beer and wine are flowing, and Reno entertains us with stories of his adventures from all around the world. Javi, seated next to me, occasionally squeezes my hand or rubs my knee underneath the table.

"Is Reno your real name?" I ask before taking a sip of wine.

He shakes his head.

"Why are you called Reno?" I ask.

The conversation stops. Javi lets out a laugh as Reno stares at me.

"Let's just say it came from a night I don't remember but no one else can forget," he says in a deadpan voice.

I guess my eyes got really big, because seconds later, the entire table erupts in laughter.

"That's for another day when I know you better," says Reno with a warm smile. "Don't want to give everything away on our first day together. Where would the mystery be then?"

At midnight, Ines and Gloria stagger off down the beach. Reno and Javi are in separate hammocks swinging between palm trees. They're drinking beer and looking up at the stars. I overhear them discussing the meaning of life.

"Ines and Gloria left," I say as I grab a beer for myself and head toward them. I'm about to sit down near Javi when he suddenly gets out of the hammock.

"That was an amazing dinner, Sirena," Javi whispers as he passes me heading into the house. "All those side dishes? You obviously know how to cook."

Javi's right. The food was good, and I prepared most of it without even thinking about it. I knew what to do. I've learned something about myself. I didn't have any significant knife skills, so I don't think I was a chef. But the food I made, though simple, was delicious. While I contemplate the deeper meaning of good culinary skills, Javi returns and takes my hand.

"There's something I've been wanting to show you," he says. "I've been waiting until you were feeling better. I had hoped that Reno might be able to help us decipher something."

"What are you talking about?" I say, my forehead wrinkling.

Reno sits up in the hammock and jumps out. "The doctor is in, mate. What may I help you with?"

Javi holds up a phone and looks over at me.

"You had this phone in your pocket when I found you. It was dead, but I was able to charge it. Perhaps the answers you're looking for are on this phone. Unfortunately, I'm unable to open it. I need a password."

He puts the phone in my hand. I turn it over several times before I shake my head. It doesn't look familiar.

"I don't recognize it," I say. "How do we know it's mine?"

"It was inside the zippered pocket of your jacket in a waterproof case. The case must have been slightly compromised, though. There was some condensation inside."

"Let me see it," says Reno, walking over and taking the phone from my hand. He examines the device and presses a few buttons.

"What do you think?" says Javi.

"Never met a phone I couldn't break into," says Reno, smiling and shaking it next to his ear. "Of course, there's always a first time. You say she had it with her in the water?"

Javi nods.

"And how long was it in the water exactly?" says Reno.

"We don't know," says Javi, "but it was a while."

"I'll do what I can. Give me forty-eight hours," says Reno, holding the mystery phone in one hand while grabbing a beer with the other. "I like a challenge."

CHAPTER TWENTY-EIGHT

Andre

Four months have now passed since Becca and I went on our anniversary cruise. As I expected, the cops are no closer to figuring out what happened. These small-town cops are clearly not equipped to solve murders. Despite all their investigating and even checking in with Beacon Cruise Lines, they've come up with nothing unusual. Their entire investigation to find Becca is 100-percent centered in Connecticut. Way to go, guys!

I always thought cops weren't that smart. They're all badges and guns. Even Detective Contessa has finally stopped haunting me on a daily basis. I guess life goes on. He has new crimes to solve, which has taken the heat off me.

To keep things interesting, I turn the tables. Now, I call Contessa several times a week and ask *him* what's happening with Becca's case. What's *he* doing to find my wife? Putting him on the defensive for doing a shitty job takes the spotlight off me. It won't be too long before Becca is moved to a cold case and becomes a distant memory. Lily and I can finally be together and live our best life.

Lily and I don't talk very often. It's too risky. I call her once every few weeks to make sure she's not losing her nerve. So far, it seems like she's holding it together. I keep reminding her that we agreed to wait one full year before starting to officially date.

"But that's so long," Lily whines over the phone one night. "I'm getting older by the minute."

"You're twenty-six," I say, rolling my eyes.

"I'm almost twenty-seven. How about ten months? That's almost a year."

I shake my head. Sometimes Lily is so myopic. She doesn't see the larger picture. We're talking about our freedom. What's two months?

"Trust me," I say softly. "It's not worth jeopardizing things by moving too soon. We're talking about a difference of eight weeks. Haven't I been right about everything so far?"

She and I go back and forth before Lily finally lets it go. I can't see her face, but I know she's pouting. One of us has to be the grown-up and hold the line, or we'll both end up in jail.

On the career front, things are going better than ever for me. After Becca went missing, I was the lucky beneficiary of a groundswell of support and sympathy. Everyone gave me encouraging advice and insisted they were saying prayers for my wife and me.

"Poor man," they whisper as I walk by. "He loved his wife so much. It's such a tragedy. They just went on an anniversary cruise. I say prayers for them every night."

I'm an atheist, so that kind of religious sentiment falls on deaf ears, but it's the thought that counts and I always thank them anyway.

Then there are those people who have slightly vilified poor Becca.

"They're saying his wife took off on her own," some whisper.

"I heard she ran away with another man," say others, but always in a whisper.

"Poor Andre, it's just so awful. It's too soon right now, but eventually we should fix him up with someone. I have this cousin who just got divorced and she would be . . ."

I only know all this because I was standing by the elevator and overheard two women from the media department discussing my situation at length. As the two walked out of the company coffee room, they didn't see me standing there, but I sure as hell heard them. I guess if Lily starts getting on my nerves, I'll have other options.

I arrive home from work to a big empty house tonight. Walking in, it occurs to me how nice it is having the place all to myself without the wife of doom-and-gloom lying on the couch eating popcorn and complaining. I can spread out and leave things wherever I want. I can eat or drink without anyone's disapproval. I can sit naked on the couch with a bowl of ice cream on my lap if I want to. For the record, I don't, but I could, and somehow that's enough.

While I heat up some takeout lasagna from the Woodmere Market, I mix myself a gin and tonic, pop in a lime wedge and sit on the couch to catch the nightly news. As usual, the world is a mess, filled with depravity and destruction. I turn it off in less than five minutes. I don't want that kind of dirty, toxic energy getting into my head. I've got enough going on managing the police without adding global annihilation to my otherwise busy schedule.

As I dig my fork into the lasagna, my phone rings. It's Stella, again. She's made a habit of calling me every night to "check in." At first it seemed thoughtful and supportive. Now it's just plain annoying. I take a deep breath and put on my happy face. Well, not too happy. My wife *is* missing, after all.

"Hey, Stell. What's going on?"

"Anything new from Contessa?"

I take a moment to answer because I have a mouthful of cheese and pasta. When I finally swallow, I pretend her question got me choked up.

"I'm sorry," I say, sniffling once or twice. "Just hearing Contessa's name makes me want to scream. Those cops don't know what they're doing."

"I didn't mean to upset you," she says. "God, I miss her so much. I've been thinking . . ."

Here we go.

"I think we need to get the press more engaged again," says Stella. "In the beginning, the local media was all over Becca's story, but when nothing turned up, they moved on. We need to activate them again."

I take a sip of red wine. It's delicious, a smooth pinot noir with chocolate undertones. I make a mental note to order a case before turning my attention back to my wife's friend.

"How do we get the press interested?" I say while dishing myself another half-portion of pasta.

"We've got to find a champion," says Stella. "It should be someone who took an interest in Becca's disappearance when it first happened."

"Like who?"

"I don't know. We could offer them an exclusive with us," she says. "We say we'll *only* talk to them. In exchange, they keep Becca's story alive and hopefully take ownership of it."

I put my fork down. I never considered Stella to be particularly bright. However, this idea is actually a good one, *if* I wanted to keep the story alive, which I don't.

"That's interesting," I say. "But who would we go to? And more importantly, what have we got that we could share with this reporter that would get them interested?"

There's silence on the line. Thankfully, I've managed to stump her.

"What about a human-interest story about Becca and her life?" says Stella. "We could talk about her volunteer work and her friends and family. We could talk about how even with her fibromyalgia, she soldiered through each day, and then this happened."

Being in the creative advertising world, what Stella just said doesn't sound like great copy to me, but I play along. She needs to think I'm 100-percent game to do *anything* that might bring my wife back to me.

"Okay," I say. "If there's the slightest chance it might lead to finding Becca, I'm in. I still have this feeling she's out there somewhere waiting for us to rescue her. I don't want to let her down."

"We won't. And remember, I'm always here for you, Andre. You know that. We're going to find her if it's the last thing we do."

That's where you're wrong. We're definitely never going to find her.

"Thanks, Stell. You've been so amazing throughout this whole ordeal," I say. "I don't know how I would have gotten through it without you."

"That's what best friends do," she says.

"Becs and I had a storybook romance, you know?" I say, deliberately choking up so she can hear it over the phone. "The minute I met her, I fell in love. Even after ten years of marriage, it sounds corny, but every day was like a fairy tale. Most people never have what we had. I used to think we led a charmed life."

There's a distinct silence on the other end of the phone. Had I been painting with too heavy a brush? The reality was that Becca and I were not blissfully happy. She was sick all the time, and I was sick of her. Stella would know that. Becca told her everything.

The cat's already out of the bag, so I decide to double down. I blame any negativity Stella may have heard from Becca on her fibromyalgia.

"She didn't feel well a lot of the time," I say, "which sometimes affected her outlook. But we were soulmates."

There's another long moment of silence.

"You mean you '*are*' soulmates," she finally says.

"Right. Becca and I *are* soulmates," I say. "Always. Now and forever."

After another longish pause on Stella's end, I wonder if she's buying what I'm selling.

"Stella?" I say softly. "I should have asked you before. How are *you* doing?"

"I'm fine, Andre," she says in a business-like tone. "I'll do some checking and come up with names of a few reporters. I'll get back to you."

CHAPTER TWENTY-NINE

After that slip-up on the phone with Stella, I remind myself to be more careful with what I say to her. Who knows what kinds of secrets and inner feelings my late wife shared with her best friend. It's possible Becca told her *everything* that went on between us. Did she tell Stella how I got really pissed off a few months ago when Becca started moaning about the numbness in her legs? I didn't talk to her for weeks. Some things are meant to be kept private.

Nobody understands what it was like being Rebecca Gifford's husband. We met the old-fashioned way: in a bar. She was hot, athletic and up for a good time. One of the things that attracted me to her was her sense of adventure. She was a person who'd take calculated risks and try things other women might not. She rode motorcycles *and* a mechanical bull, though not at the same time. She tried skydiving, something I would never do. She loved to travel, cook exotic foods and go dancing. When we'd go out, she'd dance for hours. Then there was her laugh. When she'd start to giggle, sometimes she just couldn't stop. It would get everyone around her laughing. She was a lot of fun back then.

It wasn't only her personality that sucked me in. When we first got married, Becca was a good financial partner to me as well. As a kindergarten teacher, she had summers off and great medical benefits. She loved her classroom of kids, and they adored her. Those were years one, two and three. Seven through ten weren't nearly as much fun. I started to get bored.

She and I had wanted kids of our own, but then she got sick, and kids got put on the back burner. It started with some aches here and there. Then it morphed into headaches and increased pain. By the time our sixth anniversary rolled around, my wife had taken to her bed and pretty much stayed there.

She went to a million doctors at significant expense. She was tested for rheumatoid arthritis, lupus, Lyme disease and a whole host of other little-known illnesses. She was depressed, and supposedly had pain and tingling all over her body. That's about the time she stopped taking care of herself. What was I supposed to do? I was healthy, traveling all over the country on business and my career was catapulting forward. I wasn't about to sit home and be her handmaiden.

It was all reasonably tolerable while she was still working. But after numerous leaves of absence from her job, she finally resigned. She had been out of work more than she was in. She said she didn't want her kids to suffer. Saint Rebecca, as I liked to call her.

I started thinking, what about me? I woke up one day and was married to an invalid. That's not what I signed up for. Sure, I know shit happens over thirty or forty years, but we'd only been married a few years and already I was moving into a caregiver role. None of the doctors knew what the hell was wrong with her. But according to my wife, she was unable to hold down a job or do much of anything.

To be fair, she had some good days when she was up and out. But it seemed to me that she reserved all the good days for her girlfriends, Stella in particular. I got the leftovers. I got to pick her up off the floor and put her into bed when she'd cramp up.

I was working my ass off all day in the city in a high-pressure advertising job. I'd come home and find my twenty-nine-year-old wife slumped on the couch covered in blankets, eating chips and drinking Diet Coke.

It was around this time that hair and makeup became an afterthought for her. Plus, with her mainly sedentary lifestyle, she started packing on a few pounds. Becca wasn't fat, but she got flabby, and that smokin' bod I'd married, I hadn't seen that in years.

It was coming up on Becca's birthday a few years ago. I'd gone into a department store planning to buy her a handbag I'd seen her looking at in a magazine. I remember she showed it to me and commented how nice it was. It wasn't cheap but it *was* her birthday, so I decided to get it. I ripped the page out of the magazine and drove over to the Trumbull Mall.

That's where I met Lily.

They didn't have the bag I wanted, so I started looking at other handbags from the same designer. After examining a dozen, I realized I knew nothing about ladies' bags. I looked around for some sales help. They're never around when you need them but in your face when you don't. With no help in my vicinity, I spotted this knockout platinum blonde standing several feet away examining a leather backpack. She had a similar body type to my wife, only the blonde was younger, more toned and a little thinner. I remember thinking, *That is a woman who takes care of herself*.

"Excuse me," I said as I held up a black leather bag, "I'm trying to buy a birthday gift for a friend. What do you think of this one?"

When she smiled, I nearly fell over. From the first second, I was hooked like a fish on a line. I didn't mention that I was married to the "birthday friend." Why ruin a perfect moment? It was winter and I had gloves on, so she couldn't see my wedding ring. We chatted amiably for quite a while about fashion and gift giving. Finally, I asked her if she'd like to go to Starbucks with me for a coffee.

I remember holding my breath waiting for her answer. If she said no, my big fantasy about this dream girl would be over. I wasn't going to stalk her. That's not my style. But then, she said "yes," and I could barely feel my legs as we walked through the mall to get our lattes.

After we got our coffees, to avoid taking off my gloves, which would have revealed my wedding ring, I suggested we sit outside and chat. It was winter, but it was a warm day and the sun was shining. I figured if she got to know me first, she might overlook the whole wedding ring issue. We sat on a bench talking for almost two hours. For me, it felt like two minutes.

After a while, I could see she was getting cold. I brought up the idea that we meet for dinner in a few days, and she gave me her number. It took everything in me not to dance as I walked away from her that first day.

The following week, I suggested we meet at a restaurant that was very far from where Becca and I lived. There'd be no chance I'd run into anyone I knew there. When I got to the restaurant, Lily was already there waiting at a table.

"Is it possible you're more beautiful tonight than you were at the mall?" I said as I approached her.

She flashed that amazing smile again, and I knew I had to have her. This was out of my control now. We were meant to be together.

We began sleeping with each other after our second date. By the tenth meeting, I knew I had to come clean about being married. Putting it off would only make things worse.

"Lily, there's something I need to tell you," I said, lying naked next to her in her apartment, adrenaline pumping through my body.

"Are you going to tell me I'm hot, again?" she said, licking her lips and touching me in ways that were so distracting. "'Cause I already know that."

I sat up in her bed and looked at her.

"You are, but I really need to talk to you. It's important."

She rolled over and sat up.

"Okay. What's on your mind?"

I could tell from her casual tone she had no idea I was about to rock her world with some devastating news.

"Lily, I haven't been completely honest with you," I said.

She laughed. "We all have secrets, Andre. Take me, for instance. These tits? They're not real."

At first I was a little put off by her admission. Her breasts were one of her better assets. By not mentioning it, she *had* technically deceived me. But given what I was about to dump on her, I decided to overlook the fake-breast thing. They were still extremely nice, real or not.

"There's no easy way to say this . . . I'm married." I held my breath.

She looked at me incredulously and then let out a snort.

"Duh," she said. "You think I didn't know that? It's not my first time at the rodeo, you know."

"But how did you . . . ?"

"That first night when I met you out at that restaurant, I saw you standing by the entrance before you saw me. I watched you slip your wedding ring off your finger and put it in your pocket before you came over to the table."

"You knew I was married this whole time? You're okay with it?"

She tilts her head. "Nobody's perfect."

CHAPTER THIRTY

A few weeks later, I get a call from Ed, my wife's stepfather. Since Becca disappeared, I'd typically talk to Becca's mother every day or two and give her an update. So, it was unusual to get a call from Ed. In fact, this was the first time he'd ever called me.

"I know you've got a lot on your plate right now," says Ed, his voice shaky and almost inaudible, "but there's something you need to know. My beautiful wife, Martha, died last night. They think it was a heart attack. I don't know how I'll manage without her. Will you let Stella know? Martha thought of Stella as her second daughter."

Wow. I didn't see that coming. I actually felt slightly sad. Becca's mother was all right. She was pretty young, too, just turned seventy-one. After I give Ed my condolences and hang up, I take a moment to remember Martha.

That's when it dawns on me that her unexpected passing is actually a good thing, a fantastic thing. Besides Stella, who's annoyingly obsessed with finding my wife and has become a thorn in my side, the only other person who was super invested in locating Becca was her mother.

"I went to see a psychic today," Martha said three months after Becca disappeared. "He told me that Becca's alive. He said he feels her presence is still here on earth. He thinks she's somewhere in Connecticut near the water."

I remember thinking, *He's got the water part right, Martha, but that's about it.* Now, with my mother-in-law deceased, I'm fairly certain Ed will not continue carrying the torch on Becca's investigation. He and Becca weren't that close. He married my mother-in-law five years ago, and we only saw them on holidays. From my perspective, Martha's death meant that the Philadelphia branch of the Find Rebecca Gifford Club was effectively disbanded and closed. One less thing for me to worry about.

Also, with Martha gone, that meant Lily and I could resume our relationship far more easily. I had always worried about how Martha would take it when a new woman came into the picture.

Lily and I only talk on our secret phones occasionally, but I can tell she's getting itchy.

"I might as well become a nun," she complained during our last call. "This isn't the way I thought things were going to be, Andre. I have needs, too, you know."

"Trust me, it's not for that much longer," I said, trying to coax her off the ledge she'd climbed out on. "We're so close."

"I'm not getting any younger," she said. "I have no social life whatsoever. All my friends have boyfriends or husbands. I'm always the third wheel and I'm sick of it. What am I waiting for, Andre? You tell me."

I did some fast talking and made a lot of promises. By the time we finished, she was calmer. I tried to explain how great it was that Martha died.

"If I started dating again," I told her, "Becca's mother would have been the hardest person to win over. Even after a year, Martha would have found it suspect that I'd stopped carrying the torch for her daughter."

"Who cares what her mother thought?" said Lily.

"It's not about what Martha would have thought," I said. "I don't want to draw any unnecessary attention to us. With Martha conveniently dead, we don't have that problem anymore. You can thank the universe for that."

There was silence on the phone for a few long seconds.

"You didn't do anything to her, did you?" said Lily in a frightened whisper.

"No. What kind of person do you think I am?" I said, with as much indignation as I could muster.

Later, as I had promised my buddy Ed, I called Stella. She had known Martha since she was eighteen, and they had grown even closer since Becca disappeared. I think Martha and Stella talked every week.

"Oh, my God. What is happening in this world?" says Stella between sobs. "How can she be dead? Martha was so alive. I'm in shock."

Shock? Martha was a smoker whose diet consisted of ice cream, hamburgers and French fries. She didn't exercise, had high blood pressure and was prediabetic. I'd say 'shock' is a bit of an overstatement.

I look at my watch. There's a college football game about to start that I want to watch. I've got to get Stella off the phone. To wrap up the call, I start making stuff up.

"The doctor said it could have been brought on from all the stress about losing her daughter. Ed said Martha couldn't sleep and was having palpitations all the time. Sounds like Becca going missing put Martha over the edge."

Stella sniffles a few times. "I can understand that," she says as she starts to cry again. "I'm so stressed out, too. I miss Becca all the time. We used to talk to each other ten times a day, you know."

I think it was more like fifty times a day, which in my opinion is pathological and annoying.

I was really hoping to avoid this trip down memory lane. Now, I've got to pretend to cry or it will seem strange.

"I know," I say, making my voice catch ever so slightly. "Life isn't the same without my girl here."

I let out a primal groan before continuing. "I miss her every minute of every day, Stell. And I'm not giving up. We're going to find her. We've got to."

As expected, Stella starts weeping and carrying on. I look at the clock and tap my foot. My game starts in three minutes.

"I can't talk anymore, Stell. I'm too upset. I'll call you tomorrow."

. . . And the Oscar goes to . . .

I heat up a frozen burrito, crack open a beer and settle in for what will hopefully be a good game. I need a mental break from Becca, Martha, Stella and Lily.

It's nearly the end of the first quarter when my phone dings. It's Stella, again, only this time she's on FaceTime. I mute the TV, and rub my eyes to make them red just before Stella's face pops up on my phone.

"Sorry to bother you. I'm still so upset about Martha, but that's not why I'm calling. Remember how we talked about getting more press attention to keep Becca in the news?"

I nod.

"I was waiting until I had more to tell you, but I reached out to this reporter at the local cable news channel a couple of weeks ago," she says. "You may have seen him on TV."

"I don't watch cable news," I say looking over at my burrito that's getting cold and my game that is continuing without me.

"The reporter's name is Tommy Devlin. He kind of looks like a Ken doll. You know, Barbie and Ken?"

I nod again. "Okay."

"He's a bit of an arrogant asshole, but he strikes me as the type to leave no stone unturned. That's what we want, isn't it?"

"Yeah," I say.

"He was familiar with Becca's case, and I filled him in on a few more details," she says. "He was the same reporter who covered that investigation about the mother with three kids who disappeared in Newcastle two years ago."

I shrug. I have no idea what she's talking about.

"You know, the murder/suicide where they found the wife with her husband dead in their car in Portland, Maine?" she says, trying to trigger my memory.

All I really want right now is to watch my game.

"Oh, yeah, I remember that story," I say, hoping to get rid of her. "Sad."

"When I filled Devlin in on Becca's case, he said it *might* be an interesting story to cover. He said it 'could have legs' and that he'd poke around and see what he could find out if we give him the exclusive."

"How long ago did you contact Devlin?" I say, making conversation while watching an instant-replay clip on TV.

"About two weeks ago. We met at his office, and I gave him photos and a whole ton of background stuff with lots of details about Becs and her life."

Without the sound on, which totally ruins it, I watch the quarterback make an incredible touchdown pass and stamp my foot.

"And Andre, there's one more thing," says Stella. "Part of the deal is, Devlin gets an interview with you."

CHAPTER THIRTY-ONE

Sirena

Javi's gone off to town for supplies. It's not often that he leaves me alone. He worries that someone will try to hurt me, and he wants to protect me. I reminded him that I'm not made of glass and insisted he go. Sometimes, it's nice to be alone, and it gives me time to practice my Spanish.

"I won't combust, Javi," I said playfully. "You've got to start leaving me by myself more often. Nothing's going to happen."

Each day I walk farther along the beach and breathe easier. The sun is so healing, and when my toes are in the sand, I feel a connection to the earth. Sometimes I have to laugh because I don't know who the hell I am or how I got here, but I'm so freakin' happy. Though I can't remember much of anything about my previous life, in a weird way, I don't care.

However, over the past few weeks, many more images and faces have flashed through my mind. Sometimes it's when I'm awake. Sometimes they come in a dream. I try to remember them, but they're always fleeting, and then they're gone.

This week has been different. A lot more pictures are sliding into my mind, and they're coming more frequently and staying longer. It's almost like my brain is a drain that's been clogged — the water can't get through. Then slowly, as the opening gets bigger, more water starts rushing in.

I've noticed that some of the faces I'm seeing, I've seen before. Javi thinks it means those images are more important to me than others. Each day, additional memories push through.

"You can't rush it, Sirena," said Javi when I vented my frustration. "The brain is very complicated. It will happen in time. Besides, is it so bad here with us right now?"

I smiled at him, because he's been amazing. As Javi and I get to know each other, our days are easy and filled with so much joy. I don't remember who in my life I've loved before, but I don't think anything could compare to what I feel now.

Today, Javi will be gone for the better part of the afternoon. He's searching for a replacement part for his boat. As a surprise, I'm going to prepare a special dinner for him. As I start peeling the vegetables for tonight's feast, the face of an older woman appears before my eyes. She's got short white spiky hair, and she's smiling. I like her, but I don't know who she is. Seeing her sparkly blue eyes in my mind, I have the feeling she's someone important to me. As I close my eyes to allow my brain to conjure up another memory, I hear the sound of a motor out front.

I peer out the window and see Reno coming toward the house on his motorcycle. He pulls right up to the door, turns the engine off and places his silver helmet on the seat.

"Buenas tardes," I say, standing in the doorway and giving him a wave. "Javi's not here."

"You've been practicing your Spanish," he says as he walks over and gives me a hug. "Cómo estás?"

"How am I? Palm trees, ocean breezes, tropical birds and even the occasional dolphin," I say, looking out at my surroundings. "What do you think?"

"Amen, sister. That's why we're all here." He walks over to the outside table and sits. "We got ourselves a little piece of paradise."

I nod and sit at the table across from him.

"Drink?" I say, ready to get up and fetch one.

"In a minute. First, there's something I wanted to show you." He reaches into his pocket and pulls out the broken phone Javi found in my jacket. "This baby was pretty fried even with the waterproof case. I screwed around with it for a couple of days. She was a bitch."

Disappointed, I give him a half smile. That phone was my only link to the past.

"Thanks for trying," I say. "We knew it was a long shot. I really appreciate you taking the time to . . ."

Reno tilts his head and stares at me with mild indignation.

"Hold on there. I'll admit this assignment was challenging. But, I've never met a device I couldn't hack. I had to make a few modifications. After I played around with it for a while, I was able to get it partially working."

"Oh, my God." I break into a full smile. "I love you. Did you find anything?"

"I'm a card-carrying geek, but I'll spare you the technical intricacies of how I pulled off this minor miracle. For all intents and purposes, this phone was DOA. In order to get it working at all, I had to jimmy-rig the device so it would turn on. I used a different kind of battery to circumvent the main component. However, that makes it very unstable. It was the only way."

"And?"

"I was able to recover a few pictures, a video, a couple texts and some random documents," he says smiling.

"That's amazing. Can I see?"

We go into the house, and he plugs the phone into the wall and boots it up. Erratic flashes crisscross the badly cracked screen, but nothing appears.

"It's not working," I say, chewing on my thumbnail.

"Give it a minute. Remember, this phone has been beaten up and drowned like a rat. You'd need a minute, too."

I nod. I can relate. Breathing in and out a few times, I wait for the phone to do something. Finally, there's a weird beep, the phone flashes a few times and the home screen appears.

"It's on," I shout.

"I tried clicking on some of the icons, but nothing connected," says Reno. "I also tried looking up the factory info about this phone, but all of that's gone, too. There's not much here, I'm afraid."

"Can I see what you did find?" I say, leaning over his shoulder.

"There are about a dozen pictures and one video," he says. "They appear to have been taken shortly before Javi found you. Do any of these look familiar?"

I take the phone in my hand and squint. The screen is so cracked and mangled that it's nearly impossible to make out the pictures underneath. There's a photo of a woman with long dark hair and bangs. She's sticking her tongue out and making a face. I smile.

"I feel like I know her," I say, shaking my head, "but I don't know from where."

There are other pictures. One of a flower garden and another of a small deer nibbling on a shrub.

"These mean anything to you?" says Reno.

"No," I say as I scan through the remaining pictures. When I get to the last one, my breath catches. It's the older woman with the short spiky white hair and twinkly blue eyes.

"I know her. I've seen her in my mind, and in my dreams."

Reno nods. "That's good. That's progress, then." Using his phone, he takes a screenshot of the young woman with bangs and the older woman.

"Now we've got copies in case this baby dies," he says, putting his phone away.

"Thank you."

"There's one more thing I wanted to show you," says Reno. "I also found a video. I listened to it five or six times. I'm not sure if we have the whole thing. But maybe it will mean something to you."

While holding the phone, I feel it getting very warm. Reno takes it from me, pushes a few buttons and hands it back.

"Have a look now. See if anything rings a bell."

I start the video. It shows a night sky. It's hard to see anything through all the cracks on the screen, but suddenly, a half-moon appears. A female voice is chanting. I think it might be my voice, but I sound strange.

"Stel-la, Stell. I'm making this video for you. Look at all the stars, look at that big old moon. Oh, my God, Stell, I've had so much champagne. I can't feel my face or my feet. But I'm having the best time ever," the female voice says while the shaky video stays fixed on the moon. "Tomorrow, we dock in Fort Lauderdale, and then I'm going shopping."

If it *is* me on the video, I sound drunk.

The female voice continues. "I don't know if you can see all the stars right now, Stell. Stars are so much brighter in Florida," drunk me says. "You should totally come down here. We should do a girls' trip."

There's a faint bang or slam sound on the video.

"Oh shit, he's coming. I gotta go."

Suddenly, the screen goes completely dark.

"Stop the video a second," says Reno. I pause it. "Now, this is where it gets kind of weird, Sirena. I'm not sure what happened to the picture. From this part on, it's only audio, and it cuts in and out. Maybe it will still mean something to you."

With the phone getting even hotter in my hand, I start the video from where we left off.

"I think I've had enough to drink," says drunk me. "I feel kind of sick."

The audio is now only unintelligible sounds. It's impossible to understand.

"How can you ask me that question?" says the man on the audio just before the sound gets garbled again. We listen for a few seconds until the words become clear again.

"Let's get you over to the railing so you can breathe in some air and get your bearings before we try to go to the cabin," says the man.

More garbled words.

"I feel really weird," drunk me says now.

I look over at Reno. There are more garbled words, and then we hear the man say, "You're safe with me."

The last thing we hear is my voice.

"Look at all the stars. It's like I'm flying."

Right after that, there are two loud guttural grunts. The audio ends just before the phone dies.

CHAPTER THIRTY-TWO

"What do you think that means?" I look at Reno hoping he can interpret what we just saw and heard.

He shakes his head and shrugs. "Don't know what to tell you," he says. "We presume this phone is yours. The woman's voice on the video sounds a lot like you, but who knows for sure?"

"What do you think just happened there?" I say. "Is it just a stupid video of two drunk people, or was it something more?"

"I've got to be honest with you. I'm not sure."

With the hot phone still in my hand, I hear Javi's truck pull in.

"Let's show Javi the video," I say.

After we unload the groceries, the three of us crowd around the table. I'm holding the damaged phone.

"The phone is getting super-hot," I say to Reno. "What does that mean?"

"It means we need to do this quickly," says Reno.

I activate the video. We all watch and listen to the whole thing, all two minutes and thirty-nine seconds of it. Just as it's ending, the screen flashes and crackles. Smoke pours out of the phone, and I drop it on the table.

I look up at Reno. "What the hell just happened?"

He exhales sharply. "I knew that was a possibility. But it was the only way I could get it going."

"Can we get the video back?" says Javi, standing.

"I don't think so," says Reno. "This thing is officially dead."

"There's no way you can recover it?" I say. "Or maybe try to . . ."

Reno shakes his head. "It was a gamble, but I took it so we could get into the phone."

"Shit," says Javi loudly. "Something weird happened on that video, but what exactly?"

Not long after, we walk Reno outside, and I thank him for all he did.

"Sorry about the crash-and-burn ending," he says as he swings his leg over his motorcycle. Seconds later, he revs his engine, waves and sails out of the driveway.

Javi hands me a beer and the two of us sit on the front porch and gaze out at the calm sea.

"Does anything on that video sound familiar to you?" he says.

"No. Maybe it wasn't even me?"

"The date of the video was from the same day I found you," says Javi. "This phone was inside your pocket. And the voice sounded like yours. Although you seemed a little under the weather."

With the video probably gone forever, Javi and I write down everything we heard and saw so we don't forget anything.

"There was a half-moon out and she/me was talking to someone named Stella," I say. "She mentioned Florida and stopping in Fort Lauderdale."

"That's right," says Javi. "And the man said something about getting over to the railing to breathe in some air before going to the cabin. They must have been on a ship of some kind."

As I look at Javi, an image of a ship's cabin flashes before my eyes. I cover my face with my hands. The memories are so mixed up.

"What does this all mean?" I say through my fingers.

Javi takes my hands from my face and holds them between his. Tears have already sprung from my eyes. I'm so confused.

He looks at me, and I can tell he's processing all the information we've just heard.

"I think . . . you were a passenger on a cruise ship," he says, thinking out loud. "In that video, you were with a man at night on the deck. Maybe he was your husband or a boyfriend or maybe you just met him?"

"It sounded like they were a couple on a trip together," I say, as if the person on the video wasn't me but some stranger. "Maybe they met on the ship?"

"I don't know," says Javi. "If that was you, you were making a video for someone named Stella. It sounded like the man knew Stella, too, and didn't like them being on the phone together. You said so on the video."

"Maybe this Stella person was also on the ship?"

"Could be, but probably not. Why would you make a video of the moon for someone who's already on the ship?"

"You're right. So this woman we heard on the video, me, is on a cruise with a man and makes a video to share her experience with some other woman named Stella."

"I think that's correct," says Javi. "Stella could be your friend or even your sister. If the man doesn't like them being on the phone together, that may be why you stuck the phone in your pocket when he appeared. You didn't realize it was still recording."

"That's why we lost the visual part and the sound quality changed."

Javi nods. I turn and face him squarely. "What do you think happened at the end of the video?"

Javi puts his head back, takes a swig from his beer and slams the bottle on the table between us. His eyes are angry.

"I think, my beautiful girl, that man was the person who threw you off the ship into the water and left you to die."

The enormity of his words leave me numb. All these months, I had assumed my being in the ocean was most likely the result of a freak accident. In a million years, I never imagined that someone had actually tried to kill me, even though Javi thought it was possible.

The thought of murder makes my head spin. Had I done something terrible and this was my payback? Was I working for some criminal enterprise and they put out a hit on me? Who would have hated me enough to do that?

"Why would someone want to kill me? Maybe I was a terrible person who did horrible things?" I say.

Javi stands, lifts me up and holds me.

"We've been through this," he whispers into my ear. "You were not a bad person. I don't believe that."

"But how do you know for sure?"

Javi swivels his head and looks into my eyes. "How do you know that I'm not a bad person?"

I smile at him. "So tell me, are you?"

"I think I'll let you decide that," he says. "It's the man on the video who's the bad person. Don't forget, he tried to kill *you*, not the other way around. You were clearly intoxicated, and it seemed like he was trying to make you more so. I think he planned the whole thing."

I shiver. I had imagined that my life before Puerto Rico had been calm, quiet and normal. Now it appears there was a lot of bad stuff going on before I ended up in the water.

"What do we do now?" I say softly, still clinging to him.

"It's like I said when I first found you, and the reason I didn't go to the police. We must keep you safe," says Javi, stroking my hair. "Now with that video, we know for sure someone did try to kill you. But we don't know who or why. My guess is, they believe you're dead, and that's how I want it to stay until we figure things out. Until we know who it is, you won't be safe. They may try again."

I look into his eyes and feel his love wash over me.

"What do we do next?" I whisper.

"Since the day I found you, I've been checking the newspapers for any reports of fishing accidents or missing people. But now that we know you were on a ship about to stop in Fort Lauderdale on a certain date, that narrows down the field tremendously. We start there."

CHAPTER THIRTY-THREE

Over the next few days, Javi and I scour the internet looking for information on recent cruise ship passenger deaths or missing persons. Surprisingly, we learn that they're not that uncommon. You never see those kinds of statistics in travel ads when they're trying to lure you onto an exotic cruise, but apparently they do happen.

After doing a fair amount of research, we find out that nearly twenty people per year go overboard on cruise ships. The total *deaths* each year on ships clock in at around two hundred people. The question is, was I meant to be one of them, or was what happened to me an accident? Javi is convinced in my case it was not an accident.

He makes a bunch of calls to the Fort Lauderdale police, media and some unnamed people he knows in "strategic places." I don't ask. He's got trusted people in Florida who are going to check and see what cruise ships were in Fort Lauderdale the week he found me.

Fort Lauderdale is a big port. There could have been a lot of ships there at the same time. After a few days turning over many stones, we find no reports of anyone going missing from a cruise ship near Florida during a six-month period. We hit a dead end.

This afternoon, Javi's going into town to get a haircut. I ask to join him.

"If you go out in public, and the wrong person sees you," says Javi, "they might come here to finish the job. I won't take that risk. You're too important to me."

The whole thing sounds like a terrible movie. In my heart, I know he's not completely wrong. So, I agree and stay behind to plant some herbs in pots. When my gardening is done, I start getting things ready for tonight's dinner.

To entertain myself while I prepare the meal, I turn on the little TV in the corner of the living room for some mindless noise. Javi has a satellite dish on the roof that picks up channels from all over the world.

Flipping through several dozen shows, I finally settle on a news program that's broadcast from somewhere near New York City. There's a story about a six-year-old child prodigy who's able to play the violin like a master. The little boy is so tiny, and I find myself mesmerized by his performance.

Before I know it, all my vegetables are chopped, and I take the fish out of the fridge to marinate it. As I'm unwrapping the mahi-mahi that Javi caught yesterday, the show on the TV changes. The new one is called *Crime Busters*. The first segment is about a missing child kidnapped by a noncustodial parent. The host explains that when children are taken, it's often a parent who is involved.

As I attempt to cut up a fresh coconut, a new segment on the TV begins. The knife I'm using is very sharp, and the coconut is extra tough. As I slice through the dense fruit not fully in control of the knife, an announcer's voice projects from the TV.

The host is talking about a missing persons case in Connecticut. The camera pans to a man sitting alone in a chair. The man has sandy-brown hair, a close-cropped beard and light eyes. He's handsome and looks like he works out. I want to say he looks familiar, but he doesn't, not really. But when he speaks again, I know I've heard his voice before. I put the knife down and walk over to the TV.

The caption under the man says "Andre Gifford, Husband of Missing Woodmere, Connecticut woman."

"My wife's been missing for months now," says Andre Gifford. "You can't imagine how devastating it's been for me and all the people here who love her."

"*Crime Busters* is watched by thousands of people. Why don't you tell our audience exactly what happened," says the *Crime Busters* host. "Let our viewers be your eyes and ears."

The camera moves to a close-up, and I see tears in Andre Gifford's eyes as he shakes his head.

"That's just the thing," says Andre. "We've got very little to go on. My wife just vanished from our house one day. That's why it's been so frustrating for everyone involved. The police have no leads to follow up on. It's like she disappeared into thin air."

The host leans forward. "Keep talking, Andre. Someone in our audience may know or have seen something."

Andre Gifford pauses and presses his lips together before he speaks. Oddly, it's the pursing of his lips that strikes a familiar chord with me. I move even closer to the TV.

"My wife and I had just celebrated our tenth wedding anniversary. We were so happy. We'd just returned from an amazing vacation. The first morning after we got home, I went to work in the city like I always do. Before I left, I poured my wife's morning coffee into a cup, and told her I loved her."

"Go on," says the host.

"I had a normal day at work. When I got home that night, everything had changed. She was gone."

The camera pans back to the host. "According to the police reports my producers received, there was no sign of a struggle in your home. Mrs. Gifford's car was still in the garage, correct?"

The camera's on Andre Gifford again. He jerks his head away and nods as if it's taking his entire concentration to keep from falling apart.

"I came home at my usual time, and she was nowhere in the house. The police have ruled out a kidnapping because everything in our home was intact. The only thing missing was her purse and her weekend bag."

"So could it mean she left on her own?" says the host.

Andre shakes his head. "No. That's not possible. We were very happy and had big travel plans ahead of us. My wife had been ill for a number of years. Recently, she'd been doing so much better. She was looking forward to the future. I feel certain that someone came to our house and took her against her will or convinced her to go with them or drugged her."

"Is there any evidence to support that theory?" says the host.

Andre shakes his head. "No. That's what I mean. There are no leads. But here's what I want your audience to know. My wife is the most wonderful person. I want her back more than anything and will do whatever it takes."

I feel myself starting to tremble, which startles me. I'm having a physical reaction to this story from Connecticut. There's something familiar about this man's face and voice.

I'm inches from the TV when a picture of a woman splashes across the screen. I literally jump backward and knock over a chair when I see a photo of myself in a wedding gown. The title under the picture says Rebecca Gifford Wedding.

I feel lightheaded. My heart is pounding so hard that I have to grab on to a piece of furniture to steady myself. Taking a deep breath, it dawns on me what I've learned, and now I'm terrified.

My name is Rebecca Gifford.
I'm married.
I think my husband tried to kill me.

CHAPTER THIRTY-FOUR

Sirena/Becca

When Javi's black Jeep finally pulls up in front of the house, I'm waiting outside, wringing my hands and walking in circles. Seeing my photo and learning about my life on TV has opened up the floodgates. Now, random images have started to coalesce. They still don't make total sense, but something is taking shape.

My first instinct was to go online and find out more. I didn't have the right password for Javi's computer, so I had to wait until he got back.

"Sirena," he says with a smile as he leaps out of the Jeep holding a large basket filled with food and wine. "We are going to have a feast tonight."

As he starts unloading boxes from the back of his car, I go over to him. He looks at me and must see the worry on my face. One of his eyebrows shoots up.

"You don't like my haircut?" he says.

"Something's happened," I say, my voice quivering.

He turns and faces me. "What?"

"I saw something on the TV," I say, grabbing his arm. "I think I saw me."

For the next few minutes, I tell him about all the things I learned and the moment when I saw my wedding picture.

"I think . . . I'm married." I look into his concerned eyes, and I can't stop my tears. There are tears in his eyes, too. "My name is Rebecca Gifford."

"Tranquillo," he says softly, taking me into his arms. "You're absolutely sure?"

I nod into his chest. Without saying a word, we bring the groceries into the house and Javi sits me down at the kitchen table.

"Wait here," he says before he goes into the bedroom. "There's something I need to show you."

When he returns, he sits down next to me and places something in my hand. I look down at my open palm. It's a gold wedding band.

"What's this?" I say.

"I probably should have given it to you sooner. I was waiting until you were stronger," he says. "You were wearing this when I pulled you out of the ocean."

I pick up the ring and place it on my ring finger. It fits. I slide it off and look at the inside for an inscription. "B & A Forever" is etched inside.

"This is my wedding ring," I say numbly.

He nods. "Let's go online and see if we can figure this out," he says.

We sit side by side in front of his computer.

"You do it," I say, squeezing his hand. "I'm too nervous."

Javi types "Rebecca Gifford missing woman Connecticut" into Google.

Seconds later, several dozen listings pop up on the screen about missing Connecticut women.

There are a number of postings about my case. We read every single article and watch two videos before either of us speaks. When we're done, Javi looks at me.

"What doesn't make sense is what Andre Gifford is saying. He said he went to work in the morning in Connecticut, and that you were gone when he came home that night. There's no way you could have floated all the way down to Florida from Connecticut. That's over a thousand miles. You would have drowned."

"Agreed," I say, anger bubbling inside me. "I don't understand. According to all these articles, Rebecca Gifford disappeared a week after you found me. How could that be?"

"It couldn't," he says, pressing the spot between his eyes with two fingers. "You were definitely on a ship in the video we listened to on that phone. So why is that not mentioned in any of the articles? They all say you disappeared in Connecticut."

Javi gets up and circles the room.

"But we checked," I say. "No one was reported missing by any cruise ship around the time you found me. That man, Andre, said he arrived home from work in New York City and discovered his wife was gone."

"The timelines don't add up," says Javi, his eyes now on fire. "If memory serves me correctly, the Andre Gifford we just read about and saw online sounds a lot like the voice we heard in that video on your phone."

Suddenly, an image of Andre Gifford sitting across a table from me appears in my mind. Feeling like I'm suffocating, I run out of the house and down to the water's edge. Javi follows me, and when he catches up he wraps his arms around me.

"We'll figure this out," he says. "I promise. I won't let anything happen to you."

The tears burn slightly as they slide down my cheeks. My face feels hot. I'm about to bury my head into Javi's chest when he abruptly pulls away and changes the subject. I know what he's doing. He's trying to distract me so I don't fall apart.

He pulls a bandanna from his pocket and instructs me to wipe my eyes.

"We need to talk," he says.

"What?" An icky feeling settles in my stomach. Those words are so familiar.

"We need to talk," he says again.

More images pass in front of my eyes... a little girl, then an old woman followed by that same younger woman with the bangs, the one whose picture was on my phone.

"Are you all right?" says Javi, putting his hand on my cheek. "You're burning up."

I stare at Javi, my mouth open as pieces of the puzzle fall in place. A vision of Andre Gifford is right in front of me, but he looks different from the man I saw on *Crime Busters*. He's younger and doesn't have a beard.

Suddenly, everything starts to spin, and my legs go from under me. I'm about to hit the ground when Javi's strong arms catch me. He carries me back into the house, places me on the couch and goes to the sink to get some water.

"Drink this." He holds the cup to my lips as he brushes my hair back. I sip slowly as more and more images pass through my mind as if they're on a reel. I can't piece them all together, but I'm starting to remember.

I grab his forearm. "I think I know what happened."

"Tell me."

"When you said, 'we need to talk,' I remembered, that's exactly what he said."

"Who?"

"Andre Gifford, my husband," I say slowly, enunciating each word as I look away. "I can see him clearly now. He took me on a cruise for our anniversary. It was a surprise. I can see him walking toward me holding two champagne flutes. We're outside on the deck of a ship. It's dark, and he's smiling. I'm looking up at the half-moon... and then suddenly I'm flying through the air."

I cover my face with my hands as the movie in my head finishes.

I look up at Javi.

"My husband was the one who threw me off the ship."

CHAPTER THIRTY-FIVE

Becca

After my epiphany yesterday triggered by the *Crime Busters* TV segment, Javi held me the entire night. I kept asking him what I could have done to make my husband throw me off a moving ship. It seemed incomprehensible to me.

"Why would anyone do that?" I kept asking while wondering if I had done something to deserve it. "Maybe it *was* an accident?"

Javi pulled me to him and stroked my hair. "Until you remember more, we won't know. Why would you think *you* did something? He's the one who tried to kill you. Always remember that."

When we wake up this morning, the sun is shining. We go for an early morning swim. Neither of us say anything about Rebecca and Andre Gifford. I think we both want to preserve the perfect world we've created — the girl with no past and her handsome angler.

I had been a woman with no name and no history rescued by a mysterious man from South America. I've thanked Javi over a hundred times for saving my life. But every time I do, he swears to me that I was the one who saved him. He never explains what he means by that.

Now that I know part of my own truth, I want to understand Javi better.

"Why do you say I saved you?" I ask, sitting across the breakfast table from him.

"Do I say that? It's because you bring me so much joy. You've saved me from a life of boredom."

I give him a side eye. "There's more to it than that. You know some of my secrets, but I know none of yours."

Javi takes his last sip of coffee, puts his cup on the table and clears his throat.

"I told you why my family moved to Buenos Aires and how my father was killed by agents of the corrupt Venezuelan government."

I nod. "There's more, isn't there?"

He looks up at the ceiling fan and sighs.

"Like you, I was married once," he says softly. "She was a beautiful Argentinian girl named Delfine. She was sweet and kind like you. I loved her with my whole heart. You remind me of her in many ways."

"Where is she now?"

"Those people I told you about, the ones who murdered my father? They eventually came after me, too. We had a boat that slept eight docked in the main harbor. I was about to travel down the coast for a few days to take care of some financial business. Delfine was six months pregnant and begged me to let her come along. 'One last trip before the baby comes,' she had said."

Javi stops and takes a deep breath. His eyes are misty.

"You don't have to tell me if it's too hard," I say.

"No, it's time you know. I couldn't say no to her. Delfine was going to meet me at the boat and take the trip with me. I was supposed to be there at noon, but there was so much traffic, and I was late. I tried to call her to tell her I'd be there soon, but she never answered her phone. When I finally pulled into the harbor, there were fire trucks and police everywhere. Plumes of black smoke hung in the air. All I could smell was burning gasoline, and Delfine was gone."

His face twists into a mask of anguish and a tear trickles down one of his cheeks.

"Those men who killed my father, they were looking for me. They put a bomb on my boat. I was the target, but my wife and my unborn child were the only ones there when it went off. The bomb was meant for me."

Now it's my turn to comfort him. I get up and put my arms around his neck as he sobs.

"I'm so sorry, Javi. To live with something like that — it's terrible."

He wipes his eyes.

"Now maybe you understand why I've been so protective of you. There are some very bad people in this world, Sirena. I lost Delfine, but I will not lose you, too."

"Those men who tried to hurt you," I say. "Are they still looking for you?"

He smiles ruefully. "We're talking about South America. Governments change there as often as you change your clothes. Fortunately, the bad people who had a grudge against my family have disappeared for the most part. I don't believe I'm in danger anymore, but to be safe, I'm still very careful. That's why I moved here to Puerto Rico. It's far from Buenos Aires, far from everything I know. I still hope to go back one day."

"We both had bad people wanting us dead," I say.

"Yes, but my bad people are probably gone, and yours, we don't know. What we do know is that, not long ago, your husband tried to kill you. Until we find out why, you're not safe."

"We could go to the police."

"Not yet. First, we have to find proof that he tried to kill you. Without that, it will just be his word against yours. Once we know why and how, then you can go to the police. But you'll have to leave me out of it."

"But you're the one who saved me. You could testify that you found me in the water a week before Andre reported me missing."

Javi takes my hands in his.

"I don't think I'm in danger, but I'm not 100-percent sure. After Delfine was murdered, I went looking for the people who did it. I knew who was behind it. I was able to end the life of two of them, but there were still others. I disappeared from Argentina eight years ago. I get reports from friends of my family keeping me apprised of what's going on. Most of the other people responsible for Delfine's death, the ones who were looking for me, are now dead. I believe there's still one more person left. I have friends looking for him. Until I know he's dead, I can't risk exposure. Also, I wouldn't want to put you in more danger."

"Why would I be in danger?"

"Those people looking for me," he says, "they would try to hurt you as a way to get to me. That's how they operate."

After hearing Javi's story, I agree to wait on contacting the police. The truth is, I don't know what I would say anyway. I don't have any evidence to prove that Andre tried to kill me. I still can't remember very much. Although every hour I seem to recall more, which is disturbing and exhilarating at the same time.

After our intense discussion, Javi wants to walk alone on the beach. I give him his space. While he's gone, I sit at the computer searching for any information on the disappearance of Rebecca Gifford — me. I find numerous pictures from an assortment of news articles the week after I went missing. They're mainly from local Connecticut papers and cable news stations. I print them out and put the articles in chronological order. From what I can tell, my disappearance was initially treated as a kidnapping by the police. But then, a day or two later, the cops learned that my "leather weekend bag" and my handbag were missing. Everything checked out about Andre and me returning to Connecticut after our cruise. That's what led law enforcement to suspect I may have taken off on my own. The thing is, I don't remember having a weekend bag.

I zoom in on a picture of Andre and me from our cruise. According to the article, we were on the Beacon Star sailing out of Port Canaveral, Florida, headed to the Caribbean, stopping in Fort Lauderdale, Puerto Rico, St. Thomas, St. John and then our last stop, Miami. According to several articles, Andre and I got off the ship in Miami and flew home.

I check a few more news sources and find another Connecticut paper that had published several pictures of Andre and me taken on the cruise. There are two shots of both of us. One is a selfie that looks like it was taken right after we boarded the ship in Port Canaveral. A vision of me posing for that picture pops into my head. I remember Andre and I standing on the top of the walkway smiling. The sun was shining and we were so happy. I was wearing a bright pink-and-orange dress.

An avalanche of memories suddenly spills into my consciousness. As random things start flooding my mind, I become overwhelmed. I remember now. Andre bought me that dress as a gift. It was part of my anniversary "surprise." I was so happy when he gave me the cruise tickets and presented me with that dress, sunglasses and hat. It meant he still loved me.

I scroll down to the next picture. It's another one of Andre and me. I'm still wearing that pink-and-orange dress, although this time we're not on the ship. We're standing by a sign that says Las Olas. That's Fort Lauderdale's main shopping street. There's a picture of me, but I don't remember ever being there. It's funny, I remember that first day but nothing else.

In the photo, Andre and I are in the distance facing each other, kissing next to the Las Olas sign. My hair and the skirt of my dress is blowing in the wind. I stare at the picture, trying to remember that moment, but I can't, no matter how hard I try.

I enlarge the photo and look at Andre's head, then zoom in on his legs. Then I do the same with my picture. I'm wearing sunglasses and that straw hat with the pink ribbon. Zooming in on different sections of the photo, I look for anything to help me make sense of this horrifying mess.

I'm about to shut down the computer when suddenly I see it. It's so tiny that I almost didn't notice, but there it is. On the inside of my right ankle is my little flower tattoo. Something's wrong. To make sure I'm not crazy, I check my own ankle. The flower is still there. It's a one-inch tattoo of a rose with two leaves on the stem. There's no color, just the outline in black.

I remember now, I got it in college. Most people don't even know I have a tattoo because it's that small. I thought if I made it really tiny, my mother wouldn't notice, but she did. My mother. Oh, my God. I can see my mother now. All those images of the woman with the short spiky white hair, they were her. Mom. She must think I'm dead.

Remembering my mother fills me with such joy that I almost forget about the tattoo in the picture. Almost. Looking down at my ankle again, I remind myself to stay on task, and I once again enlarge the rose tattoo in the picture.

It's all coming back now. I got the tattoo with my best friend, Stella. I can see her face. She's the girl with the bangs that I kept seeing in my mind. Stella. Stell. We got the tattoos together to symbolize our friendship.

As I stare at the picture of Andre and me holding hands in Fort Lauderdale, there's no doubt in my mind. The woman in that photo with my husband, that is *not* me.

CHAPTER THIRTY-SIX

Most people wouldn't have noticed, but that tattoo is something permanently on my body. The rose on my ankle has two leaves on the stem, one on either side. But the tattoo on the woman in the photo — the person everyone *thinks* is me — has three leaves on the stem.

I scroll for other pictures of my husband and me and find two more from the anniversary cruise on another news site. The first thing I notice is that both pictures are shot from a distance and from the side. In fact, in one of them, you can't see my face at all, only my long red hair and hat. Andre's facing forward in each shot, but I'm not. I zoom in on my ankles and sure enough, there's an extra leaf on the tattoo in both photos. That's proof that the woman in the pictures isn't me.

I'm desperate to tell Javi what I've discovered and run out of the house to find him. He's far down the beach, barely a speck. I know his walk and the way he ambles when he takes a step. Bursting over my discovery, I start waving my arms and running toward him. As I run along the sand, I suddenly remember, in my previous life I had been sick. I had fibromyalgia and hadn't been able to run like this in years. As each second passes, more memories clamor for my attention.

Javi finally sees me and starts running in my direction. If there was music playing, it would look like some romantic scene from a movie. Javi is running much faster than me. In less than two minutes, out of breath, we nearly collide.

"Are you all right?" He grabs my shoulders as he bends over to catch his breath. "What's wrong?"

"I'm fine," I say, gasping for air. "I found something, and I've remembered so much more. You're not going to believe it."

"But you're okay?"

I nod.

"You scared me, Sirena," he says, relief spreading across his face. "Please don't do that again. My old heart can't take it."

Still out of breath, I tell him about my illness and the tattoo as we walk hand in hand back to the house. Once inside, I hold up my ankle next to the computer screen with a close-up of the picture of the woman with my husband.

"See, there are three leaves on her tattoo, not two."

"Son of a bitch," Javi mutters. "This husband of yours and that woman, they planned this. They worked the whole thing out. This was no accident or a crime of passion. Your husband crafted the whole thing well in advance of the trip, and that woman helped him."

"I think you're right."

"What kind of monster would do something like that to my beautiful girl?" he says, taking my face in his hands.

"I love you," I say softly as I start to cry.

"No tears," he says. He wipes my tears away with his thumbs. "I think I've loved you since the day I pulled you out of the water."

He kisses me. Knowing this beautiful man loves me and has my back tells me what I need to do. I just have to figure out how.

"A person can't just dump his wife over the side of a ship and get away with it," I say, walking across the room from him. "We have to do something. He needs to go to jail for what he did."

"We still don't have the full story yet. Until then, we must exercise patience to get the outcome we want. Reacting to a situation without a well-thought-out plan could backfire."

"Javi, that man tried to kill me," I say. "In fact, he thinks he *did* kill me, and now he's living his best life. Doesn't he have to pay for that?"

Javi nods. "In time. Your memories are only just starting to return. We must wait until we know everything. Besides, what would you say to the police? How did he try to kill you? What proof do we have?"

"The tattoo is proof that the woman in the picture isn't me," I say.

"It doesn't prove he tried to kill you," says Javi. "And how are you going to find out who the imposter is? The tattoo on her ankle was probably temporary. It would likely be gone by now, so your only proof will have disappeared."

I throw my head back in frustration and groan.

"Tell me, what do you *want* to happen?" he says.

I grit my teeth. As I speak, my voice is cold and hollow.

"I want Andre to go to jail for my murder," I say.

"That presents a problem because here you are. You're very much alive. They can't arrest him for your murder if you're not dead."

I parse Javi's words, knowing there are elements of truth to what he says.

"But you found me in the ocean when he says I flew back to Connecticut with him."

"Then he would be convicted of lying to the police, not for your murder."

I nod and wrack my brain for another way forward.

"Tell me about this illness you were talking about before," Javi says as he sits down in front of his computer. "What was it called again?"

"Fibromyalgia."

A fleeting memory of me in an MRI machine and of someone drawing my blood fixes in front of my eyes. I remember taking a lot of pills and spending days and weeks in bed. I also remember pain in my joints all the time.

"It says here," he says, reading from the screen, "fibromyalgia is a chronic condition causing widespread pain in the body's muscles, tendons and soft tissue."

"Yes, that's right."

"It can also cause fatigue, depression, anxiety, as well as burning and numbness in hands and feet. You had all that?"

I nod. "Sometimes. I took a lot of anti-inflammatory pills, but they didn't always work."

"You have pain now?"

I smile. "A twinge here and there, but I thought I'd just pulled a muscle. Living here with you, eating clean and healthy and getting a lot of exercise, I feel really good."

"No depression or anxiety?"

"None."

He pushes back from the computer and sighs. "Good."

I shake my head in frustration. "If I go to the cops now, he'll just deny it. He'll blame everything on the fibromyalgia and depression and say that I obviously ran off. He'll paint me as a crazy person."

"It's quite possible," says Javi.

As I wander around the room trying to recall more facts, I remember something else. Andre was not always sympathetic to my health problems. In fact, I often sensed his disapproval and irritation whenever I had a flare-up.

"He didn't want a sick wife, so he got rid of me," I say. "He needs to pay for that."

He smiles at me like a teacher explaining a problem to a confused student. "Let's establish some goals first. We'll get him, I promise," says Javi, taking my face in his hands. "But first we need a plan that also protects you."

He's right. We have to be as meticulous and cold-hearted as Andre was when he planned my death.

"Come," says Javi, grabbing my hand and leading me toward the door. "It's starting to rain. Let's go sit out on the porch and enjoy the nature around us."

He's trying to distract me again. I pull my hand back and look at him, my eyes searching for his soul.

"I promise, you'll have your justice," he says. "As you know, I can be a very vindictive man if someone hurts the person I love."

Now that the pieces are coming together, I feel liberated. Instead of sitting on the porch watching the rain, I leave Javi and run outside and dance in it. I hear Javi laughing from the dry safety of the porch while I spin and twirl with joy.

Soaked and dripping when I finish my dance, I join him on the porch.

"It makes my heart happy to see you so filled with joy," he says. I sense something else going on behind his eyes, but I'll let him tell me when he's ready.

For the next few weeks, I try to enjoy my life in the little blue beach house. Each day my head is filled with thousands of memories and images, and they keep coming. I remember my mom and dad and the house I grew up in. It was a little white house with green shutters and a flower garden out front. I want to call my parents and hear their voices and tell them I'm okay. Then, I remember my father died a long time ago, and it makes me sad. For a few minutes, he was alive, and then he wasn't. I feel myself grieve all over again.

I can visualize the college I went to in New Hampshire. I met my freshman roommate that first day. She had a nest of messy brown hair piled on top of her head and became my best friend for life, Stella McCrystal.

People used to call her Stella McCrazy back then, because she was. She got that name because her clothes were always slightly askew and wrinkled, and she would do anything on a dare. When it came to our college misadventures, I was usually the adult in the room. But, when all was said and done, Stella had a heart of gold and has never, ever let me down.

I'm smiling as flickers of Stella come back to me. Suddenly, there's a pit in my stomach when I realize what my former world must look like. My mom, Stella and my other friends probably all think I'm dead. My ears ring with rage. It's like hearing a million crickets at once. I'm so angry.

When Andre threw me off that ship, he didn't just hurt me, he hurt the people who love me, too. My poor mother must think I'm dead. I'm her only child. What kind of person would do that to someone's mother? Mom was always so nice to him, too. As I consider all the people Andre's actions have impacted besides me, I realize I haven't examined my own feelings about being murdered.

My marriage wasn't perfect. But now I think it was the stress that came from Andre's disapproval that made my health deteriorate. I'd push myself through the pain when I wasn't feeling well. That's what happened with my teaching job. I did it for as long as I could. His irritation with my illness was written all over his face. After a while, being with him was like walking on eggshells. I was so afraid of being alone that it clouded my judgment. But I'm strong and healthy now, and I'm not going to be intimidated by anyone.

One thing I know for sure — my husband's going to pay for what he did, but he'll never see me coming.

CHAPTER THIRTY-SEVEN

For the next few weeks, I spend most of my time digging online for more information about my disappearance and the ensuing investigation. Occasionally, Javi tries to distract me with a fishing trip or a walk on the beach, but I've been ignited. I'm a woman on a mission, and I won't stop until it's over, until I get him.

Every night, I share what I learn with Javi, who takes it all in but says little. A huge part of me wants to pick up the phone and call Stella or my mom and tell them I'm okay, that I'm alive. But Javi says we should wait, so we know where the danger lies.

"Find out where the sharks are swimming before you go in the water," he says on more than one occasion.

He's right, so I wait and watch.

One day, after spending a few hours Googling my case, I put all the players into a spreadsheet. It's been nine months since Andre threw me into the sea like a bag of garbage. There have been no new developments in my case. The articles and media coverage have become pretty thin. In fact, within the last few weeks, there's only one reporter who's written anything about it. The journalist's name is Tommy Devlin, and he's with a local Connecticut TV station and has a column that appears in a local newspaper.

I look up Devlin's picture and biography. He's forty-five and has had a lot of jobs. Some were with pretty big news organizations. That's probably why he looks so proud of himself in his picture. His bio sounds that way, too. I wonder why he's working in local news after having a stint at CNN years ago. Maybe he's not as good as he thinks he is, which makes him perfect for me. Devlin is my man.

I start small by sending the reporter a few tiny, cryptic messages to see if I can get a rapport going. I don't tell Javi. He's so protective of me, but the thing is, Javi didn't get thrown off a ship by someone he was married to. That does something to your head. Andre's premeditation under the guise of an anniversary cruise is something I can't get over. And truthfully, I don't want to get past it. I want him to pay.

After so many months of me missing and no repercussions for my murder, I figure Andre's feeling pretty untouchable right now. My objective is to rattle his cage and put him on edge. When people are nervous, they make mistakes.

I create a couple of bogus Gmail accounts and attach those emails to fake social media accounts. In one afternoon, I've created a presence for Magnolia Starship, a little nom de plume to pay homage to what was supposed to have been my watery grave.

But wait, there's more.

From my newly created social media accounts, I send a one-line message to ace reporter Tommy Devlin. It's short and sweet and gets right to the heart of the matter. I don't have time for innuendo.

Did Andre Gifford kill his wife?

The following morning after Javi goes out to look at a new pickup truck he's thinking of buying, I log in to my new Gmail accounts. Sure enough, there's a response from Tommy Devlin.

Who is this?

My first reaction is that he isn't a very good investigative journalist . . . *Who is this?* I could do better than that, and I never worked at CNN. That explains why the bigger news companies are in Devlin's rearview. I suspect that there's no *Boston Globe* or BBC in his future, either. But I don't want a reporter who's particularly sharp. I need someone I can manipulate. More than ever, I'm convinced Devlin is my man.

I don't respond right away. But after an hour, Magnolia Starship replies.

Have you looked carefully at Rebecca's husband? You've missed something important.

I figure that's intriguing enough to get Devlin to at least take a second look at Andre.

Over the next few days, Devlin and Magnolia Starship exchange several messages. I give him very little, just enough to keep him going. I let him know I'm a friend of Becca's, and after five days of dangling carrots, I go for the punch.

Is it possible Rebecca Gifford never returned to Connecticut after the cruise?

A wicked smile spreads across my face when I hit send. I know how that last message will land. From everything I've read about the case, and I've read it all a hundred times, my husband was ruled out early in the investigation. The entire investigation was relegated to the New York/Connecticut metro area, not off the coast of Florida.

Ten days after I sent the first message, I see Devlin's latest article. The headline reads:

DID REBECCA GIFFORD VANISH INTO THIN AIR?

The article reviews the entire timeline of me going missing. I guess Devlin can't come out and say "her husband did it" without any hard factual information. If he asks publicly whether the police had looked at the cruise, then he's essentially accusing Andre of lying. It was Andre who told everyone I returned home. There were no other witnesses. The only thing Devlin can do is what he did. I'm satisfied for now as I reread his article.

> *. . . if there's no trace of Rebecca Gifford anywhere in Connecticut, the police must go further back in the timeline. Prior to disappearing, Ms. Gifford was on a cruise in the Caribbean with her husband. Could she have met someone on that trip who wanted to do her harm? From this reporter's perspective, more questions need to be asked by the police. They need to cast a wider net.*

When I see this, I know Andre is squirming like a worm on a hook, and I'm loving it. It's not the justice I want, but it's a start.

I post something online in the comments section under Devlin's article. By the next day, a few other people have chimed in, agreeing with the reporter. Some have even gone for a full-blown conspiracy theory. I put up a few more comments to fan the flames. My posts are even more outrageous than the others. Soon, there's a mini pile-on with even crazier ideas.

The seeds of doubt have been planted.

The next day, I go online to see if there are any new articles about my investigation. I spot one that is several months old. I hadn't seen it before and click on it.

When I read the headline, I'm shattered.

My mother, Martha, died of a heart attack months ago, before my memories started to return. My eyes fill with tears, which trickle down my face. I had desperately wanted to reach out to my mother and tell her I was alive. Now I know it wouldn't have mattered because she was already gone.

A fury rises within me. Not only did Andre try to kill me, but he also deprived me of the last few months with my beautiful mom. I can never forgive him for that.

CHAPTER THIRTY-EIGHT

Andre

In the many months since my wife disappeared, I've thrown myself into my work at the agency. Despite the stress of Becca being gone, I've made great strides with the Chick'n Lick'n account. I came up with a kick-ass tagline, and the client loves me. You might say I walk on water.

My bosses keep telling me to take it easy and carve out some time for myself. I remind them that being at work is far better than going home to an empty house filled with ghosts. These days, I'm in the office on weekends, too. I'm the wounded warrior throwing everything I've got into my job because I have nothing else left. Not great for me but fantastic for my employer. There have been rumors about me getting promoted and maybe making partner. It's all coming together. I'll make partner at Hardy & Engel, and Lily and I will be together. Sweet.

The police don't call as much anymore, but I get an update every other week or so. They've set up a tip line for people to anonymously call in. From what they tell me, they've received some pretty whacky reports, none of which have materialized into anything. And they won't.

I get a call from Detective Contessa this Friday morning. He wants to stop by tomorrow at the house and give me an update in person. I explain that I'm on deadline with a pitch. I tell him that I'm planning to work in the city over the weekend and suggest we do the update on the phone.

"It will only take twenty minutes," he says. "I'll come by early."

The next morning, I'm up at 6:30 a.m. I throw on a pair of jeans and a navy golf shirt for my audience with Contessa. I know he's going to grill me. He always does. I can handle it. I was born ready for guys like him.

I put on a pot of coffee, figuring I should be a little hospitable to the lawman. After all, he *is* in charge of my wife's case. I need him on my side. At seven thirty the doorbell rings. Contessa's right on time. I do appreciate punctuality.

"Detective Contessa," I say with a deliberate brave smile fixed on my face.

He walks past me into the foyer as I close the door.

"Let's go into the kitchen," I say. "I just made some coffee."

I've already placed two mugs on the kitchen table along with milk and sugar. He sits down as I fill our cups.

"It's good," he says after taking his first sip. "Thanks for making time to see me today."

"Finding Becca is my priority. I'll do anything I can to help."

"You roast your own beans?" says Contessa, sipping from his mug.

"No."

"I use one of those pod machines."

"Takes the guesswork out." I look at my watch. "So, what did you want to talk about? Is there news on Becca?"

The detective shifts in his chair. "Mind if I get a little more?"

I refill it, now regretting that I offered him a beverage. I take my seat while obviously looking at my watch again. "I really do need to catch the 8:45 train."

The detective folds his hands in front of him and locks in on me.

"I'll get to the point, Andre," he says. "As you know, we have numerous theories as to what happened to your wife. First, we chased down the 'abduction from the house' angle. We're still not ruling it out. But since there was no forced entry and no history of unsavory characters in your lives, that's moved to the bottom of the list."

I put my cup on the table and lean forward. "What about someone grabbing her off the street?"

Contessa nods. "It's possible but unlikely. She wasn't a kid, and it would have happened in broad daylight. Somebody would have seen something."

"Not if they pulled up next to her on the street, pointed a gun at her and forced her to get into a car."

"Anything's possible. It's still one of the theories we're chasing down," says Contessa.

Where is this cop going with this?

"Andre, I'll be honest with you. Your wife's disappearance has always been a puzzle to me. I don't like it when I can't solve a puzzle. Because of that, we decided to retrace all of Becca's steps during the weeks leading up to her disappearance."

His robotic death stare is starting to freak me out.

"I know you've got a train to catch, but this will only take a few minutes," says Contessa, finishing his coffee. "We did some investigating into your wife's movements in the weeks prior to her disappearance.

"And?" I say.

For the love of God, please get to the point, Detective.

"All dead ends," says Contessa. "Nothing we saw shed any new light on your wife's whereabouts. I just wanted you to know that we're still working every angle possible."

I let out a silent sigh of relief, pick up my black leather backpack and look at the time again. "I'm afraid I really must leave now, or I'll miss my train."

We walk outside together. His car is parked next to mine in the driveway. I'm about to get into my car when he suddenly turns and faces me.

"There was one more thing that's been puzzling me," says Contessa. "We got some videos from the TSA in the Miami airport of you and your wife on your way home. You both were looking at the Departures screen. I presume you were trying to find your gate."

"Probably," I say as I toss my backpack onto the passenger seat. "I don't remember, but I'm sure we did look."

"Your wife wears glasses. She's nearsighted, isn't that right?"

"Yes, she wears glasses but mainly for distance."

"That's what I thought. But in the TSA video, it looked like your wife took off her glasses to read the Departures screen up on the wall. If she's nearsighted and needs glasses for distance, why do you think she'd do that?"

183

CHAPTER THIRTY-NINE

I offered Contessa no explanation regarding my wife's distance vision or lack thereof. Of course, the reason the woman on the video removed her glasses is because Lily has 20/20 vision. Those prescription lenses were blinding her and affecting her balance. She complained about it the entire time we were traveling.

Thankfully, when I didn't have an answer, the detective dropped it and hasn't brought it up since.

In the meantime, Lily's been on my ass about lifting our "moratorium of silence" as she calls it. We haven't physically seen each other in months. We talk on our special phones but have had no in-person contact, except for that one time.

It was about a month ago. Lily had been freaking out saying she couldn't "take it anymore" and "what kind of life is this for a young woman?" She said other girls her age were going out and having a good time while she was sitting home watching *The Real Housewives of Somewhere*. I had to do something to keep her from combusting, so I suggested a one-time-only meetup.

We met at a public beach in Cape Cod that I'd been to years earlier. It was off-season, so I knew there wouldn't be many people around. It's also two-and-a-half hours from where I live and in another state. Chances of running into anyone there who'd recognize us was slim to none.

I took a calculated risk. I had to. I was afraid Lily would start shooting her mouth off and we'd both end up in orange jumpsuits. She's not cut out for this cloak-and-dagger stuff.

Maybe that's why I'm so crazy about her. She's so real. What you see is what you get. She says what she thinks even if sometimes she sounds batshit crazy. The problem is, I had essentially taken away what made Lily tick. She is first and foremost a sexual being oozing sensuality. You can taste it when she walks into a room. That's what drives her. With only girlfriends to spend time with for a year, she was off her game. Lily is so different from Becca, who spent most of her time in front of the TV complaining about her aches and pains. They're nothing alike.

If I'd heard that word *fibro-fucking-myalgia* one more time, I wouldn't have waited for the cruise. I would have strangled her in our bed, or hit her over the head with the iron, and gladly done the time.

I continue to check in with Detective Contessa regularly to keep tabs on him. In fact, it's on my calendar to call him every Wednesday. Maintaining the appearance of the concerned, devastated husband is of paramount importance. When the investigation was fresh, Contessa and I spoke several times a day. But once the leads dried up, and he had nothing to share with me, I hardly heard from him. Frankly, he should be mortified. A thirty-five-year-old woman disappears from her home in Connecticut and the police have nothing? They're a joke.

Next month we're coming up on a year, or as I like to call it, the finish line. Lily and I have been talking about putting our dating profiles up on Match. We won't do it at the same time in case anyone ever checks. She put hers up last week, and I'll do mine in another month. I'm committed to waiting the full year before we publicly connect. I'm in the branding business and appearance is everything.

I also won't put my profile up on the dating sites until I get the blessing from Stella and some of Becca's other friends. I want *them* to encourage me to do it. I think Stella's almost there. She still comes over once or twice a week to check in on me and bring me the odd meal or a box of donuts.

"How are you doing?" says Stella when she stops by my house unannounced, which I hate.

"Hanging in," I say, making myself tear up. I've become really good at this insta-cry thing. I can turn on the water anytime I need to. If a relative, friend, cop or insurance agent walks through my front door, the dam breaks within seconds.

"I mean really," says Stella. "How *are* you?"

I nod sadly and look away. "It's been a tough year. I'm not going to lie to you, Stell. I still miss her so much. I feel lost without her."

I see her getting weepy, so I turn up the pressure on my own eye faucets and away we go. We both start bawling, and she hands me a tissue.

"You know, Andre," she says, "maybe it's time for you to get out, meet people, socialize a little."

I shake my head and wipe away my manufactured tears.

"I can't. My heart wouldn't be in it."

"Becca wouldn't want you to sit around and be sad all the time," says Stella. "She'd want you to move on and build your life again. She'd want you to be happy."

And there it is, my "get out of jail free" card. My wife's best friend is urging me to get myself out there to meet women and have a good time.

"I can't go out with another woman after Becca," I say, planting the very specific seed about me dating.

She doesn't say anything right away, and I wonder if I pushed her too soon. But after a few moments, she rallies.

"You don't have to date right away, but you're still young," she says. "You're only in your forties. Honey, you've got a long life ahead of you. Don't give up on it now."

I ask to change the subject as if the mere thought of being with another woman is too overwhelming a concept for me to consider.

Over the next couple of weeks, whenever she drops by, I surreptitiously lead her into bringing up the dating idea again. After the third time, she gives me a hard sell. This time, I respond a little more positively.

"Maybe you're right, Stell. Maybe I should get out and meet some people. All I've done for the past year is talk to reporters and the police and go to work. But I don't know how I'd even start."

Her eyes light up. "I can help you. I'm an old pro at dating sites. I'll show you how to put everything up . . . if you want me to."

I tell her I need to sleep on it. The next day, I call her and say that I'll give it a try . . . if she really thinks I should.

Tonight, Stella's coming over to help me create my profile on the dating sites. Once that's up, I'll spend two or three weeks meeting a few other women for coffee to make things look legit. Then, when enough time passes, I'll "meet" Lily for the first time.

"How does this sound for my profile blurb?" I say to Stella after doing some wordsmithing. "Successful creative director in advertising biz enjoys sports, travel, hiking, movies, concerts and nature. Looking to meet like-minded woman for good conversation and shared experiences."

"That's nice, Andre," says Stella. "It's engaging and normal, not intimidating or weird. I'd answer that one, especially with *your* photo attached to it."

I deliberately blush and look away.

Is Stella hitting on me? Was this whole dating thing just a ruse on her part to get me into bed with her?

"You're a handsome guy, Andre," says Stella. "Loads of women will want to meet you. I promise. You'll see."

She doesn't take it any further than that, so I let it be. All that matters is that I've received the stamp of approval from my wife's best friend to go out and meet women. You don't have to tell me twice. After that night, I put the wheels in motion.

Over the next few weeks, I meet up with six different women at local coffee shops. They're all nice and in their thirties. One of them named Audrey, is pretty hot. Andre and Audrey also has nice alliteration. For a nano-second, I think about asking her out to dinner. Then my better self reminds me that I must not complicate my situation.

Adding a girlfriend, on top of a girlfriend, on top of a dead wife would be a poor decision. However, I keep the woman's name and number and tell her I'm still getting over the loss of my wife. I leave the door open in case Lily and I don't work out. You never know.

After each meeting with a different woman, I dutifully report back to Stella so we can do a postmortem together. She and I both agree, none of the ladies I've met so far are right for me.

It's time to introduce Lily.

She and I have agreed to play it straight going forward. She'll use her real name, Lily Flagg, and meet me in her real blonde hair. It will be a completely legit operation with the blessing of Becca's friends.

I reach out to Lily on Match, and we begin a texting conversation. I remind her on the phone that all texting must be benign in case anyone ever subpoenas the files. We start out slow. After a week, I suggest we meet for coffee. Before our first date, Stella comes over and reviews Lily's profile and reads our text exchanges.

"She seems nice, I guess," says Stella, looking at Lily's pictures. "She's very pretty. She reminds me a little bit of Becs."

I sit back and stare at Stella as if that thought never occurred to me.

"I hadn't seen it, but you're right. There's a slight resemblance." I push the computer away from me and make a forlorn face. "Maybe this whole thing is a mistake."

Stella looks at me and places her hand over mine, holds it there and gives it a squeeze.

What is this? Is Stella coming on to me?

"Nobody said this was going to be easy," she says, "but you've got to put yourself out there. It's been a year now. It's time."

"A year doesn't feel so long to me," I say as she squeezes my hand again.

I "let" Stella convince me to keep my meeting with Lily Flagg. And surprise, surprise, it's a match made in heaven.

I call Stella after my first date with Lily.

"I liked her," I say. "She was nice. I think Becca would like her, too."

Stella seems cautiously optimistic that it went so well.

"I'm happy for you. I know Becs would want this. But, at the same time, don't rush into anything."

Make up your mind, lady. I should date or I shouldn't? Or is it that you want me for yourself?

After two months, Lily and I are a thing. We're dating out in the open with the approval of everyone I know. Neighbors, friends and colleagues all seem to want me to have a next chapter.

Three months after our first "meeting," Lily moves into my house, and we make plans to marry. All I can say is thank God Becca's mother is dead. She wouldn't have approved of me moving on so quickly. She would have caused problems and asked too many questions. Every now and then I pinch myself. It's all worked out just the way I'd planned. I've pulled off the perfect murder. How many people can say that?

Then, one night, Lily and I go out to the movies. We're waiting to buy popcorn when we bump into Detective Contessa with his girlfriend, Donna, a cute blonde. I'm a little surprised the detective has such good taste in women and wonder if he interrogates her while they're in bed.

"Andre," he calls out as he walks toward me.

Contessa was the last person I expected to see tonight. We introduce our girlfriends, but I say nothing about Becca. Mentioning it would be awkward in front of my date.

After exchanging a few pleasantries, I notice Contessa is memorizing every inch of Lily. I'm about to make my excuses so we can leave when he suddenly looks at his watch and says his movie is starting.

"Good to see you, Andre," the detective says as he walks off. "I'll be in touch."

I don't trust that cop.

CHAPTER FORTY

Becca

It's hard to believe that it's been eighteen mainly blissful months since Javi saved my life. Being here in Puerto Rico has been grounding and filled with so much love. I've even planted a garden and am in awe of the tropical nature all around us.

Who would have guessed? After all that happened, I'm living a happy life with a man who puts me first. I never had that with Andre. In the beginning, he put me up on a pedestal, but that didn't last long. When we were dating, he'd dole out the compliments, and I'd be riding high. Then, slowly, he started to take me down. A little insult here, a tiny dig there. Even before I got sick, Andre liked things *his* way. We'd watch the movie he wanted, go to the restaurant he liked. I'd even fix my hair the way he suggested, when all I really wanted to do was put it up in a ponytail.

I don't think I ever looked at our relationship clearly back then. I chose to see our marriage through rose-colored glasses. It's a nice way to go through life, but rose-colored glasses hide an awful lot of sins. I can't believe I thought we had the perfect marriage. Clearly it wasn't.

I continue to monitor the progress of my missing persons investigation. From what I read, there's not much going on. Still, I ingest every piece of data I find, and I continue sending provocative messages to that reporter, Devlin. I need to keep him interested in my case.

Despite my efforts with Devlin, the coverage on my case is almost nonexistent. The police have never found a body, received a ransom note or had other suspects under the microscope. The public consensus was that Rebecca Gifford probably took off and left her poor husband to clean up the mess. It's stunning, really. I'm the victim, and I've been turned into the villain. Andre must love that.

My friends still want to find me. But it seems a lot of people feel sorry for Andre in a different way now. Instead of him being the husband of a murdered woman, he's become the jilted husband of a conniving and duplicitous woman — me. This new theory sends me into orbit. That asshole tried to kill me, and now the public sympathy is on his side? You can't make this stuff up.

According to Woodmere.org, an online Connecticut community board, a woman has moved into my house with Andre. I figured that would eventually happen. He has way too big an ego *and* libido to sit idly by mourning me for too long.

"I want to go to the police," I say to Javi over dinner. "Andre's getting away with this."

"We're not there yet," Javi says. He takes a bite of an ear of corn. "You want him to go down for murder. For that to happen, we need proof."

"But nothing's happening."

"If you present yourself to the police now, our life here is over," he says. "We'll have no privacy. The press will be all over us. You'll never get what you want, and Andre will remain free."

I listen to his sage words and know he's right. I take solace in the fact that I'm living in paradise with my soulmate. And I'm healthy with not a single ache or pain. That's worth a lot.

"The last few years Andre and I were together," I say to Javi later that night in bed, "I was getting sicker and sicker. Meanwhile, he was getting more irritated and disinterested. But here with you, I feel fine."

"I think you feel fine, too," he says, cradling me in his arms.

***

On the two-year anniversary of Andre's attempt to kill me, I find a human-interest story online written by Devlin. There's a video embedded in the article. When I press play, I can see it's been shot in *my* living room in Connecticut. Devlin is doing a one-on-one interview with Andre. I cringe as I begin to watch it. My blood boils with every word he utters. The worst part is Andre comes across as kind, thoughtful and deeply wounded. How is he getting away with this?

Watching that interview fires me up. I'm more determined than ever to make him pay for what he did to me. Connecticut doesn't have the death penalty, but Florida does. I want him to be arrested for my murder in Florida. Beacon Cruise Lines is headquartered in Miami, and he technically attempted to murder me in the waters off Florida.

While most of my memories have returned, there are still occasionally some minor gaps in my timeline. But the jigsaw puzzle is slowly coming together. The things I most want more clarity on are the few days Andre and I spent together in Orlando and on the ship *before* I went overboard. Those are still hazy.

I remember being so excited to go on that cruise. I'd never been on one before. The whole idea seemed very glamorous to me. I remember Andre insisting he carry me across the threshold of our cabin. At the time, I thought it was completely out of character for him. He might have done something like that when we first got married, but the last five years of our marriage, there wasn't much romance. That's why I was so startled and, if I'm honest, a little delighted when he actually picked me up.

I had hoped the cruise marked a new beginning for us and a shift in his attitude since he initiated the trip. I still had some numbness in my arms and legs, and my balance was a little off. But I was determined to have fun on the ship, so I kept my mouth shut and ignored it. The first night on the ship, we had a late dinner in an Italian restaurant and then went to the casino.

I concentrate on the dinner to remember more. That night, the wine was flowing . . ., and our waiter had a funny accent making him impossible to understand. Andre had to ask him three times to repeat the specials. I had a lot of champagne that night. I drank much more than I normally do. The rest of the evening on the ship is spotty, and that's frustrating.

I look at the time and put Andre and the Beacon Star out of my mind for the moment. Tonight, we have friends coming over for dinner. Javi's out fishing for the main course while I prepare some appetizers and side dishes. As I cut up a few mangoes, an old woman's face appears in front of me. She's got short dark hair and bangs. She's wearing oversized glasses, like mine, but they're green or blue. I get the sense that she and I talked about how neither of us could wear contacts. But I don't know how I know her. I must have met her on the ship.

After mixing up the vinaigrette dressing for the avocado-and-vegetable salad, I reach for a container of olives. That's when it comes together for me. The old woman's name was Olive. I congratulate myself, put down my knife and sit at the kitchen table to focus my energy on her. Where did I meet her, and why is she important?

Commanding my brain to deliver answers, I finally get one. I met Olive on the ship in the restaurant. She was very old and . . . told us she was terminally ill. She said she had come on the cruise to die in style or something like that.

I push my chair back from the table and stand. I can see her quite clearly now. She said her doctor told her she didn't have much time left. She loved cruising, so she cashed in whatever she had to go out on a high note. I was surprised because she looked perfectly healthy.

"This will be my last hurrah," I remember her saying. I felt sad for her. Sad because she was sick, but also because she had no one to be with. I said something about it to Andre after she left. He wasn't as interested in her as I was. I thought she was quirky and funny. He found her "annoying." Typical Andre.

I put the salad in the fridge and start mashing the chickpeas for the homemade hummus. As I pour sesame oil into the bowl, Olive's face flashes in front of me again. I can see her sitting next to us in the restaurant on the ship in a blue kaftan. I remember wondering why Andre didn't like her, because she was so nice. When I asked him later, he insisted it was only because he wanted to be alone with me. I was so stupid. I wanted to believe that, so I dropped the conversation.

Now, I can see what was going on. He wanted to keep me away from people so he could easily replace me without anyone noticing. But here's the thing. Olive was old, but she was sharp as a knife. After all the champagne I had and then being thrown overboard, I don't remember that night very well, but she definitely would. She's my proof.

As I take the coconut pie we bought at the Farmers' Market out of the oven, the sweet buttery aroma instantly takes me back to that night on the ship. Andre and I had pie for dessert. We were at a table in the restaurant talking with Olive. What is her last name? I remember thinking her whole name reminded me of cocktails. Olive for martinis and her last name is like . . . a whiskey.

I go to the sink and splash water on my face, hoping it will jog my memory as I make a mental list of different whiskey brands. Jameson? MacCallum? Johnny Walker?

Johnny Walker. That's it. Her name was Olive Walker.

Somehow, figuring out her name allows the other pieces to fit into place. I smile. It's all coming back. Olive was into Instagram and took pictures of everything, especially food. She and I took a few selfies together when Andre walked away. I'm sure she'd remember me. She didn't miss anything. I'll bet she'd notice if another woman with the wrong tattoo took my place.

CHAPTER FORTY-ONE

Tonight, I put on something festive for our dinner party by draping a yellow, green and orange sarong around my body. Tucking it in just the right places, I finish the look by placing a flower behind my ear.

With my chores finished and the table set, I have a few spare minutes to jump on the computer. It's become my routine to check every day to see if there are any new stories about my case. I do a Google search from this past week, and a video of a Detective Contessa from Woodmere PD pops up. He's giving a statement to the press.

"We will always continue to look for Rebecca Gifford," says the detective, who is the lead investigator on my case. "Mrs. Gifford disappeared two years ago. The fact that her whereabouts are still unknown has been extremely difficult for her family and friends. Unfortunately, throughout this investigation, we've hit a lot of dead ends."

Because you're looking in Connecticut. Try looking in Florida.

When the camera zooms in on Andre, I can't breathe. A petite blonde woman is standing next to him before he steps forward to the microphone.

"The search for my wife has been long and traumatizing for those of us who love her. Despite this difficult and heartbreaking time with no answers, I've been able to get through it with the help of family and friends. After Becca vanished, I was so lost. The grief was overwhelming, and I didn't think I'd ever be whole again. But with the encouragement of my wife's friends, I kept going and eventually met Lily."

Andre reaches for the blonde woman's hand and pulls her over to him.

It's her. I feel sick.

"While I will never stop looking for Becca, it's time for all of us to begin healing. Lily has helped me through the bad times and brought light where there had only been darkness. Lily's become my rock. I know Becca would want me to move on with my life. She was that kind of person. She'd want only the best for me."

A reporter steps forward. "Are you and Ms. Flagg getting married?"

My husband looks sheepishly at the blonde before responding.

"Having Lily in my corner is more than enough. But to answer your question, I have asked her to marry me, and she's said yes. According to the laws in the state of Connecticut, there is a wait time before I could legally do that. In the meantime, I know Lily's looking out for me, and I'm very grateful for her support."

When the video stops, I can't move. I'm stunned by Andre's unabashed audacity. He's already replaced me with her. I think back to that night on the ship. Images of Andre and I walking on the deck holding champagne flutes play in my mind . . . .. He kept refilling my glass . . . .. I was so drunk when he left me out on the deck . . . . I started making that video to send to Stella, the one that Reno found.

It's all coming back to me now. I was looking up at the moon when I heard a loud bang. Andre was coming out on the deck through a side door. I didn't want him to see me on the phone, so I stashed it in the pocket of my windbreaker. I must not have stopped recording when I zipped my phone into my pocket.

When Andre approached me, I was wobbly and seeing double. He held me up and we walked over to the railing to look at the moon and stars. He lifted me off the ground, and I thought he was being romantic.

Oh, my God. That's when he threw me over.

A tear runs down my cheek. None of the memories have ever come together like this before. I had glimpsed bits and pieces over the months but nothing linear that made sense. Now I understand everything.

"What's happened?" Javi walks in the front door carrying a large piece of mahi-mahi on a wooden cutting board. He puts the fish down and takes me in his arms and holds me.

I can't speak. I shake my head and cry harder.

"Take your time," he says.

"I remember," I say, barely squeaking out the words. "I remember everything."

I show Javi the video of Andre and the next Mrs. Gifford.

Javi grinds his teeth. He does that when he's angry.

"That man is pure evil," he says.

"I know."

"Show me that video again. I want to see something."

Javi sits in front of the computer, and I start up the video. When we get to the part where Andre introduces Lily, Javi stops the player.

"I thought so," he says, leaning closer to the screen.

"What?"

"Look at that woman's face, the shape and the placement of her eyes, nose and mouth."

I scrutinize Lily's picture but don't connect the dots.

"Look at her face, Sirena. She looks like you," he says. "Your hair is different, but the placement of your features and shape of your face are very similar. Other than the hair, you could be sisters. You know what I think? That woman was on the ship. I think she was the one on the Beacon Star pretending to be you."

I'm about to respond when we hear our guests coming up the walk.

"We'll talk about this later," he says as he takes my hand and puts a smile on his face.

Throughout the evening, Javi's revelation is all I can think of. Lily Flagg may have been the person in the pictures with the wrong tattoo.

By the time Reno, Ines, Gloria and the others leave, it's past midnight. Everyone had a good time, but all I could think of was Andre. He planned my death for months and deliberately took me over to the railing to throw me overboard.

While Javi walks our guests to their cars, I start cleaning. So overwhelmed by feelings of betrayal and rage, I'm unaware that I'm slamming things in the kitchen.

"Don't be angry with the pots and pans," Javi says as he walks into the house. "You want to talk now, or wait until morning?"

"There's nothing to say."

"There's a lot to talk about. I've been giving it some thought. An eye for an eye?"

I look at him and blink. "I'm not throwing him over the side of a ship, if that's what you mean."

He smiles. "I would never expect you to do that."

"So, what are you proposing?"

He takes my hand. "Andre needs to pay for what he did to you. As you've said, an attempted murder charge is not enough, and it would be hard to prove, so it would probably mean no charges. The way I see it, Andre did everything he could to ensure you died. That would be murder. It was only by the grace of God that you *didn't* die. He believes he succeeded. Would you agree with those statements?"

"Yes."

"Then, he needs to receive the appropriate punishment," says Javi. "Your husband must be convicted of your murder and spend the rest of his life in prison."

"But how can they convict someone of murder without a body?" I say.

"You don't need a body. I've consulted with a criminal attorney through some back channels."

"What? Who?"

"It doesn't matter. The less you know, the better. Your name and mine were kept out of the inquiry. What I can tell you is this. A person *can* be convicted even without a body."

"You're sure?"

"If there's enough circumstantial evidence for the jury to conclude the victim is dead and the defendant is guilty, they can convict. If the prosecution comes up with a theory and lines up the circumstantial evidence to support a murder, it can stand on its own."

"Then let's do it."

CHAPTER FORTY-TWO

Stella

After Becca was gone for a year, it was me who encouraged Andre to rejoin the human race. He seemed so lost. I didn't think Becs would want him to live that way. I thought I was doing the right thing. But now, I'm not so sure.

He seemed so sad and lonely. All he did was go to work and sit at home. He never went out or saw any of their old friends. I stopped by all the time because I thought Becs would want me to. I still miss her so much that it physically hurts when I think of her.

A missing person is a terrible thing for those of us who are left behind. When you don't know if someone's alive or dead, it eats at you, and your imagination takes over. There's no closure. Not knowing is way worse than being told she's dead . . . I think.

Sometimes, I wake up in the middle of the night in a panic that she's being held as a prisoner somewhere, that she's hurt or worse. I have to turn my mind off when it goes there. The thoughts are too horrible.

When Andre surprised Becs with that tenth-anniversary cruise, she was so excited. Things between them had grown a little stale. Because she didn't feel well a lot of the time, they didn't do many things together those last few years. She thought the cruise was Andre's attempt at reigniting their marriage. She was really happy he did that.

From my perspective, it seemed like they had a very romantic trip. The pictures and texts Becca sent to me were so happy and silly. She even texted that she physically felt better than she had in years. She sounded good.

Honestly, when I look back on it, I think Andre's expectations of Becca contributed to her attacks. He can sometimes be a little arrogant and demanding. I know Becca felt the pressure. But when he surprised her with the cruise, I thought it would be a turning point for them.

God, I miss her. We were like two peas in a pod. Even after we both got married, our friendship never changed. Then I got divorced, and she was there for me. For seventeen years, we'd start every day by talking to each other and end it the same way. Honestly, I think Andre was somewhat jealous of our friendship. I also thought he was a little insensitive to Becca's medical issues. I never told her that. Maybe I should have.

Becca didn't want to be sick. It just started happening one day. If I have a headache, toothache or even just a cold, it makes doing regular things harder. But I know my minor pains will eventually go away. For Becs, her pain lingered, and it always came back. It sucked for her.

At first, it was occasional pain or numbness, and there would be long gaps between flare-ups. Eventually, it started happening more often, lasted longer and didn't go away. That's when her depression started.

She tried to figure it out and went to all kinds of doctors. Nobody knew what was wrong with her, but that didn't stop them from prescribing things. Sometimes they helped, but only for a little while.

Becca also tried homeopathic solutions. She did massage, acupuncture, cupping, hydrotherapy, psychoanalysis, hypnotism and physical therapy. Andre thought all that stuff was expensive bullshit. And like the pills, they helped at first, but none of them worked for long.

When Becca gave up her job teaching kindergarten because of her fibromyalgia, Andre was very critical. She'd tell me about some of the things he'd say. Sometimes, it seemed like Andre thought she was making up her symptoms for attention. I've known Becca for most of my life. When she had an attack, that girl was down for the count. If she was making that up, then she deserved an award. I saw the anguish on her face when she had a flare-up. Why would she lie? Becca was never an attention whore. And she loved teaching and her kids more than anything.

Eventually, her principal called her in. Becs had missed a lot of school days. While he loved her, they both agreed her absence wasn't fair to the children. Becca told me that her kids needed a teacher who'd be there every day. The principal told her they'd love to have her back when she got her health sorted out. That was her goal, to go back to teaching.

Losing Becca has been like having my arm cut off. Best friends like her only come along once in a lifetime. Now it's been two years since she disappeared.

About a year ago, I started getting strange messages about Becca. It was from someone calling themselves *Justice League*. The messages came through via my email and text. The first thing I wondered was how someone had my personal contact information.

Throughout the investigation, I've received loads of messages from random people containing conspiracy theories and other whacky ideas. Usually, I'd delete them, or if I thought they had any merit whatsoever, I'd send them to Detective Contessa.

At first, I didn't know what to make of the messages from *Justice League*. Was this just another crackpot trying to insinuate themselves into a police investigation? I told Contessa about it, and he said it happens all the time, regular citizens trying to get inside an investigation. I don't know why I did, but something told me to save all the messages from *Justice League*.

The first email was fairly benign. It didn't say much of anything other than asking me if I knew what happened to Becca. But by the third and fourth messages, *Justice League* started questioning certain settled elements of the case. Whoever they are, they were trying to get me to look at Becca's investigation from a different perspective.

It was a Tuesday when an email came in with a picture attached of Becca and Andre. I'm not sure why, but something clicked for me. I'd seen that picture countless times in local newspapers and on TV. It's a side shot of Becca and Andre standing near the Las Olas sign in downtown Fort Lauderdale. It must have been breezy because Becca's long curly hair is blowing around her head.

You can't see much of her face, but you can tell she's smiling as she gazes at Andre. His head is turned toward the camera. He's got a big goofy grin on his face and they're holding hands. Like I said, I've seen that picture plenty of times, but this time, there's a caption with it.

I spy with my little eye something that's not quite right.

I shake my head, annoyed at myself for getting sucked into some wacko's sick game. I close the email and am about to shut off my computer when something stops me. I open up the picture again and take a closer look.

"I spy with my little eye something that's not quite right," I say out loud. I think *I Spy* was one of the books that Becca used to read to her kindergarten class. What the hell does that mean? I scour every inch of the picture, looking for anything that doesn't belong. To be honest, I go down a rabbit hole.

For thirty minutes, I examine every pixel, but nothing in the picture seems wrong to me. I tell myself if *Justice League* sends anything else, I'm going to delete it without opening it. I feel an itch and swat at a mosquito on my lower right calf. I reach down to scratch.

As I curse the little bloodsucker, I see a welt forming right above the rose tattoo on my ankle. Instantly, I get weepy. I remember the day Becs and I got them. Some people have friendship rings or bracelets. We liked to be different, so we both got identical friendship tattoos — a single rose with two leaves on the stem. A leaf on either side symbolized us, young women about to bloom.

Sitting there scratching, I'm about to close the email and be done with *Justice League* when I take one last look at the picture of Andre and Becca.

That's when I see it. How did I miss it?

It takes me a moment because I have to enlarge the photo again. But when I do, my heart stops for a second. Looking at a close-up of Becca's ankle, I have a clear view of her rose tattoo. Holy shit.

I spy with my little eye something that's *definitely* not quite right.

"The stem on her tattoo has three leaves," I shout out into the empty room. For a second, I think I'm losing my mind and double-check my own tattoo. Yes, there are only two leaves.

That woman in the picture, the one holding Andre's hands?

That's not Becca.

CHAPTER FORTY-THREE

After I recover from my shock over the cryptic email and photo, a million thoughts run through my mind. The woman in the photo is definitely *not* my best friend. So why is she dressed like Becca and holding Andre's hands in Fort Lauderdale?

Honestly, my brain is now on serious overload. Too many competing thoughts are fighting for center stage. I take a few deep breaths and light a lemongrass candle, hoping it will calm me down.

The woman standing in front of that sign with Andre, dressed like my friend, is not Becca. So why is Andre standing there with her? And more importantly, why did he pretend it was Becca? He's seen that picture. If it wasn't his wife's photo, why didn't he say anything? None of this makes any sense.

For the next hour, I come up with a gazillion half-baked theories, most of which I discard because they're ludicrous and impossible. My leading contender is that they met someone in Florida who looked like Becca. Maybe they decided to take a photo as a joke to see if anyone would notice. I let that notion sit with me for a while until I decide it's ridiculous. If my best friend wasn't missing, maybe that could have happened. But Becca is the subject of a murder/kidnapping/missing persons investigation. That changes a joke to something far more sinister. I don't know what to think.

Frustrated and coming up with nothing plausible, I pick up my phone to call Andre. I'll ask him to solve this mystery. I'm about to connect the call when I stop myself. With several alarming thoughts running through my mind, I call the one person I can think of with no agenda other than finding my best friend — Detective Contessa.

I'll admit, I'm a little hysterical when Contessa picks up the phone. I start talking really fast and in circles. He's patient and offers to stop by my place in an hour. While I wait for him to arrive, I dig online for all the photos of Becca that have been circulating since she disappeared. Other than the one that Justice League sent me, none of the others support my theory.

And what exactly *is* my theory? I don't have one. I just know something isn't quite right. If that woman in the photo isn't Becca, then maybe the timeline on her disappearance is wrong, too. My brain is so fried by the time the doorbell rings that I trip over my own feet as I run to open the door.

"I'm so glad you're finally here," I say, out of breath as Detective Contessa comes in.

We sit down in my living room and I show him the emails and picture of Andre and the unknown woman pretending to be Becca.

"You're absolutely positive Becca has two leaves on her tattoo?" says the detective, his eyes scanning the photo.

"Yes, absolutely sure," I say, "A hundred percent positive."

As I explain the whole story of how Becs and I got the tattoos, and the very personal meaning behind them, I can see Contessa processing the data.

"There's no chance she might have added a leaf at some point over the years?" he says.

I knew he'd ask me that question. So I didn't sound like a crazy person, I found a picture on my phone that I'd taken two months before Becca went on that cruise. She and I had gone for a spa day one Saturday. Midway through the afternoon, in our robes, we headed up to the café to get some juice. I took a picture of her holding her cup of green liquid while she gave a thumbs-up. Her ankle is captured in the picture.

"Look," I say, enlarging that photo. "See? Look at her ankle. Two leaves, not three. That picture was taken two months before they went on the cruise. Look at the date."

Contessa takes the phone from my hand and stares at the picture.

"Will you send me this?" he says.

"You think I'm right, then?" I say.

He presses his lips together. "I don't know what it means yet, but you've raised a logical question. Why *don't* the tattoos match? I'll have a little talk with Andre and ask him about it."

"Please don't bring me into it, Detective. I need to keep an open line of communication with him. I don't want to get shut out or do anything to keep me from finding my friend."

"Got it," says Contessa. "I'll tell him I was looking at a collection of photos and noticed it myself. Let's see what he says. There could be a perfectly reasonable explanation."

I peer at him. "There could be. But what do *you* think this means?"

"Don't know yet," he says, scratching his nose. "But it could change the direction of the entire investigation."

I start to cry. I promised myself I wouldn't, but I can't stop. "Do you think it's possible Becca is still alive?"

Contessa shakes his head in frustration. "Anything's possible. This picture's been circulating throughout the entire investigation. What made you suddenly notice the tattoo today?"

I open my email and show him the file containing the correspondence from Justice League. He reads through all of them and asks me to send him copies.

"Somebody out there knows something," he mutters. "They're trying to help us."

"Who do you think it is?"

"Hard to say," says Contessa. "There are thousands of amateur detective clubs and online chat groups that like to solve mysteries and cold cases. Could be one of those."

"Or?"

"Or it could be someone who knows the truth about what happened to your friend," says Contessa as I walk him to the front door. "Whoever Justice League is, one thing is pretty clear. They want to help."

CHAPTER FORTY-FOUR

Andre

Standing before the whiteboard in my agency's conference room, I'm in the middle of doing a kick-ass presentation to a new auto client. As I succinctly answer their questions, I glance down at my phone sitting on the conference table. I've got a voicemail from Detective Contessa.

It's been two freakin' years. Doesn't he have other cases to stick his nose into?

I'm so distracted from seeing the detective's name that my answer to my client's question comes out sounding idiotic. Fortunately, one of the agency's partners is sitting in and picks up my fumbled ball.

Soon, things get back on track and everyone's nodding and shaking hands. Despite my momentary brain freeze, it appears the client likes the pitch, which means my boss is happy.

"What happened to you in there, Andre?" says the partner as we walk out of the room together. "You need to bring your A-game for these presentations, buddy."

As the partner walks off in the opposite direction, I remain in the hallway listening to my voicemail.

Contessa has a question for me and wants to stop by my house tomorrow. I thought this was a cold case now, and Contessa was no longer assigned to it. I suppose I have no choice. When I get home from the city, it's dark. Lily's already in the house drinking white wine. She picked up Chinese food on her way over, and we're planning to watch a movie. Unlike Becca who was usually in a reclined position when I got home, Lily's got the music blasting and is prancing around the living room like a cage dancer in a strip club.

"Hey, baby," she says as she spins over to me and sticks her tongue down my throat. "I got the lo mein with pork that you like."

I put my backpack on the table, pour myself a glass of wine and take a big gulp.

"What's wrong?" she says, still twirling and swinging her hips.

Lily can read me. I think that's what attracted me to her. She sees right through my bullshit. I tell her about the voicemail from Contessa.

"What do you think he wants?" she says, suddenly not so happy.

"He said he had a question for me."

"He couldn't ask you over the phone?"

"I don't know, Lily. That's all he said."

"We're supposed to go to that music festival tomorrow."

Does she not see the bigger picture here? She's bitching about attending a concert when I've got a cop breathing down my neck about my missing and possibly dead wife?

She must notice the incredulous expression on my face because she shifts gears immediately. Walking over to me, she puts her arms around my neck and presses her sinewy body into mine.

"You're too stressed out," she says, rubbing my upper back. "You had that big presentation today, and then you got that awful voicemail from that mean detective. I wish he'd just go away. You want me to give you a massage, babe?"

Actually, what I want is for you to remember that we murdered my wife. We have to be buttoned up when it comes to the police.

"A massage sounds good," I say, thinking with my lower body instead of my head.

I leave a message for Contessa to meet me at 10 a.m. tomorrow. It's early enough to salvage the afternoon and keep my girlfriend happy.

Not long after Lily and I "met" on the dating site, I went out to lunch with Stella at the local diner. Stella was the one who had advocated for me to get back in the dating game. But when I told her I'd met someone special, she didn't seem very happy. I found Stella's emotions hard to gauge. After all, she's the one who originally helped me create my dating profile.

"You met someone you like?" she said with no enthusiasm and looking down at the menu as if she was studying for an exam. "That's great."

"What's wrong?" I said, noticing her supportive words didn't match her expression.

She finally looked up at me with tears in her eyes. "I guess I knew this day would come. You're a handsome, successful man, Andre. Of course someone would want to be with you. I just didn't think it would happen so fast, that's all."

"I never thought there would be anyone else in my life," I said softly.

"I still miss her so much," she said. "It hasn't gotten any easier."

I reached for her hand and squeezed it. "I know."

For the rest of the lunch, we talked about Becca. Eventually, I moved the conversation to the new woman in my life, Lily. I even showed Stella a picture of her.

"The blonde," said Stella. "Wow. I remember when you first showed me her picture. I always thought you were partial to redheads."

"Becca's irreplaceable," I said, pretending to get all choked up. "I'm not looking for a cheap imitation of my wife. Lily's very different from Becca, but you'd like her."

Stella smiled at me like a protective mother comforting a nervous child.

"If she makes you happy, Andre, then I *know* I'll like her."

Once I had Stella's blessing, getting everyone else onboard was a piece of cake. If Becca's best friend bought into it, others would, too. Slowly, I started bringing Lily out to a few social events and she held her own. One thing about Lily, she's not afraid to talk. It's both a blessing and a curse. That's why I have to stay on top of her to make sure she doesn't slip up.

Lily's already met most of Becca's old friends. Given that, I didn't think there was any reason for her to leave the house when Contessa stopped by. I'm a grieving widower trying to move on with my life the best I can.

Of course, there's no actual proof that my wife is dead. When there's no body, you have to wait seven years until you can petition the courts for a "presumption of death" order. That's how long I have to wait to cash in Becca's million-dollar life insurance policy. We took them out on each other a month after we got married. At that point, I hadn't even thought about killing her. It was dumb luck that we got the policies. I've only got five more years until the big payoff.

A million bucks will be awfully nice after everything I've been through. Murdering your wife and getting away with it is extremely hard work. The details I have to remember are staggering. Sometimes I feel like my head is going to explode.

When the doorbell rings, I put on my game face and walk to the front door.

"Morning, Andre," says the detective as he steps into my foyer.

We go into the kitchen. Lily is standing by the coffee maker pouring herself a cup. I look at Contessa. His face remains unchanged.

"Detective, I believe you've already met my fiancée, Lily," I say. "We bumped into each other at the movies. Remember?"

"Nice to see you again," says Lily, cool and calm as she walks over and sticks out her hand. Contessa doesn't blink and shakes her hand like it's no big deal.

"Andre told me you've worked so hard trying to find Becca," she says. "It's such a sad story. I wish I'd known her."

As Lily chatters on, it occurs to me that Contessa hasn't said a word. Maybe this meeting isn't going as well as I thought?

"Can I offer you a coffee, Detective?" I say, reaching for an empty cup.

Contessa's face twitches slightly and then relaxes as he focuses on me and then on Lily.

"No, thanks," he says. "I would like to have a word with you privately, Andre."

"Lily and I are engaged. I don't mind if she stays."

"It's up to you," he says.

We sit down at the kitchen table.

"You said you had a question for me?" I say, looking him in the eye.

Directly across from me, Contessa leans in. "Did your wife have a tattoo on the inside of her ankle?"

"I think she did," I say. I glance at Lily standing against the wall biting her thumbnail.

"You *think* she had a tattoo, Andre, or you're sure she did?" says the cop.

"I'm pretty sure she had a tattoo on her ankle. Yes."

"You don't *know* if your wife had a tattoo?" he says, getting slightly confrontational.

I sit back and fold my arms. "Yes, my wife had a tattoo on her ankle," I say in the most patronizing tone I can muster.

"And what kind of tattoo was it?" says the detective, his eyes still locked on mine.

I would swear this man never blinks.

"It was some kind of flower," I say.

"Let me get this straight," says Contessa. "Your wife of ten years has only one tattoo on her entire body, and you're not sure what it is?"

"It was a flower, a rose."

"Okay," says the detective, now smiling. "You had me worried there for a minute, Andre."

"Was that your question?" I say.

"Yes. I wanted to make sure I had everything straight," he says. "That's all."

Feeling myself starting to sweat, I get up and cross the room.

"If that's all, let me walk you out," I say.

As I open the front door, he stops me.

"Let me ask you one more thing, Andre." He pulls a piece of paper out of his pocket. "That tattoo of the rose on your wife's ankle, did it look like this?"

I look down at the drawing in his hand. There's a sketch of a single rose on a stem with a leaf on either side. My eyes don't hide my surprise. The picture he's holding is exactly like Becca's tattoo.

Where the hell did he get that, and why is he showing it to me now?

"I'm sorry," I say, swallowing for effect. "I'm a little overwhelmed seeing that image. That's definitely Becca's tattoo."

I look up at the detective's hardened face, trying to figure out what he's after.

He's not buying my act.
Shit.

CHAPTER FORTY-FIVE

Becca

For the next few weeks, pretending to be Justice League, Javi and I send several more emails to Stella. In each one, we raise specific questions about my disappearance. I'm dying to pick up the phone and tell my best friend that I'm alive. But Javi begs me to wait.

"Only a little longer, Sirena," he says, rubbing my shoulders while I stare at the computer screen. "We have to make sure he'll be arrested. In order to do that, we need to get the police to extend the investigation down to Florida, to the Beacon Star."

Javi's overly cautious, but I can't blame him. If things were reversed, I'd feel the same way.

"I don't understand Andre at all," I say to Javi as we compose another Justice League email. "If he hated me so much, why didn't he just get a divorce?"

"That is one of life's great mysteries," says Javi as he types.

"There would have been fights and tears, but he could have had what he wanted without the incredible charade and murder charge hanging over his head. I don't get it."

Javi pushes "Send" and another Justice League tip is on its way to Stella. We're working blindly on this. We don't know if Stella told the police about the Justice League emails or if they're having any meaningful effect on the case. What I do know is how resourceful and dogged my best friend is. Once Stella bites into something, she never lets go. If anyone can keep this ball moving, it's her.

"What if the police hack into our email account and trace it back to us?" I say. "Would we be arrested?"

Javi laughs. "For pointing out that your husband threw you over the side of a ship to try to kill you? I don't think we'd be arrested for that."

"But we're meddling in a criminal investigation."

He nods. "And you have every right to do so."

"Shouldn't I have called the police and . . .?"

"My love, we've been over this. You were not well for a long time after I found you," says Javi, brushing a lock of hair out of my face. "Until your memories started to return, you didn't know who you were or what was going on."

"But when I did know, shouldn't I have reached out to them then?"

He shakes his head. "Who can say when you got your memory back? We weren't sure where the danger was, so I disagree. Your safety was my primary concern. Besides, they'll never trace the emails to us."

"How do you know?"

"Because I didn't get out of Venezuela, make it to Argentina, live through an assassination attempt and not learn a few tricks along the way."

"What do you mean?"

"All of our communications have been encrypted. They bounce off servers from all over the world. Reno's a techno genius. He saw to that. Everything we've done is untraceable. We're totally safe."

Javi stands me up and takes me in his arms and holds me.

"No one's ever going to harm you again," he whispers before kissing me.

Later, after we make love, Javi and I go outside and climb into the double hammock together. As we rock in the warm breeze, we go over our plans.

"You think he's really going to pay for what he did to me?"

"That is my intention," says Javi.

"Is the circumstantial case strong enough?"

"That all depends on what kind of case the prosecution builds and what else they uncover in the process. We're going to help them build their case."

CHAPTER FORTY-SIX

Andre

A week after the encounter at my house with Contessa, he leaves me a message saying he needs to speak with me again.

"You look like you have a tan," I say jovially to the detective as he walks into the Woodmere PD conference room.

"I took a little trip down to Florida earlier this week. Weather was beautiful."

My stomach knots, but I steady myself. "Yeah, Florida is great. Why am I here? Did you find something new about Becca?"

"During my trip, the Beacon Star happened to be in the port in Miami. So I stopped by to have a look at it," says Contessa. "Nice ship."

"It's a beautiful vessel," I say, wondering where he's going with this.

"We got permission from Beacon Cruise Lines to board the ship," says Contessa. "They put all their security people at our disposal."

I find myself squirming in my chair to avoid looking into his death stare.

"Can you get to the point?" I stand, my annoyance clearly showing. "You want to tell me how spending time on a cruise ship in Florida helps find my wife in Connecticut?"

Contessa looks at me like I'm incredibly dense.

"Like I've told you before," he says, "when there's no information to follow *after* a crime occurs, we're forced to go in a different direction. When you can't move forward, your only option is to go backward. We needed to examine what happened *before* Becca vanished."

"It's been two freakin' years, Detective. I don't see how that helps at this point. For the millionth time, we came home from the cruise and then the next day I went to—"

"While I was on that ship, I asked the security personnel for all the videos taken during the week of your cruise. They usually get rid of them after six months, but apparently, if there are any incidents on the ship, they keep those videos in storage for up to three years."

I look at my watch and clear my throat. "I've got to leave soon because I . . ."

Contessa raises his open palm to me. "I looked at all the videos from the restaurants, as well as the daily boarding and departure areas. I was able to access BCL's reservation system, and they were able to match up your dining times with the videos. It was impressive. It made it so much easier to put together a linear picture."

I sigh. "And what did you learn, Detective?"

Contessa stands and smiles ruefully. "It looked like you and your wife had a very good time. There were videos and still shots of you and Rebecca getting on and off the ship in Fort Lauderdale, the U.S. Virgin Islands, Miami. I also saw pictures of you two dining in several restaurants on the ship throughout the week."

"That's what one typically does on a cruise," I say. "You get on and off the ship and you eat. You didn't need to go to Miami to find that out."

"That's what they tell me. I've never been on a cruise myself. I'm partial to land. I get a little seasick."

"Can you get to the point?" I say. "I have an important meeting in the city this afternoon."

"Absolutely. Another thing I was able to view was a video of you and your wife from the airport. The two of you were boarding a flight at the Miami International Airport on your way back home."

He's milking this.

Contessa walks to the other side of the room before turning and facing me.

"Remember how I told you Beacon Cruise Lines keeps records from a ship for up to three years when there is an incident on a particular sailing?" says the detective.

I take a deep breath. "Yes, I remember."

"Turns out that something *did* happen on your cruise, Andre."

Shit. Does he know about Becca? He's either going to handcuff me right now and read me my rights, or walk me out to my car.

"I don't recall anything of note happening on that cruise," I say, trying to remain cool. "We had a fantastic week, and then we came home."

The detective crosses his arms in front of him and stares at me.

"Do you remember meeting an elderly woman on the ship named Olive Walker? She was a tiny lady with big, blue-framed eyeglasses."

Of course I remember who Olive Walker was. I was going to kill her until she saved me the trouble.

"I'm afraid I don't recall her," I say. "Becca and I met so many people on the ship, and it *was* over two years ago. It's possible we met her."

"It was a long time ago. But Mrs. Walker sat with you and Becca in the restaurant more than once."

"We dined with a lot of people, Detective. That's how it goes on cruises. People are friendly."

"She was over ninety, and apparently, the lady became quite ill while onboard the ship."

I feel like a dog toy caught between Contessa's paws. The man is playing with me. I change course, deciding it's in my best interest to be a little less oppositional. I soften my tone and tell him I vaguely remember an old woman sitting next to us at dinner one night.

"That's right," says the detective, nodding. "That's exactly what the video shows."

He tells me that we were caught on camera sitting with Olive Walker a second night, and other videos recorded what looked like a few exchanges of words in the hallways throughout the week.

"We met a lot of people," I say, throwing up my hands. "Is there anything else? I really have to go."

On a power trip, the cop ignores me and keeps talking.

"Like I said, BCL keeps records whenever there's an incident," says the detective. "You were aware that Mrs. Walker had a catastrophic event on the ship late one night."

"I don't recall that," I say.

"That's funny, because we have videos of you standing outside of her cabin holding a bottle of champagne while the emergency crews were still there."

Stay cool. I didn't touch her.

"Now I remember," I say, smiling. "She was a nice older woman. When Becca and I met her, she told us that she had a terminal condition and didn't expect to make it to the end of the cruise. She wanted to go out with a bang. I guess she did."

"Seems that way," he says, shaking his head and looking distressed. "We don't treat older people very well in this country, do we?"

I look at my watch for the tenth time. Contessa's choosing not to take the hint, so I take a step toward the door.

"I have got to get into the city. If there's nothing else . . ."

"You've been very helpful, Andre. I've taken up a lot of your time. I'll be in touch if I have any other questions."

We both walk toward the door. I put my hand on the knob and am about to open it when Contessa blindsides me.

"There was one *other* thing that's been bothering me from those videos," he says.

My heart beats faster. *He's fishing. He didn't say anything about videos from the back of the ship. He's got nothing.*

I turn the knob but pause. I need to know what he's got. "What was that *other* thing?" I ask.

He smiles. "All the pictures of you and your wife getting on and off and moving around the ship were shot from a distance."

"Okay?"

"Were you aware that your wife went shopping on the ship?"

"Are you fucking kidding me?" I say, raising my voice. "My wife has been missing for over two years, and you want to know if she went shopping on the cruise? What if she did? How does that help find her?"

I start to open the door, but he stops it with his foot.

"According to the ship's records," says Contessa looking down at his phone, "a Rebecca Gifford purchased a pair of Prada sandals in size seven on the second-to-last day of your cruise."

I told Lily not to go shopping. That's what those charges were when we settled up at the end.

I force a smile. "What can I say? Becca liked nice things. It was our anniversary. I guess she treated herself to some shoes. It's not a crime."

He scratches his head. "The thing is, Andre, the Beacon Star boutique is rather small and has a lot of security cameras to prevent shoplifting. We got some close-up pictures of your wife trying on sandals."

"What are you trying to say? That Becca stole something? How is that even relevant after she's been missing for two years?"

Contessa reaches into his breast pocket and pulls out several black-and-white photos. They're pictures of a woman's legs putting on shoes. Some are close-ups.

"There's no complaint of anything being stolen from the shop," Contessa says as he slowly hands each picture to me one at a time. "But we did get a clear shot of your wife's legs. In particular, her ankles. You want to explain why your wife's rose tattoo has three leaves on the stem?"

"What?" I examine the photos slowly to buy time to think.

Fucking Lily and her artistic expression. I warned her about that.

"According to Stella McCrystal," says Contessa, "she and your wife got the exact same tattoos together while they were in college. Ms. McCrystal said there were only two leaves on the stem, not three."

CHAPTER FORTY-SEVEN

A week later on a Saturday, Lily and I are in my kitchen having lunch. I've just cracked open a beer when we suddenly hear the crunch of tires on gravel. I look out the window and see three Woodmere PD cars speed into my circular driveway.

Lily and I look at each other.

"Why are the cops here?" she says, peering out the window again.

"I told you messing around with that tattoo was going to screw us up," I say, venom in my voice. "You just had to add another leaf."

"The drawing was unbalanced," she hisses.

"Says who?" I hiss back.

"I've taken art classes," she says as the doorbell rings.

I walk to the front door with Lily behind me. Contessa's smug face is visible through the window on the side of the door.

"Looks like you brought the cavalry with you," I say, smiling as I open the door. "Where's the fire, Detective?"

Contessa steps forward, his face expressionless.

"Andre Gifford," he says firmly, "you're under arrest for the murder of Rebecca Gifford."

As he continues with instructions regarding my rights, I become enraged and start to talk over him.

"I'll have you fired," I say as another officer cuffs me. "You'll be unemployed in a week. You'll lose your pension. You'll be sorry. Do you know who you're screwing with?"

"You can't do this," Lily shrieks as they start to lead me out of the house. "You're making a big mistake. Andre's the victim here. You don't even know if his wife is dead."

"You can't arrest me for murder without a body," I shout as they march me to a police car.

"What should I do?" screams Lily, still standing in the doorway with Contessa.

"Call Shapiro, my lawyer," I shout over my shoulder. As I turn to get into the car, I see Lily's face freeze — an officer is placing her in handcuffs.

"Andre," she shouts, "what's happening?"

The next few hours are like a bad dream. In different cars, Lily and I are both taken down to the police station, booked, fingerprinted and photographed. As soon as I'm allowed, I place a call to my lawyer.

"Andre," he says, "I'm very sorry to hear you're in this situation."

"The cops have nothing," I say. "For two years they've bungled Rebecca's investigation, and now they're trying to pin it on me so they can close their case. It's a total miscarriage of justice. When can you get me out of here?"

There's silence on the other end of the line.

"Andre, you need to stay calm," says my lawyer. "Let me make a few phone calls, and then I'll be down to the police station to clear up this misunderstanding."

Frustrated, I'm led down the hallway to another room. As I walk, I hear Lily shouting from somewhere.

"I had nothing to do with her death," she says. "You have to believe me. I've never even met her."

"Shut up, Lily," I shout as loud as I can, hoping she can hear me. "Say nothing until you have a lawyer. Plead the fifth."

After my outburst, the two cops escorting me pull me down the hallway with a fair amount of force. As I pass a doorway, I catch a glimpse of Lily sitting at a table inside. She sees me and nods.

"I'm not saying anything until I have a lawyer. You got that?" she says to the officer sitting across from her.

An hour later, Shapiro shows up at the police station. In his fifties, though he looks younger, he's still got a thick head of black hair and seems partial to expensive Italian suits.

We get a private room and go over the particulars. I tell him I still have no idea what the police have.

"It looks like this whole case is based on a bunch of bullshit," says Shapiro. "Honestly, it's so frivolous and flimsy that I can't believe the prosecutor would even look at it, let alone try it in court."

"A judge signed off on my arrest warrant," I say, starting to lose it. "They must have something."

"That doesn't mean it's going to stick," says Shapiro. "From where I sit, it looks like nothing. An extra leaf on a one-inch tattoo? Are they kidding me? It's fucking ridiculous is what it is."

"And yet, here I sit," I say. "You got to get me out of here, and Lily, too."

Shapiro nods. "I'm working on it. There will be bail required, and we'll have to use your house as collateral."

"Do what you have to do. What about Lily?"

Shapiro looks down at his notes.

"Andre, in my professional opinion, you and Ms. Flagg should each have your own attorney. It's to protect you both."

"But Lily and I are going to get married. She wouldn't do anything to hurt me."

"I'm sure she wouldn't, but still, it's inadvisable to use the same attorney with such serious charges hanging over you."

Let's just say Lily didn't take it well when she found out I was hiring a lawyer to represent *only me*. I was able to make bail using my assets. Lily was eventually able to raise the money with the help of relatives but had to spend a few more days in jail than I did.

When she finally got out, she was spitting mad.

"You left me in there," she fumed as we sat alone on a park bench. "How could you do that to me?"

"I didn't 'leave' you in there," I say. "My lawyer said we should both have our own attorneys. It just makes good legal sense."

She folds her arms. "For you, maybe. Just remember, I wasn't the one who tossed your wife off a ship. All I did was give you an alibi. If you think I'm going down for murder, and you're going to walk away, guess again."

I put my hand on her shoulder.

"Lily, this is exactly what the prosecution wants us to do," I say, gently caressing her arm. "Shapiro says they've got nothing. So the video showed a woman with a tattoo that had an extra leaf. Becca could have added it herself."

"But she didn't."

"The more I think about it, I remember Becca talking about getting another tattoo and adding something to the one she already had."

"Really?"

I roll my eyes. "C'mon, Lily, pay attention."

Her eyes get big. "Oh, I see," she says. "You just made that up."

"They've got nothing else besides that. That's their only ace in the hole? Think about it. A quarter-inch leaf?" I take her hand. "My lawyer thinks if we can discredit their theory, the DA will probably drop the charges, or the judge may even throw out the case. But whatever happens, we've got to stick together."

She looks into my eyes and nods. "Okay. But don't leave me out there to dry. Just remember, if I go down, you go down."

CHAPTER FORTY-EIGHT

For the next six months, Lily and I prepare for the trial. We're being tried together but retain our own counsel. Over and over, my lawyer attempts to get the case dropped, but the DA won't budge. He says he'll "take his chances and let a jury decide."

It's safe to say that my life right now is a shit show. I took a leave of absence from my job, but at least it was with pay for the first six months. Right after I got arrested, the partners were extremely supportive and offered me any help I needed. But as time went on, more not-so-flattering stories appeared in the media about me. I guess carrying me on their payroll and holding my job open got old and expensive. Last week, my employment was terminated.

"Once this is all over, Andre," said the HR director of Hardy & Engel, "we'd absolutely love to have you back. You did great work for us, and we really hate to lose your creative talents. But unfortunately, we have a business to run. I'm sure you understand."

Actually, I don't understand. I've worked for this fucking agency for eighteen years. One little thing goes wrong and you cut me loose?

I was also advised by my attorney not to fraternize with Lily before the trial.

"She's my fiancée," I said to Shapiro.

"It's better for you to keep everything professional," said Shapiro during one of our prep sessions. That advice came after a picture surfaced in a local newspaper of Lily and me having dinner in a Mexican restaurant. "In fact, I'd advise you not to spend *any* time with Ms. Flagg until this is over. It doesn't look good."

"Her name is Lily," I say, "and she's going to be my wife."

Shapiro nods. "I understand, and one day I hope to be invited to your wedding. But until the trial is over, or we can get the charges dismissed, you need to stay away from each other. It's cleaner that way."

I'm confused. "What do you mean 'cleaner'?"

"We don't know everything that the DA has," says Shapiro. "It's possible the evidence against Lily is stronger than what they have against you. We just don't know yet."

A few weeks before the trial is set to begin, I get a phone call from that local reporter, Tommy Devlin. I read some of his columns about my case. He's the same person Stella reached out to.

"How did you get my number?" I bark into the phone when he identifies himself.

"I'm doing a piece on your upcoming trial and wanted to get a comment from you," says Devlin.

"No comment," I spit back. "My lawyer says I'm not supposed to talk to the press."

"I'm offering you a public platform to present your side of the story. Surely you'd like to do that."

I think about it for a moment. From what I've read, the public opinion is that Lily and I did away with Becca somewhere in Connecticut, then we took the Beacon Star Cruise together to celebrate. The police don't think Becca ever went to Florida or got on the ship at all. That's another thing Contessa has got completely wrong. Cops are so damn stupid.

After considering his offer, I agree to talk with Devlin.

The next morning, he comes to my house. I tell him how awful it's been losing my wife and how much I miss her.

"It's been a living nightmare," I say, turning on the waterworks with ease. "You can't imagine what it's been like. Everyone thinks the husband's always the guilty party. Well, let me tell you something, not this time. I loved my beautiful wife and was shattered when she was taken from me."

"And Lily Flagg?" says Devlin.

"Lily and I met on a dating site more than a year after Becca disappeared," I say. "I had no interest in having a relationship with anyone. It was Becca's best friend, Stella, who I believe you spoke with at one time. She's the one who encouraged me to get out there and meet people. She even wrote my dating profile for me. I went out for coffee with a few women. Eventually I met Lily. Finding love again was the last thing I expected."

"It's always when you least expect it," says Devlin, obviously trying to connect with me.

"Now I find out that it was Stella who told the cops about the tattoo on Becca's ankle. She started this whole thing."

I start to rant, getting angrier by the second. I carry on about Stella being a traitor before I catch myself. Shifting gears, I wrap up the conversation with a tearful plea.

"Here's what I want you to know, Devlin. I love my wife, and I'm still praying that she's out there somewhere. Nothing would make me happier than to see Becca walk through the front door right now. If she took off on her own for whatever reason, all would be forgiven if she's alive and well. We could start over again."

"What about your fiancée?" he says.

"I haven't thought that far ahead. I just want Becca to be okay."

When the interview comes out two days later, my lawyer is not happy with me. Neither is Lily, and she calls me.

"What the hell was *that* all about?" she says. "Sounds like if Becca came back tomorrow, you'd drop me like a bad habit. Are you fucking kidding me?"

"Babe, I'm just playing their game, that's all. I was trying to get a little good press. This whole thing is being trumped up because we're together. You're the one I love. You know that."

"I'm not sure about that anymore," she says. "Things are so different now."

"Nothing's changed," I say. "I promise you, we're going to be exonerated. My lawyer says the prosecution has nothing, all smoke and mirrors. And what they do have isn't enough for a murder conviction."

"I didn't murder anybody," she says. "All I did was put on a wig and go on some shitty cruise."

I take a breath. "C'mon, babe, remember our plan. It's you and me forever, right?"

"Somehow, it doesn't feel that way anymore," she says.

"My lawyer thinks the trial will be over in a few days, if it doesn't get thrown out before it starts. After that, we'll do all the things we talked about. I'll sell the house and we'll move somewhere else. You want to go to California?"

"I've always wanted to live in LA. I thought I might try being an actress. You really mean it?"

"Of course. Would I ever lie to you?"

CHAPTER FORTY-NINE

The murder trial will be starting shortly. Despite solid arguments from my legal team throughout the jury selection process about dropping the case, the obviously biased female judge didn't buy it, and the prosecution is moving full steam ahead. While today is officially the first day of the trial, my attorney continues to feel confident that he can still get the charges dismissed. He's filed all sorts of motions, and we're hoping for good news at any time.

In the weeks leading up to the trial, the public's interest in our case ramped up a fair amount. We're not front-page news, or regular fodder for cable news, thankfully. But I've been told the story is being selectively picked up by news organizations in other parts of the country.

For the longest time, Becca's disappearance stayed a local story. Then that asshole Devlin started peddling it like a haberdasher at a Turkish bazaar. Now, when I'm out in public, people gawk and whisper when I walk by. It's become so bad these last few weeks that I rarely go out. Thank God for Amazon and Uber Eats. Lily's in the same boat, but I worry that she won't hold it together. She has thinner skin than I thought, and I'm afraid she'll crack under the pressure.

Entering the courthouse this morning with my attorney, I spot Lily walking down the hall with her lawyer. I give her a subtle nod on my way into the courtroom. I sit at one end of the defense table, and Lily takes a chair at the other end. Our two attorneys sit between us.

"You're still sure they've got nothing?" I whisper to Shapiro as I slide into my chair. "We've got a woman judge. That's not going to work in my favor."

"That was unfortunate," says Shapiro, writing something on his notepad. "It was the luck of the draw. But don't worry, I don't think the prosecution has enough to sway a jury. There are so many holes in his case, it's like a piece of Swiss cheese. Most of what they've got is unsubstantiated and wide open for reasonable doubt. I'm not worried."

Despite the fact that Shapiro is a well-regarded criminal defense attorney and seems confident that we've got this, it's hard to relax when you're the one on trial for murder. If he loses this case, he goes home to his wife and kids. If I lose the case, I go to prison.

As the courtroom fills up, I look around to see if I know anyone. The first person I lay eyes on is Ed Jerome, Becca's stepfather. What the hell is he doing here? I haven't heard a word from him since Becca's mother died.

In the row behind Ed, I spot that sleazy reporter, Tommy Devlin. He's sitting between two kindergarten teachers who used to work with Becca. They both give me the evil eye, so I turn away. I don't need any of their toxic energy right now. And then of course there's Stella, or should I call her Judas? She's not in the courtroom because, apparently, she's going to be a witness for the prosecution. I passed her in the hallway on my way in. She wouldn't even acknowledge me. That bitch stabbed me in the back, called the cops and started this whole thing. Now she can't look me in the eye. I think she did it out of spite because I never put the moves on her. That's what she always wanted. Seems like all the roaches have crawled out of the woodwork to be here today.

I look around the courtroom. It's noisy and crowded with not a single empty seat. When Judge Rachel Pollen enters the room, the place becomes instantly silent, and the court is called to order.

I lean over to my attorney. "All still good?" I whisper, my nerves starting to get the better of me.

"I've got this," Shapiro says softly. When I hear those words, I give myself up to the universe, sit back comfortably in my chair and stretch my legs. Let the games begin.

The prosecution makes their big opening statement. They start out by trying to weave a tale that makes sense, one that has a beginning, middle and end. From the confused looks on some of the jurors' faces, they're not getting the logic in what the prosecutor's saying.

When you think about it, the prosecution has a hard sell. They've got no body, and no real motive to hammer away at. They bring up the life insurance policies, but Becca and I both got those ten years ago. It's too long a time frame, so Shapiro doesn't think that particular point will be damaging. Now the prosecutor tells the jury that he's going to prove that Lily and I killed Becca in Connecticut before going off on a cruise vacation. From the looks on the jurors' faces, it doesn't look like they're buying it.

It's Shapiro's turn. He gets up and walks over to the jury. He's polished and gives off confidence, speaking with eloquence.

His first sentence pokes holes in the prosecution's tenuous fantasy theory. I know I killed my wife. But honestly, after hearing Shapiro's opening remarks, I start to question if I really did do it. I look at the jurors' faces again. They're eating up everything my lawyer says. I guess Shapiro was right — he's got this.

There is no death penalty in the state of Connecticut. Thankfully, that's always been off the table. Still, doing a long stint in prison doesn't sound appealing to me. When Shapiro finishes his opening remarks, he comes back to the table and gives me a subtle wink as he sits. That's when I let out a relieved breath. Shapiro is driving this bus, which means Lily and I will be all right. I push my chair a little further back to give my legs more breathing room.

With opening remarks complete, the prosecution introduces what appears to be a long list of meaningless evidence. They go on and on, but none of their points line up. Like I've told myself a hundred times, they won't be able to pin this on me because I executed the perfect murder.

At 12:45 p.m., the court breaks for lunch. Shapiro and I go into a private conference room. One of his associates is waiting there for us with box lunches. While I eat my turkey-and-cheese sandwich, Shapiro goes over the witness list for this afternoon.

"I think they're going to call one or two of Rebecca's friends to the witness stand," says my attorney. "The testimony from Stella McCrystal is essentially what the prosecution's entire case is predicated on. What she'll tell the court may look suspicious, but in my opinion, there's no meat on the bones."

I take a bite of my sandwich. It's rather good for a box lunch.

"Tell me about it," I say with a full mouth. "Can you believe this whole trial is over a freaking leaf on a tattoo?"

"It's preposterous," says Shapiro, checking his messages on his phone.

"Like I told that detective, Becca was always talking about getting another tattoo. I never noticed she added a leaf. It was so small, who'd ever see that?"

"My point exactly." Shapiro blots his mouth with a paper napkin. "It's simply not enough to convict, not by a long shot."

I notice there's some flesh-colored residue left on his napkin. Interesting. I think my lawyer wears makeup.

After a few more minutes prepping, we head back into the courtroom. Once we're seated, I glance over at Lily. She's as white as a ghost and looks like she's going to throw up. That's probably because we think Stella will be the first to testify. Stella's testimony will cover the ankle tattoo. Our lawyers got copies of the pictures from the prosecution early this morning. That's what's upsetting Lily. All eyes will be on her.

After all, Lily's the one who had the tattoo on her ankle. Thank God it washed off. At one point, she had suggested getting a real tattoo. I reminded her that a real tattoo would be permanent and incriminating and, in general, a terrible idea. I'll admit Lily's an extremely hot woman, but she's no criminal mastermind. Instead, I insisted we go with a stenciled drawing and trace it with a black Sharpie. It looked real enough, and it washed off in a few days.

Stella takes her seat on the witness stand and is sworn in. She looks nervous and refuses to look in my direction. Hopefully, her anxiety causes her to make a fool of herself and lose all credibility. To think how I'd trusted and confided in her. She was such a train wreck that I even considered sleeping with her out of pity. Then she goes and double-crosses me.

Stella starts out by explaining to the court how she and Becca got the same tattoos and with two leaves on the stem "representing their enduring friendship."

Give me a freakin' break. What is this, high school?

"Ms. McCrystal, would you show the jury your tattoo?" says the prosecutor. Stella lifts her left leg and rests her ankle on the railing in front of her. Reaching down, she rolls up her pants leg, exposing an extremely white leg and fat ankle.

No wonder she's single. Nobody's tapping that.

"Here's my tattoo," she says, pointing to the flower on the inside of her leg. "See, only two leaves on the stem. Becca's and mine were identical. That was the whole point."

The prosecutor then puts up a large image on the overhead screen. It's a close-up of Stella's tattoo.

"It was our special friendship thing," Stella says as she takes her leg down. "Becca wouldn't have changed hers without telling me."

"Objection," says my lawyer. "Speculation. This is purely Ms. McCrystal's opinion, your honor. Not a fact."

"Sustained," says the judge.

The prosecutor moves a little closer to Stella. "Did Rebecca ever mention that she was thinking about changing her tattoo?" he says.

Stella doesn't answer right away. She chews on her lower lip. I've seen her do that before. It means she's nervous. Good.

"She talked about it, but not about adding leaves," she says slowly.

"What exactly did Becca say?" says the prosecutor. "And when did she say it?"

"It was about a year before she disappeared. She wondered if we should get some color added to the rose and make it red or pink and the stem and leaves green."

When the prosecution finishes with Stella, I can't tell what the jury is thinking. It didn't sound like a grand slam to me. Now, it's Shapiro's turn at bat.

"Ms. McCrystal, according to your testimony, Rebecca Gifford *did* consider altering her tattoo."

"Yes," says Stella, "but it was just girl talk, nothing serious. And we never said anything about adding a leaf. That never came up."

"On the contrary, it sounds like Becca had thought quite a bit about the tattoo and wanted to make some changes."

"No, that's not what I said. It was just a random passing comment," says Stella. "People say stuff all the time that they never actually do. I've talked about dying my hair blue or pink and that ain't gonna happen."

There's a bit of chuckling in the courtroom before Shapiro continues.

"But you said Rebecca considered adding color to the tattoo," says Shapiro. "That would indicate that she gave altering it a fair amount of thought."

Stella's mouth puckers up.

She's annoyed because Shapiro is twisting her words. Nice.

She leans forward. "Do you want the truth here, or a false story you're inventing for the jury?" she says, spitting out each word like bullets from an automatic pistol. "Becca may have thought about changing her tattoo, but she also told me she'd only do it if I did it, too. And that's the truth. I'm telling you right now, she never changed it."

CHAPTER FIFTY

That afternoon the testimony drags because of a lot of legal mumbo jumbo. The judge finally calls it quits at 4:30. Walking out of the courtroom, I catch Stella's eye and give her a nod just to piss her off. She mouths an obscenity, and I respond with a polite smile. I'm winning this. The prosecution hasn't established their case. I know it, she knows it and the jury knows it.

When my attorney walks me out to the front of the courthouse, there are about eight or nine reporters and photographers waiting for us. We stop. Shapiro says some encouraging words about how convinced he is that I've been wrongly accused. He tells them that he expects me and Lily to be fully exonerated.

"The fact of the matter is, it's *not* always the husband," he says to the reporters. "Sometimes it is, but not in this case. My client has endured the terrible loss of his wife and now is being subjected to this baseless trial. It's nothing short of ludicrous and, frankly, cruel. This is a witch hunt. The state's attorney wanted a high-profile victory, and they'll stop at nothing to get it."

I say nothing and put on a sad and weary face. I also tee up my tear ducts in case a little weeping is needed. Before I have a chance to parade my acting chops, Shapiro pulls me away from the reporters and walks me to a waiting car.

"Get a good night's sleep, Andre," he says as he puts me in the back seat. "Tomorrow's going to be a long day. According to the witness list I received, the prosecution has called various staff from the Beacon Star. They'll be on tomorrow's lineup."

"Who?" I say.

"Don't worry. I've vetted all of them. All they're going to say is that they saw you with Becca during the cruise. That's it. No one can identify Lily as having been anywhere near that cruise ship. They've tried to paint you two as monsters, but it's going to fall flat. Trust me."

As my car pulls away from the curb, I see Lily getting into another vehicle several feet away. I make the sign of a phone with my hand so she knows I'll call her. We're almost at the finish line. I don't want her losing her nerve now. After I'm acquitted for murdering my wife, they won't ever be able to try me again thanks to double jeopardy.

By the time I get home, I'm starving. I heat up a frozen Italian dinner. While it's in the oven warming, I call Lily on our special phones.

"Hey," I say softly when she answers. "I've got some pasta cooking. What are you having for dinner?"

"How can you be so calm, Andre?" she says. "Who gives a shit about dinner? We're on trial for murder. Did you see all the reporters who were there today? It was a freakin' circus."

"Relax. Shapiro says we've got this. He thinks the judge might still throw out the case for lack of evidence."

"When's that going to happen?" she says, the pitch of her voice getting higher. "They keep talking about that goddamn tattoo. I can't take it anymore."

"Just do what your attorney tells you. We'll get through this," I say, trying to lower her temperature. "Remember, I love you, Lily."

I hear her sigh and make a tsk-ing sound. "I love you, too. How did things go so wrong? There wasn't supposed to be a trial. You said all I had to do was go on a free cruise, and you'd take care of the rest."

"And I will. Stick to our story, nothing more, nothing less," I say. "Shapiro thinks this will all be over this week, maybe even tomorrow. If the prosecution doesn't have anything besides that tattoo, he's pretty sure the judge will call it for us."

I hang up the phone and sit back on the couch with a nice glass of pinot noir. I'm beginning to think that life would be easier without women. Every woman I've been involved with has caused me nothing but aggravation. It was Lily's stupidity with that tattoo that brought all these legal problems down on my head. I'll never forgive her for that. And now, she's losing her nerve. I could see it in court. Instead of being an asset, she's becoming a liability. What do I do about that?

I ponder this conundrum over several glasses of wine until the answer becomes clear. After the trial is over, I've got to get rid of Lily — permanently. As hot as she is, she's become a massive loose end for me. I'd have to make it look like an accident. I could take her hiking, or loosen the brakes on her car.

***

The next morning, Shapiro's car picks me up and we head to the courthouse. As he and I walk into the building, I spot Tommy Devlin texting while leaning against the cream-colored marble wall. I go directly over to him and get right in his face.

"I thought you were on my side," I say in a hoarse whisper. "You twisted everything I told you. This would have been an insignificant trial that would likely have been thrown out until you blew it up in the press. Now I'm getting calls from reporters in Chicago and Texas."

Devlin stands up straight, towering over me, and puts his phone into his pocket.

"What did you think I was going to do?" he says in an equally loud whisper. "Thought you could manipulate me with your ridiculous story? You thought you'd weave a sad tale and I'd print it verbatim like I was your puppet? Let me tell you something, Gifford. I've been a crime reporter for over twenty years. I know a bullshitter when I see one, and, buddy, you're full of shit."

"I gave you that interview so you could help me find my wife," I say as Shapiro tugs on my arm. "You've turned this into a circus. I'm going to sue your news organization."

Devlin smiles. "Good luck with that. You only agreed to talk to me so you could use me. You wanted me to write a fairy tale about your perfect marriage. But everything you said felt hollow to me. I checked you out. I could tell you didn't give a shit about finding your wife, and I had to ask myself why. I wrote my first opinion piece with healthy skepticism and my editors loved it. The readers liked it, too. That article was picked up by all of our affiliates around the country."

"Andre," says my attorney, tapping me on the shoulder. "C'mon. We've got to go in."

Shapiro pulls me away from Devlin, which in hindsight was a good thing. I was about to grab that asshole by the throat and bash his head against the wall. Since I don't need any additional trouble right now, I'll have to save Devlin's retribution for another day.

We file back into the courtroom. As I take my seat, I notice Lily at the other end of the table. She looks tired, like she hasn't slept. Yeah, she's a liability.

People fall and slip off mountains all the time.

CHAPTER FIFTY-ONE

Over the next few days, the prosecution puts the most ridiculous "expert witnesses" on the stand. They trot out several of my former work colleagues, a tattoo artist, and a couple of Uber drivers.

Mr. Tattoo, a man in his forties or fifties, sports a long salt-and-pepper ponytail. Not surprisingly, every inch of the man's body is covered with drawings. From where I sit at the defense table, it looks like Mr. Tattoo's arms, legs and neck are fully tatted up. He couldn't add another one if he wanted to. He's even got a teardrop on one of his cheeks and a dagger with blood on the other. Classy. He identifies the drawing of the rose and testifies that particular image is especially popular with women. He says that image appears in many of the books people use to choose their tattoos.

"I've done that flower a hundred times," says Mr. Tattoo, smiling. "It's what I like to call an 'entry' tattoo. You know, for people who've never been inked before. It's small and sweet. Even your grandmother might go for one."

"And does this rose always have two leaves on the stem?" says the prosecutor.

"That's the way it's usually shown in the ink catalogs."

The prosecutor takes his seat and smiles. He seems confident he's made a solid point and is taking a private victory lap inside his head.

Shapiro gets up to do the cross.

"You said the drawing of the rose is usually shown with two leaves," says Shapiro. "But do people ever ask you to make modifications to standard tattoos? Do they ever ask you to change colors or turn a smile into a frown or add a leaf?"

Mr. Tattoo grins. "Look, man, I'm an artist. I don't just trace pictures from a book. If someone shows me a picture of a tattoo but wants me to change it, then that's what I'll do. The customer's always right. A lot of times they even leave it up to me."

"Do people ever come to see you and ask you to add to their existing tattoos?" says Shapiro.

"All the time," says Mr. Tattoo.

Shapiro takes his seat next to me and gives me an encouraging smile. I wouldn't call his cross-examination a slam dunk in my favor, but he's effectively raised the possibility that Becca could have very easily added a leaf, and no one would have thought it strange or even noticed.

After Mr. Tattoo finishes, the prosecution calls a few people from my former ad agency. My former colleagues all testify that I was at work the entire day after going on the week-long cruise. They also said that I showed them pictures of my trip, including shots of Becca. They all swore that I left the office to go home around five on the day she vanished.

I lean over to Shapiro. "What's the point of his line of questioning?" I say. "I *was* in the office that whole day, that's never been disputed. Why did he call all my former colleagues in?"

"Because he's got nothing," whispered Shapiro, rolling his eyes. "He's blowing smoke. I'm going to ask for a motion to dismiss after lunch."

The next witness is the Uber driver, the one who drove Becca and me to the airport on our way to Florida. I remember I talked with him about sports all the way to the airport.

"... and you picked up Andre and Rebecca Gifford at their house in Woodmere, Connecticut, and drove them to Kennedy Airport?" says the prosecutor.

"That's correct."

"I'm holding a picture of Rebecca Gifford. Will the jury refer to exhibit 53," says the prosecutor as he hands the picture to the Uber driver. "To the best of your knowledge, is this the woman you took to the airport?"

The Uber driver looks at the picture of Becca.

"It was, like, three years ago, but I remember her long red hair. You don't see that very often. But it was a while back, so I couldn't say for sure it was her."

"Then it could have been any woman with long red hair?"

"Not any woman," he says. "Looking at this picture, the woman here is about the same size and looks like the woman who was in my car. That's about the best I can tell you."

The next witness is the driver who brought Lily and me home from the airport after the cruise. He's shown the same picture of Becca and gives a similar response to the first driver. He remembers the red hair, too, and thinks it's very likely the woman in his car was Becca.

One driver saw the real Becca, and the other saw Lily, but neither was sure if she was or wasn't Rebecca Gifford. I hear the words *reasonable doubt* echoing in my head.

We finally break for lunch, and I'm rushed to a private conference room with Shapiro. He closes the door and faces me.

"I can't believe Judge Pollen hasn't stopped this trial. The prosecution's case is so flimsy that even the jury looks confused as to why they've had to give up their time to hear all that ridiculous testimony."

"That's exactly what I thought," I say. "The prosecutor came up with a fairy story and is trying to jam square pegs into round holes."

"I'm going for the motion to dismiss when we go back in," says Shapiro. "You'll be home for dinner, trust me."

Back in the courtroom, the judge enters and the court is called to order. The lead prosecutor glances over at our table with a weird smile on his face. He stands.

"Your honor," says the prosecutor as he walks up to the judge and places a folder in front of her, "something new has suddenly come up. A surprise witness has come forward."

"Has the defense been made aware of this development?" says Judge Pollen, looking at the documents she's just received.

The prosecutor walks over to my lawyer and hands him a set of papers.

"No, your honor," he says. "Unfortunately, this witness literally called me last night and only arrived in Connecticut this morning. I just met with her during the lunch break. There was no time to brief defense counsel."

"Objection," says Shapiro. "We need time to review the relevance of this witness. I'm going to ask for a continuance, your honor."

"Mr. Shapiro," says the judge, "I appreciate your position, and I agree with you."

"Your honor," says the prosecutor. "Our witness is in extremely poor health. In fact, it's a miracle that she's here at all. Expediency with this witness is of vital and critical importance. I have a sworn statement from the witness's doctor supporting the urgency."

The judge reviews the documents while we all sit silently, twiddling our thumbs.

"What's going on?" I whisper to Shapiro. "Who's this witness?"

"I don't know," he whispers, "and I don't like it."

I lean forward and look at Lily down at the other end of the table. The blood has drained from her face. She sees me and mouths "What's going on?" I shrug and roll my eyes.

"I've reviewed the witness's medical documents," says the judge. "Given the unusual and urgent circumstances, I'll allow the witness to testify this afternoon. If you need additional time to prepare your rebuttal, Mr. Shapiro, you'll have tomorrow morning. We can pick up the trial again tomorrow afternoon."

The prosecutor, Lily's lawyer and mine all nod as the bailiff comes forward. There's a hush over the court as everyone looks around to see who this mystery witness is.

"The state calls Olive Walker to the stand."

CHAPTER FIFTY-TWO

The back doors of the courtroom open, and a tiny woman with a black bob and bangs wearing oversized, blue-framed eyeglasses enters. With the help of an aide and using the green cane with the faux-diamond handle, Olive Walker slowly makes her way to the witness stand. She's wearing a tan tweed suit with a gold pin on her lapel. A brown-and-cream silk scarf is draped around her neck. She coughs slightly as she sits on the witness stand.

There's an audible gasp from Lily when Olive turns and faces the court. Lily looks over at me, her mouth open. I'm literally stunned. That woman died, didn't she?

"Who the hell is that?" whispers Shapiro to me.

"Some old busybody Becca and I met on the Beacon Star," I whisper. "She's a million years old. I think she's got dementia, too. Becca and I tried to stay away from her on the cruise, but she kept finding us. She's a lonely old pest. She actually went on that cruise to die. Who does that?"

As Olive is being sworn in, Lily starts biting her nails in a neurotic way. I give her a look. She pulls her fingers out of her mouth.

"Mrs. Walker," says the prosecutor, "may I ask how old you are?"

"I'm ninety-three," she says with her strong southern drawl, "but I feel like twenty-three most of the time."

"And why did you contact my office last night?"

"I live in Nashville, Tennessee. About a week ago, I read this article in a newspaper by a reporter named Tommy Devlin. When I saw the Beacon Star mentioned in the headline, I was naturally intrigued. I've been on the Beacon Star many times. It's a wonderful ship. The crew is so lovely. I highly recommend it."

"What did you learn from that article?" says the prosecutor.

"It was about a murder trial in Connecticut. After I read about the trial and its connection to the ship, I checked my diary to see if I might have been on the same cruise as the missing woman."

"And were you?"

"As a matter of fact, I was."

"And did you remember meeting Mr. Gifford and his wife on that cruise?"

Olive folds her hands in front of her and leans forward.

"I'm not in great health, and my memory isn't what it used to be. I meet a great many people on all my cruises," she says. "I didn't remember the name Gifford. There were no pictures in the article, and I guess I just forgot about it and put it aside."

"Mrs. Walker," says the prosecutor, "what is it that made you come forward now?"

"It was the weirdest thing," says Olive. "We don't usually get local Connecticut news in Nashville. But two days ago, I got a brown envelope in the mail with a copy of a Connecticut newspaper inside. The coverage of this trial was on the front page. When I saw the pictures of the Giffords, I realized I had definitely met them on the Beacon Star. So, I contacted your office immediately."

"So you just found out about the trial this week?" says the prosecutor.

"The day before yesterday. That's why I was so late in the game coming forward. I'm in poor health, but I figured this might be the one last important thing I could do. I really liked Mrs. Gifford even though we only met for a short time. I found her to be very kind."

"Why do you think you remember them so well since you meet a good many people on your travels?" says the prosecutor.

I feel a pit growing in my stomach. What the hell is this old hag going to say now? She couldn't have seen me push Becca off the ship. No one was around that night. The only thing she could possibly know is that I was on the ship with my wife. And that's exactly what I've been trying to establish for my defense. Maybe Olive showing up here isn't a bad thing after all.

I sit back and try to relax.

"I've been on more cruises than I can count," says Olive. "Shortly before that particular sailing, I received some rather dreadful news from my doctor. He said I had a terminal condition and only a few months to live. Thankfully, he was incorrect, because that was nearly three years ago and here I am."

"We're all very glad he was mistaken," says the prosecutor with a smile as the courtroom does a collective chuckle. "Please continue."

"The reason I remembered them so well," she says, "is because Mrs. Gifford, Rebecca, was quite lovely. She had beautiful curly red hair and wore oversized eyeglass frames similar to mine. I think we even discussed how we both had good taste in glasses. I was seated next to her during dinner on what I believe was our first night at sea. She was very friendly and chatty. I liked her instantly."

Olive leans forward in her seat and clears her throat.

"On the other hand," she says, "her husband wasn't very talkative at all. He only gave short one-word answers to my questions. After a while I got the feeling he wanted the two of them to be alone. I got the message loud and clear."

"Do you see Mr. Gifford in the courtroom today?"

"Yes, sir," says Olive. The old witch points an accusatory finger in my direction. "He's right over there at the defense table."

"Thank you. You've come all the way from Tennessee to be here today. What do you want the jury to know, Mrs. Walker?"

"While I was sitting next to them at dinner, Mr. Gifford went to pick out some wine. While he was gone, his wife and I took a few selfies together. I like to post pictures of all my trips on Instagram. My handle is HotToddie123 in case anyone wants to follow me. I'll follow you back. I always follow people back."

Another chuckle ripples through the room, which irritates me.

"Go on," says the prosecutor, still smiling after the old woman's shameless self-promotion.

"Like I said, she and I took a few selfies," says Olive. "Shortly after he came back to the table, I left and went to my cabin."

"Did you have any other encounters with the Giffords during the cruise?" says the prosecutor.

"Yes, I did," says Olive. "The next night I ran into them again at a different specialty restaurant. I stopped by their table to say hello. As you can tell, I'm a very friendly person."

"I think we can all see that," says the prosecutor, smiling again and eliciting more laughter from the room.

"This restaurant had very dim lighting, but I remember thinking that Mrs. Gifford looked somewhat different from the first night we met."

"How so?" says the prosecutor, now practically licking his lips.

"Her hair and her glasses were the same, but her face was different. The way her features were laid out, they weren't as I'd remembered them. I even told her I thought she looked different. She got all flustered and said it must be new makeup or the lighting in the room."

"I see," says the prosecutor. "And what happened next?"

"I went into a lounge area and hunted on my phone for the pictures I'd taken of Mrs. Gifford the night we met. I'm a bit of a shutterbug. I snapped a few pictures of her when no one was looking."

The prosecution approaches Olive and hands her several photos and asks her to identify them. She removes her glasses, cleans the lenses and then examines the pictures for an excessively long time. Finally, she nods.

"Yes, these are the photos I took on the ship. Forgive me for taking so long, your honor. When you get to be my age, you have to double-check things. I remember looking at these pictures over and over to prove to myself I wasn't going crazy."

"And were you? Going crazy?" says the prosecutor.

"Objection, your honor," says my attorney for the first time since the old witch started talking.

"Relevance," says the prosecutor.

"Overruled," says the judge, "but can we please get to the point more quickly, counselor?"

"Yes, your honor. Mrs. Walker, explain to the court what happened next," says the prosecutor.

"I went back to my cabin to look at the selfies more carefully. I wanted to compare those first photos with the ones I had taken later."

"And what did you discover?"

Olive looks over at me. I hold her gaze and don't flinch. She looks away and focuses on the prosecutor.

"In my humble opinion, the woman I met that first night was not the same person I saw later on. Similar, but not the same."

A loud murmur runs through the courtroom. I look around to gauge the public sentiment and spot Detective Contessa standing against the back wall staring at me.

"Quiet," says the judge, banging her gavel.

"Your honor, I'd like to present Mrs. Walker's authenticated photos as Exhibits 7A–D," says the prosecutor, handing printed pictures to the clerk and the defense attorneys.

"Mrs. Walker, did you tell anyone about what you suspected?" says the prosecutor.

Olive shakes her head. "No, sir, I didn't have time. That same night I put things together, I had a seizure in my cabin. Everyone on the ship, including me, thought I was finished. But I guess it wasn't my time. They rushed me to the ship's infirmary and I spent the rest of the cruise there. They were all so nice to me. Brought me ice cream whenever I wanted."

Shapiro looks at the photos quickly and stands.

"Your honor, in light of this new information, I request time to review what has been presented today and confer with my client."

The judge agrees and the court is adjourned. As my attorney hustles me out of the courtroom, I look back at Lily. She has a deer-in-the-headlights look on her face. I catch her eye.

"Be cool," I mouth to her just before I walk out of the room.

CHAPTER FIFTY-THREE

After Olive Walker's unexpected testimony, it's now Shapiro's turn to do the cross. I thought he would slice and dice the old broad, but that ancient, weathered old bag holds her own and doesn't budge off her previous testimony. Scoring no points, Shapiro finally finishes. The courtroom quickly gets extremely noisy. Court is adjourned, and my lawyer rushes me out and into a small conference room. One of Shapiro's young male associates follows us in, but within seconds, Shapiro tells him to get out and shuts the door. The look on my lawyer's face is somber. I note tinges of panic at the corners of his eyes.

"What the hell happened this afternoon?" he says, his eyes flashing. "I don't like surprises, Andre. Why didn't we know about Olive Walker in advance?"

I throw my hands up. "She's just some old nut that Becca and I met once or twice on the ship. We tried to avoid her. I didn't even remember her name. I didn't think she was worth mentioning."

"She's got pictures of you and Rebecca. Look at them." He tosses some photos onto the table. "At first blush, the two women in these pictures look the same. But when you really examine them, there are differences. The prosecution is going to bang on this hard. Have you not been straight with me? I can't help you if you're lying to me, Andre."

"Everyone looks different in pictures. Lighting is everything," I say as I pick up the photos and look at them. "I don't see any difference between the two pictures. Frankly, I think the prosecution is using the power of suggestion. As far as I'm concerned, these are all pictures of my wife."

My lawyer opens the door and calls his young colleague in from the hallway and shows him the photos.

"Does this look like the same woman to you?" says Shapiro.

The young attorney looks at them and shrugs. "I don't know. They could be the same person or maybe not."

"We've got a solid subjective argument," I say defiantly as I pick up the pictures again. "I was married to Becca, and I'm telling you all these pictures are of my wife. If anyone would know, I would."

A knock rattles through the door and some legal aid flunky enters and whispers into Shapiro's ear. My lawyer looks at me. He's not wearing a happy face.

"We've got no one else to refute the old woman's testimony," he says, shaking his head. "This isn't good."

"Put me on the stand," I say. "Let me talk."

"No. Absolutely not."

"I want to tell my story," I say. "If they hear directly from me, they'll . . ."

"No, Andre," says Shapiro firmly. "That's beyond a terrible idea. You've got to trust me on this."

"Who's the client here? I am. I get to say if I testify, not you. I'm going on the stand. It's my decision."

Shapiro rolls his eyes and lets out an audible breath. "If you do that, Andre, I can't promise you a good outcome."

"I'm an advertising guy," I say. "My job is to convince people to do and buy things they don't want or need. Ten minutes on the stand and I'll have that jury eating out of my hands. Trust me."

Shapiro shakes his head again and lets out a short sarcastic laugh. "I hope you're right, because when we started this, I thought it was a sure thing. Now, it's become very complicated. I'd still advise against you testifying."

"Leave it to me," I say. "Olive Walker is practically senile. I can't believe the court accepted testimony from someone that compromised."

We argue further about me going on the stand, but I hold my ground. When Shapiro realizes I'm not going to budge, he agrees to review Olive Walker's testimony from today to plan our rebuttal and prepare me. I'm to arrive at his office at 8:15 tomorrow morning to prep for my testimony.

On my way home, I stop at a Mexican place and pick up a chicken burrito with beans, pico de gallo and guacamole. As soon as I walk through my front door, I pour myself a double tequila on the rocks. As I wolf down my burrito, I call Lily on the burner phone to see how she's holding up. It's do-or-die time, and I need to remind her to hold it together.

"Hello?" she says softly when she answers the phone.

"It's me. How are you?"

"You told me that old woman died."

"No one was more surprised than me when she walked into court. I swear to you, that night on the ship when I went to her cabin, one of the crew told me she'd died. There was yellow tape across her doorway."

"Clearly, she's not dead. Now what do we do? You said this whole thing would be 'so easy,' that 'no one would ever know.' You said, 'we're just going on a cruise.' Why did I let you talk me into this?"

"Babe, they've got nothing substantial," I say. "Relax."

"It didn't seem like nothing today, Andre. Did you see that detective gloating in the back of the courtroom?"

I pour myself another tequila, pop a few ice cubes in the glass and stretch out on my couch.

"Let's stay calm and unpack this," I say. "The whole tattoo leaf thing has been debunked, so we can take that off the table. The Uber drivers couldn't identify Rebecca versus you. And the handful of the prosecution's other witnesses pretty much said the same thing. Everyone said that the woman they met on our trip *looked* like Rebecca."

Lily clears her throat.

"What about Olive Walker's pictures?" says Lily. "They could bring in an expert in photography who could prove the photos are of two different people. Can't the FBI do facial recognition stuff?"

After scooping up some guacamole with a chip, I pop it into my mouth. I had no idea Lily would end up being so needy. Given that, I have to keep her focused, at least until we're acquitted. After that, she can do or say whatever she wants. No one will be able to touch me again. Double jeopardy, baby.

"I've got to go," says Lily. "It's late and I'm really tired. I have to meet with my lawyer early tomorrow morning."

"Yeah, me, too." I try to end the call on a high note. I want Lily going into court tomorrow looking and feeling good. "I love you, Lily. Once this trial is over, you and I are going to live it up. I'm going to take you to the best restaurants and hotels. How would you like to go to Morocco or Spain? Or maybe Thailand. You like Thai food? I'll take you anywhere you want to go. Your choice."

"Right now, all I want to do is go to bed."

CHAPTER FIFTY-FOUR

After spending the morning prepping with my attorney, I follow Shapiro and his associates into the courtroom and take my seat. Slowly, people file in. I look around for Lily.

The room fills, but Lily and her attorney are still not seated at our table. The bailiff calls the court to order and the judge takes her seat. Looking around the room for Lily, I see Detective Contessa is here again. His alligator-eye stare locks in on me, but his face is expressionless. I glare at him, hatred in my eyes. He blinks but shows no emotion.

What kind of sick game is that cop playing?

The bailiff approaches the judge and whispers into her ear. The judge then calls my attorney and the prosecutor into her chambers.

"What's going on?" I say to Shapiro as he gets up to leave.

"I have no idea," he says, picking up some papers and following the prosecutor out of the courtroom.

I look around again for Lily.

Where the hell is she? Did something happen to her?

I ask Shapiro's young associate what's going on.

"Don't worry," he says. "Mr. Shapiro's the man. He'll sort things out. He's the best criminal attorney in Connecticut."

"You know I'm being railroaded. You get that, right?" I say to the flunky. "This is all bullshit. I think my wife abandoned me and ran off with some other guy. She's probably living it up in Europe. She always said she wanted to live in Paris before she died."

There's a commotion at the doorway to the courtroom as my attorney, the judge, the prosecutors and several others return. The first thing I notice is that Shapiro's face is gray, his eyes slanted down. He sits next to me.

"What the hell is going on?" I whisper.

Before he can answer, the judge begins to speak.

"Ladies and gentlemen of the jury, I'm afraid there's been a change in plans. According to Ms. Flagg's attorney, she's agreed to be a witness for the prosecution. In order to give the defense ample time to prepare for this new testimony, and given that it is a Friday, we will adjourn until Monday morning."

When the judge bangs her gavel, the courtroom explodes in chatter. I don't know why, but I turn around to look for Contessa. When our eyes connect, he nods for a second and then leaves the room.

Minutes later, Shapiro and I walk out of the courthouse surrounded by a throng of reporters. Stella's standing on the edge of the crowd watching me. She shakes her head, and mouths, "Fuck you."

My lawyer grabs my upper arm and leads me through the crowd as people thrust microphones in my face.

"How could this happen?" I say to Shapiro. "A person can switch horses in the middle of the race? Let me speak to Lily. They must have confused her."

"Not here," he hisses as he walks me to our waiting car. "Do not speak until we're alone."

Once we're inside the vehicle and pull away from the curb, Shapiro begins talking.

"Lily's not confused," he says. "According to her lawyer, she doesn't want to go down for murder. Her attorney advised her to give you up, or you'd both end up in prison."

"They can't do this," I say loudly. "Her lawyer should lose his law license."

"I would have done the same if I had been her attorney," says Shapiro without any emotion. "Now we're boxed into a corner. That's not good."

I spend the entire weekend with Shapiro and several of his associates. Most of the time is spent preparing for what we think Lily might say.

"You really think the jury could convict me of murder based on an old demented woman's grainy pictures and a missing leaf on a tattoo?" I say, losing my temper. "There's no proof Becca's even dead. Don't they have to prove their case beyond a reasonable doubt?"

Shapiro lets out a sigh. "They do. And that was what I was building toward until Ms. Flagg's sudden change of heart. The fact is, we don't know what Lily is going to say. People do and say a lot of things when their life is on the line."

"If I could just talk to her," I say.

"You can't," says Shapiro firmly. "That would be witness tampering. We have to operate on the assumption that Lily is going to submarine you to save her own skin. The best I can do at this point is to discredit her and her testimony and position it as being self-serving."

"Will that work?" I say.

"I've argued that successfully in other cases where someone has flipped," says my attorney. "It won't be easy, but it can be done."

***

On Monday morning, I'm sitting next to Shapiro in court. I notice there's a lot more press here today than last week. The sensational change of events hit the news and, apparently, the public is clamoring for more. I saw a CNN and a BBC van outside. Leeches.

Tommy Devlin's sitting in the third row behind me to my right. He called me over the weekend saying if I gave him an exclusive interview, and talked to no other press, he'd give me some good preemptive coverage. I agreed.

Yesterday, he wrote an article for the Sunday paper questioning the overzealous prosecution. I'm hoping some of the jurors saw it. They're not supposed to read anything to do with this case, but I'm sure a few of them did. That should help me.

The court is called to order as the judge takes her seat.

"The prosecution calls Ms. Lily Flagg to the stand," says the bailiff.

The doors in the back of the courtroom open. I crane my neck as I watch her come in.

Lily enters dressed in a high-necked navy-blue dress. Her blonde hair has grown and is now pulled back in a low bun. She looks like a Catholic schoolgirl. All the outfits she's worn in court throughout the trial have been prim, but this one is taking it to a whole new level.

I try to catch her eye as she walks by me, but she deliberately looks away as she goes to the witness stand. After being sworn in, she takes her seat, continuing to avoid my stare.

Bitch.

The prosecutor goes through the usual questions about her name, age and profession. Then, he moves on to her relationship with me.

"Ms. Flagg," says the prosecutor, "what was the nature of your relationship with Andre Gifford?"

She licks her lips, her signature move when she wants to buy time. I've seen her do it a thousand times.

"We were friends," she says demurely.

"Was it more than a simple friendship?" says the prosecutor.

"Objection," shouts my attorney. "Speculation."

The judge gives Shapiro a weary look. "I'll allow it."

"I met Andre a few years ago," says Lily in the sweetest, softest voice imaginable. "I didn't know he was married when we met. He didn't tell me until after we'd been, you know, intimate. I would never steal someone else's husband. It's not who I am."

"Did you feel like you'd been duped?" says the prosecutor. "Were you angry when you found out he was married?"

"By the time he told me," she says, "he already had this weird hold over me. It was like I was hypnotized or something."

"Objection," shouts my attorney.

"Sustained," says the judge. "Please stick with the facts, Ms. Flagg."

"He didn't actually hypnotize you, did he?" says the prosecutor.

"No, not technically. But after we'd been together a while, I found myself doing whatever he asked. It was like I had no will of my own."

"And why was that?" says the prosecutor.

"Andre could be scary at times. He threatened to hurt me if I didn't go along with everything."

"Lying bitch," I mutter.

"Objection," shouts my attorney.

"Overruled," says the judge. "Mr. Shapiro, if you're going to object to every sentence this witness utters, we'll be here until Christmas. Please continue, Ms. Flagg."

After that, things in the courtroom went from bad to worse. Lily basically made up a lot of shit and threw me under the bus. She testified that she had no knowledge of any plans to hurt Becca.

"I knew Andre was married, but he told me he was getting a divorce. They all say that. Then one day, he invites me to go on this cruise and even bought me a new outfit and Gucci sunglasses. I don't make a lot of money, so I was pumped to go on a free cruise."

The prosecutor shows the jury pictures of the dress, hat and sunglasses.

"So you didn't know that his wife was *also* going on this cruise?" says the prosecutor.

"No," says Lily innocently. "I wouldn't have gone if his wife was going to be there. Why would I do that? That would have been weird. Andre told me that we were going on a romantic getaway. He said he told his wife he had to go on a business trip."

"So you met him on the cruise in Florida thinking everything was fine," says the prosecutor.

"Not exactly. Andre wanted me to wear a wig that looked just like his wife's hair," says Lily. "He wanted me to look exactly like his wife. He even had me draw a tattoo on my leg that looked like hers."

There's talking in the courtroom.

"Quiet," says the judge, banging her gavel.

"What did you think when he asked you to dress up like his wife?" says the prosecutor, making a dubious face that the jury can see.

"Honestly, I thought it was totally creepy," says Lily. "Wouldn't you?"

CHAPTER FIFTY-FIVE

As Lily spews her damning testimony, I furiously scribble notes to my lawyer, who seems to be ignoring me. Lily's on the stand making shit up, and Shapiro is doing nothing to stop her. She's making me out to be some kind of weirdo who likes all of his women to look exactly the same; hence, the wig and tattoo. It's total bullshit and she knows it. She was involved in every step of our plan.

"When and where did you board the ship, Ms. Flagg?" says the prosecutor.

"I boarded on the second day in Fort Lauderdale," she says. "Andre told me he booked it under his and Rebecca's name so no one would ask any questions. I never took a cruise before, so I didn't know how it worked."

"And you didn't know that Rebecca had been on the Beacon Star?"

"I only found out his wife had been there the night Andre and I met Mrs. Walker," says Lily, dabbing her eyes. "She sat down with us and started talking about our meeting the previous night. I was really confused. She acted like she knew me, but I'd never met her before."

"What did Andre say when you asked him about it?" says the prosecutor.

"That Mrs. Walker was crazy and senile and didn't know what she was talking about. He blew it off."

It's obvious Lily is trying to make the jury think I got turned on by her dressing like my wife. I look over at the women in the jury box. Mild disgust is written on some of their faces.

"Do something," I whisper to my attorney. "She's lying."

By the time Lily finishes, she's admitted that she initially lied to the police. She said it was because she thought the truth would look bad for both of us even though she hadn't technically done anything.

"All I knew was what Andre told me," she said in her continuing testimony. "He said that he and his wife had marital problems and she had recently threatened to take off and leave him. I believed him."

"After Rebecca Gifford was reported missing, you never wondered if she had been on the ship or that Andre may have done something to his wife?" says the prosecutor.

Lily looks down. "I did, but by then it was too late. I had already lied for him, and I was in too deep. I was afraid of going to jail."

"And what made you change your mind, Ms. Flagg?" says the prosecutor.

"That's easy," says Lily, finally looking at me. "A woman reached out to me last week. She said she met Andre in a bar after his wife went missing. She said that they'd been seeing each other off and on for the past few months. She saw some of the news stories recently with my name in it and wanted to know if we were still romantically involved. Turns out, Andre was two-timing me. After all I'd done for him, lying and covering for him. It took me a while to get there, but, finally, I'd had enough."

My lawyer looks over at me and rolls his eyes. "Are you fucking kidding me?" he whispers while shaking his head. "You have *another* girlfriend?"

After that, things got really dark in the courtroom, and the general mood wasn't in my favor. I guess you could say that Lily's testimony was the proverbial nail in my coffin. No matter how hard my attorney tried during the cross-examination, it was obvious the jury had made up their minds. You could see the condemnation on their faces. Lily had painted me as a first-class dick. How do you come back from something like that?

Shapiro brought in other defense witnesses, but Olive Walker's comments along with Lily's damning testimony proved to be devastating.

"I'm not going to lie to you, Andre," said Shapiro as we left the courtroom. "The women on that jury don't like you. In fact, they loathe you."

"I'm supposed to go to jail because some pathetic housewife on the jury doesn't *like* me? I didn't do anything. Doesn't the truth count anymore? I don't know what happened to my wife."

It took the jury three days to deliberate. When they finally called us back into the courtroom, I was numb and fearing the worst. Naturally, Contessa was there in the front row grinning like he'd just won the lottery. He was thoroughly enjoying watching me squirm. I'm surprised he didn't bring a bag of popcorn. I wanted to plunge a knife through his heart at that moment. He was the one who'd accelerated this whole thing with all of his annoying questions and nosing around.

Spoiler alert: the jury found me guilty. Shapiro said we'd appeal and find other witnesses to support my defense. My passport was taken away as I waited six weeks for the sentencing.

That new woman who I'd met in the bar, Audrey, she's totally hot. At least she's stuck by my side, unlike some other people. In the weeks leading up to my sentencing and ultimate incarceration, Audrey and I developed a deep and meaningful relationship. I also got to bang her a few dozen times before I went to jail. She's promised to stand by me and wait until I get out. Of course, by then, she might be too old for me, but we'll see.

Lily, on the other hand, bailed on me the minute things got too hot. When all was said and done, she was only worried about saving her own skin. Where's the loyalty? I've always said you can't trust women, especially the good-looking ones. They're the worst.

Don't get me wrong, the new one, Audrey, she's smokin'. I might even try to marry her while I'm inside. That way I might get conjugal visits and maybe have a kid or two. In some ways, it would be the perfect family. She takes care of the kids — diapers, feeding, runny noses — and when I get out they'll be practically grown.

When my sentence was issued, I was placed in a medium-security correctional facility in northern Connecticut. Because all the evidence was circumstantial and no body was recovered or any *real* evidence provided, Shapiro was able to argue for a reduced sentence. I suppose I should be grateful I wasn't tried in Florida — there I might be on death row.

I figure, with good behavior, I'll be out of here in twelve years. I'm only forty-seven now. I can make that work. I'll get myself a couple of degrees on the state of Connecticut's dime. Maybe I'll write my memoir about my unfair and unjust trial and all the women who betrayed me.

People have no idea how biased the court system is until they're in it. That prosecutor had it in for me from the beginning. I didn't have a chance. He had already convicted me.

The one thing that still keeps eating at me is how everything fell so neatly together. How did Stella ever notice the different tattoos in the first place? And who sent Olive Walker the newspapers about the trial? She lives in Nashville, which is nearly a thousand miles from Connecticut. The synchronicity of all these random things keeps me up at night.

Everything was just a little too perfect.

CHAPTER FIFTY-SIX

Becca

I had been following Andre's trial online from the moment it started. I'd spend the better part of each day sitting at the table in our little blue beach house in front of the computer. I'd follow various news sources and chat rooms reporting on the trial. I also had alerts for any live reports. I did nothing else while Andre's trial was going on.

"You're obsessed with this," Javi said as he took my hand and tried to close the computer. "We're happy now, aren't we? Can we forget about him for a little while?"

"I can't," I said. "You of all people should understand. You needed vengeance for your father's murder and for Delfine. Can't I have the same?"

He pulled me to my feet and drew me to him.

"I see the fire in your eyes," he said. "That's how I was. But it's not a healthy thing. Wanting that kind of retribution does something terrible to your soul. It eats away at you. Trust me, I know."

"And how did you feel after your father's killer took his last breath?" I said.

He looked away. "Good."

"And after Delfine's killer?"

"At peace. I honored my father and my wife, and justice was done."

"That's all I want. Justice. Nothing more, nothing less."

"Do you really want that on your conscience? You could still make yourself known right now, before the trial is over."

"And then what? Andre gets off with a slap on the wrist?" I said. "No. If I come forward, he'll go free. You know that's what will happen."

He let go of my hand, and I sat down again in front of the computer.

"I'm going fishing," said Javi, putting his hands on my shoulders and giving them a squeeze. "You do what you need to do. Each of us has our own path. I won't deprive you of yours, just as no one deprived me of mine. Whatever you decide, I'm here for you."

That conversation happened during the first week of Andre's trial. When it started, it seemed like the prosecution didn't have enough to convict. It was hard to tell which way the trial was going to go. Stella did her best. She swore that our tattoos had only two leaves. The prosecution served up that as definitive evidence that there had to be two different women on the ship. But the prosecution was never able to nail down where and when Andre committed the crime. That was the loose end that was going to sink the prosecution's case and get Andre off.

It wasn't until Olive Walker showed up that things turned around. Once she appeared, there was a domino effect, and it finally looked like Andre would get what he deserved. I read about Olive's testimony online. It seemed conclusive to me. She saw two different women on that ship and had the pictures to prove it. The defense argued that the photos were of the same woman — me. The defense tried to discredit Mrs. Walker's testimony, painting her as an old, infirm sad sack. It was still anybody's game until Lily Flagg flipped on him. I really thought he was going to be acquitted.

One thing's for sure, the way everything unfolded, I didn't see that coming. Lily Flagg was Andre's codefendant and, from all the reports, she was tight-lipped and stoic. From what I could tell, they never broke rank. I was really worried.

But I shouldn't have been, because Andre's worst angels were and are always hovering. He wasn't satisfied with only getting rid of me and running off with Lily. No, he had to have another girlfriend. I believe her name is Audrey.

When I told Javi of that development, he shook his head.

"If you go through with this, you can never be Rebecca Gifford again," he said.

"I know."

CHAPTER FIFTY-SEVEN

Becca
Ushuaia, Argentina — Eighteen months later

After Andre went to prison, Javi made arrangements for us to sail his boat to Argentina. I was worried about immigration and identification, but Javi took care of everything. I had no idea he had access to so many back channels. I guess that's what having a lot of money and escaping from Venezuela does for you.

We packed up all of our things in Puerto Rico, said goodbye to Ines, Gloria and Reno and sailed away on Javi's boat. We island-hopped all the way down to South America and hugged the coast before landing in a northern coastal port in Salvador, Brazil. It was a beautiful old Spanish colonial city. We spent a week on land after our long journey at sea.

From Salvador, Javi had everything organized. Someone else would take over his boat and sail the rest of the way down the coast to the bottom of Argentina. A car and driver took us to a private airport where we boarded a private plane to take us the rest of the way.

Finally, we arrived at our destination at the end of the world — Ushuaia, Argentina.

The city is at the southernmost tip of South America. Ushuaia is the jumping-off point for tourists going on excursions to Antarctica or heading up through Patagonia. It's also about as remote a place as you could find on the planet and is heaven on earth.

The air is clean, and the sky is blue, and everywhere you look, nature is in all its glory. Javi told me I'd love Ushuaia. The minute we arrived, I knew I was home.

It was a smooth trip because Javi had thought of everything. Before our arrival, he purchased a five-bedroom villa on a hilltop with amazing views of the ocean. The house sits high above the town, giving us the privacy we need to secure our identities, but still close enough to town to do our errands and shop.

He even had the house fully stocked with food and clothes for me in the closet. It gets a lot colder in Ushuaia than it does in Puerto Rico. As I pulled on my fleece top and wandered through our property, I marveled at where my life was now and how drastically different it is from a few years earlier.

The other thing that's been amazing is my health. Before all this happened, I was sick all the time. And if I'm being honest, I was also a little depressed. I guess that happens when your husband finds fault with everything you do. One thing I know for sure, Javier Guzman loves me and has my back, now and for always.

The first eighteen months here in Ushuaia have been filled with new beginnings. Not long after we arrived, Javi and I got married by the water. It was a small ceremony attended by some of his friends and relatives living in Argentina. For the first few months, I was busy making our home ours. Once that was done, I knew what I wanted to do. I got a job teaching kindergarten, my first love, down in the town of Ushuaia. My Spanish has improved, and the little kids understand me just fine. I'm teaching them English, too.

Everything was coming together with my new life in Argentina, but there was still an emptiness inside me. There was someone whose absence from my life was so painful.

Stella.

As much as I loved Javi and our life together in Ushuaia, not having Stella to talk to left a big gaping hole in my heart. At least I knew where she was, and that she was okay. But Stella thought I was dead. I couldn't let her go on thinking that.

I tried to imagine how I'd feel if I thought Stella was dead. It would be devastating. After months of conversation with my new husband, he came up with an idea.

"We cannot afford to reveal that you're still alive for our own protection," said Javi. "The United States has extradition agreements with Argentina. You could be arrested and taken back. My enemies could find out where I am. Neither of those scenarios work."

He was right, but I couldn't shake my feelings of loss. I needed a connection to my old life, even if it was small. Eventually, Javi came up with a plan that we both thought would be safe. Through Javi's intermediaries, we purchased a first-class plane ticket and a cabin on a ten-day all-inclusive expedition cruise to Antarctica.

Then, through a trusted attorney who had done a lot of work for Javi's family, things were put in motion.

CHAPTER FIFTY-EIGHT

Stella

It's Saturday morning. I've just finished cleaning my kitchen, and I pick up a pile of unopened mail on the counter. It's mainly junk mixed with a couple of bills and one funny-looking manila envelope from a law firm I've never heard of. I pour myself a cup of coffee and open the mysterious envelope.

> *Dear Ms. McCrystal,*
> *My name is Ricardo Montoya, and I represent the estate of your late friend Rebecca Ross Gifford. In Mrs. Gifford's will, she left a few specific items for the people she loved most, you being one of them. According to her will, of which I am the executor, it states that you and she had often talked about "going on an adventure and taking off for parts unknown." Her will stipulates that if she passed before you, she wanted to give you one last adventure on her. Mrs. Gifford authorized me to purchase a first-class plane ticket and passage on an expedition cruise to Antarctica . . .*

I read and reread the attorney's letter five times before it sinks in. I don't realize I'm crying until one of my tears lands on the paper. Pretty soon, I'm sobbing. It's been a few years since I lost Becs, but the pain is just as sharp and jagged now as it was when she disappeared.

Hearing from her this way is so emotional and overwhelming. It's like she's still alive and egging me on to go have some fun. We got cheated. We were supposed to have many more years together.

The attorney's letter instructs me to reach out to him to make the arrangements. Some people might not feel comfortable taking off for the other side of the world under such strange circumstances. But if this is my best friend's last wish for me, then I'm going.

The following day, I contact the lawyer and he arranges everything. A limousine picks me up and takes me to Kennedy Airport. From there, I take a flight to Buenos Aires, where I catch another flight to Ushuaia, located at the southern tip of Argentina. That's where I'll board the expedition cruise to Antarctica. I can't wait to see the penguins.

I'm told someone will pick me up at the airport in Ushuaia and give me a tour of the city before taking me to my hotel. The ship will leave two days later.

When I get off at the Ushuaia airport, there's a man holding a sign with my name on it. He's very polite, collects my luggage and takes me on an hour-long driving tour of the city. We finish up in front of some giant letters that spell out the city's name: USHUAIA.

Surrounded by other tourists, I take some panoramic shots of the pristine world around me. I ask another traveler to take my picture and stand in front of a giant white letter H and smile.

As I'm posing, a familiar voice rings out behind me.

"You call that a smile, McCrystal?" the voice shouts. I spin around confused. *Who said that?* I scan the twenty or so people milling around. Then I see her and my legs buckle underneath me.

"It's me, Stell," she says, rushing over and brushing the tears off her cheeks before she grabs me.

My brain can't make sense out of what's happening. Frozen, with my mouth open, I'm staring at a ghost. Even as she throws her arms around me, I can't move or think.

"You're alive?" I whisper, stepping back to look at her. Tears drip down my face. "I don't understand. Becs? How are you alive? Where have you been?"

She smiles and hugs me again.

"I've missed you so much, Stell," she says. "Trust me, I'll explain everything."

Putting her arm around my shoulders, she guides me to a gray SUV. The man in the driver's seat gets out of the car.

"Stell, this is Javi," says Becca, "my husband."

"What?" It's all I manage to squeak out.

"I'll explain everything," she says as she opens the passenger door and puts me in the front next to Javi. Becca climbs into the back.

"I have heard about the famous Stella so many times," he says as he pulls away from the curb. "I feel like I already know you. You are so important to my wife. Therefore, you are special to me, too."

I hear a baby squeal and turn around. Behind my seat, sitting next to Becca, is a little girl with dark curly hair and brown eyes.

"Yours?" I say.

Becca's face breaks into a huge smile. "Yes."

"She's gorgeous. What's her name?" I whisper, still trying to wrap my head around everything.

"We named her Stella."

***

Becca and I spend the next ten days together, and she explains everything that happened. She was the one who fed me the information about the tattoos that I gave to the police. It was also Becca who had corresponded anonymously with Olive Walker. She tipped the old woman off about the trial.

"For some reason," says Becca as she makes me an espresso, "despite what happened to me, once I started getting my memory back, I remembered meeting Olive Walker. It was probably because she was such a character. Recalling her name was another story. That took a while."

"I saw Olive in court," I say. "She was something. Body of a ninety-three-year-old, brain of a teenager."

"I knew if Olive got wind of Andre's trial, she'd put herself out there and tell the cops what she knew. She was that kind of person. Fearless."

"But how were you able to do all that without giving yourself away?" I say, then take a sip of my coffee.

"I found Olive's Instagram account. She had thousands of pictures there, mainly from her cruises," she says. "I went through all of her photos by date and found the group of pictures from the same cruise where Andre and I met her."

"Nice."

"And you won't believe this. That selfie she and I took together, it was on Instagram the whole time. So was another picture taken on the ship of Lily posing as me with Andre."

"Why didn't you just take screenshots and send them to the police?"

Becca shakes her head as she gets up to make me another espresso.

"There wasn't enough time, Stell," she says, loading up the espresso machine. "If I had sent anonymous pictures of Olive and me, and Andre and Lily, on the ship, it would have taken forever going through legal channels. They'd have to be verified, sourced, et cetera. Who knows if any of it would have been admitted? By the time I found those pictures, the trial was almost over."

Becca hands me another demitasse cup of espresso.

"If Andre had been acquitted of my murder," she says, "he would have then fallen under double jeopardy. Even if the cops figured out the meaning behind the photos proving I was on the ship, as was another woman dressed like me, it wouldn't have mattered. Andre and Lily could never be re-tried. I had to move fast."

Next to us, Baby Stella is playing with the food on the tray of her highchair. Becca gives her some sliced bananas and the baby squeals.

"How did you tip off Olive about the trial without giving yourself up?" I ask.

"Javi arranged to get a package anonymously sent to her with articles and pictures. Next thing you know, that sick old woman is on a plane heading to Connecticut. She's a force."

"Her appearance was definitely a pivotal moment in the court," I say. "I thought Andre was going to pass out when she walked in."

"That's how I imagined it," says Becca with a wicked smile.

"But even with Olive's testimony, Lily was sticking with him. It looked like Andre was going to get off until . . ."

". . . he was hoisted by his own petard," says Becca, now really enjoying herself. "The man-child was on trial for murder, and he betrayed the one person who knew all his secrets — Lily. How did he think she was going to react when she found out he had another girlfriend?"

"It was a stunning moment when they announced Lily was a witness for the prosecution. I still can't believe he actually threw you off a moving ship," I say. I begin ranting about the injustice when Becs stops me.

"Stell, he didn't get away with it. You made sure, and I made sure. Andre's sitting in jail for my murder, and that's where he's going to stay. Meanwhile, I'm alive and living a magical life here in Argentina. I'm more than okay with the way things turned out."

When it's finally time for me to go back to Connecticut, Javi pulls me aside and reiterates the importance of never divulging what I've learned on my trip to Ushuaia. I tell him he doesn't have to worry about me. Becca knows I'd die before I'd reveal her secret. We're sisters forever.

Becs takes me to the airport. On the drive over, we make plans for me to come back to Argentina in six months. I'd like to spend more time with my little namesake and her baby brother who's on the way.

As we get closer to the airport, we're both a mess. But we're not sad, because now Becs and I can communicate through encrypted apps every day, all day. We can talk and video chat whenever we want. I've found my best friend again, and I'm never letting her go.

Becca pulls the car up to the airport terminal and puts it into park. She takes a small envelope out of her bag and presses it into my hand.

"I need you to do one more thing for me," she says.

"What now?" I say with a laugh.

"I need to finish this once and for all."

I look inside the envelope and back at her.

"You don't think it's already finished?" I say.

"While he's sitting in his cell, I want him to think about me every hour of every day. I want him to lie awake at night and remember what he did to me. He's going to spend many years in prison for my murder, and I want him to always wonder. It will drive him crazy."

CHAPTER FIFTY-NINE

Andre

A medium-security prison has been my home for nearly two years now. I keep to myself as much as possible. It's the only way to survive in this place. Get out of line once, and you become a target. I try to be as helpful as I can to the guards and other inmates. I've got a regular workout routine going and am probably in the best physical condition I've ever been in.

Since I've got more education than most of the people in here, including the guards, they call me "the professor." I help people out with various things like preparing for appeals, and in exchange, they leave me alone for the most part. Even so, I still have to watch my back. This is a prison, not a country club.

I've been taking classes here and am working on a degree in theology. I don't believe in any of that spiritual crap, but I thought theology would look good when I eventually go before a parole board. I'm casting myself as the fully repented prisoner who's found God.

In fact, I've cozied up to the prison chaplain, Father Mike. I've convinced him that I'm a good person. I know he'll vouch for me when the time comes. Not only that, the chaplain has all sorts of easy jobs that require brain versus brawn. Once I established a relationship with him, he regularly asks for me on his detail. He and I have had a lot of good talks. I've vehemently denied having anything to do with my wife's demise, and I think he believes me.

I've still got it.

Everyone in prison has a job. When I work with Father Mike, it gets me out of the prison population for a few hours each day. My parole hearing is still years off. But I consider my time spent with the chaplain as building for the future. I've been thinking of also doing a degree in philosophy or social work. I'm neither philosophical nor do I care about social issues, but they'll look good when I'm trying to get my parole pass out of this place.

Audrey's still devoted to me and visits every other week, come rain or shine. That's the loyalty I'm talking about. Thank God there are women who get turned on by the incarcerated. We're planning to get married in a few months. I had to wait to get permission from the warden, but I've been a good boy in here. I think it's going to happen. Father Mike has vouched for me, too. I'm working all the angles. After the wedding, I'll be in line for a conjugal visit. I need something to get me through the next few years.

Today, I'm working on my memoir. I've got about five hundred pages written and I'm only up to the part where my wife goes missing. I haven't even started the trial portion yet.

As far as I'm concerned, that prosecutor had it in for me from the start. I shouldn't be in here. Anyone who reads my book will see that. I don't know what happened to my wife. I went to work one day and when I came home, she was gone.

Sitting in my open-door cell, I hear rumbling from the wheels of a metal cart in the hallway and look up.

Father Mike peers into my room. "Still working on your autobiography, Andre?"

"Yeah, Father, I've got a lot to say. I may have to turn it into three books."

"Looking forward to reading them one day," he says with an encouraging smile. He holds up a few books. "I'm distributing some inspirational reading materials. Can I interest you in anything?"

I nod. "You pick."

He steps into my cell, looks around and lowers his voice. "Yesterday, I received a letter in the mail for you," he says, holding up a white envelope. "It was opened by security, and for some reason, they passed it on to me."

"Who's it from?"

"The note inside had only three words written on it. 'For Andre Gifford.'" He hands me the envelope. I take out the slip of paper and examine it. Both the note and the address on the envelope are written in childish block lettering.

"No return address?" I say, flipping the envelope over.

"No, but there's a postmark," says the chaplain in a loud whisper. "Looks like it was mailed from somewhere in Connecticut." Father Mike digs into his breast pocket, retrieves a gold wedding band and holds it up between two fingers.

"Look familiar?" he says. "The inscription inside the ring says, 'B & A Forever.' I figured this must be your late wife's wedding ring, as it would be too small for you. You're not allowed to receive any hard goods in here. But I thought in this case, it would be all right. I figured you'd want to have it, to remember her. Let's keep this between us, okay?"

I smile and thank him as he pushes the metal cart down the hallway. I sit on my bed and stare at the ring in my hand.

Who sent this? And how did they get it?

I get up and pace around my cell, trying to solve the riddle. This is definitely Becca's wedding ring. But how did it get here? I know for sure she was wearing her ring on the cruise. I remember her showing it to me that night we had dinner on the ship. She definitely had it on her finger when she went overboard. I know for sure.

I look down at the gold ring in my hand.

"I don't understand. This should be at the bottom of the Atlantic Ocean," I say out loud.

My entire world now consists of a metal cot, a desk, cinder block walls, cement floors and a silver toilet. I eat, bathe and sleep with hundreds of prisoners, most of whom are violent or crazy or both. I've been convicted of murder and will remain in prison for many years. As I look at the bars on the door and the tiny window above my head, one single thought runs through my mind.

That bitch is still alive.

THE END

ACKNOWLEDGMENTS

A cruise ship always seemed like the perfect setting for a thriller because it's a symbol of a happy holiday vacation while also being a contained space. I booked a cruise in Scandinavia to figure out exactly how a murder might successfully be orchestrated and concealed on a ship. Fortunately, I was able to spend some time with the cruise director (a murder mystery fan), who gave me all sorts of information about cruise ships and the people on them. It was fascinating. Many thanks to Andre Gaffney for sharing his insights.

After that first cruise, I had some solid ideas for this book, and it all started coming together. Once I determined the murder plan could work, I couldn't get the words on the page fast enough. When I finished the first draft, I booked another cruise to make sure the theory would hold up on an entirely different cruise line. (It was a tough job, but someone had to do it!) My husband and I sailed around the South Pacific, checking if the plan for the murder would work on that ship as well. While the other passengers strolled the decks, ate in the restaurants and went on shore excursions, we looked for ways to dispose of a body. Fun!

I had a lot of help putting this book together and I'd like to thank a few people. First and always, my husband Peter Black, who helps me from beginning to end. Next, my sister Diane McGarvey, who is always one of my first readers and gives invaluable critiques. I'd also like to thank my cousin's wife, Dody Gagliano. She gave me the inside scoop on all things related to fibromyalgia, which helped me create the Becca character. Also, thanks go to my Cuban American friend Julie Garcia. She read the manuscript checking my Spanish and making sure all the Cuban references were correct. Muchas gracias.

And, many thanks to attorney and judge, Ellen Coyne and attorney, Tony Lester. Both read the legal scenes and gave me advice so vocabulary and procedures were accurate. (My knowledge of lawyers and courtrooms comes strictly from *Law & Order*.)

When the editing began, my wonderful editor and friend, Kate Lyall Grant, found all the holes and gave me wonderful direction on how to make the manuscript tighter. Thank you, Kate.

The next two rounds of editing were done by Sharon Rutland followed by Shannon Scott. They both did an amazing job picking up my mistakes and timeline issues and improved the clarity of the narrative. Merci.

And finally, I'd like to thank all the people at Joffe Books who work so hard. The wonderful cover, fantastic marketing, social media and admin support all contribute to the final product. Thanks to all of you.

THE JOFFE BOOKS STORY

We began in 2014 when Jasper agreed to publish his mum's much-rejected romance novel and it became a bestseller.

Since then we've grown into the largest independent publisher in the UK. We're extremely proud to publish some of the very best writers in the world, including Joy Ellis, Faith Martin, Caro Ramsay, Helen Forrester, Simon Brett and Robert Goddard. Everyone at Joffe Books loves reading and we never forget that it all begins with the magic of an author telling a story.

We are proud to publish talented first-time authors, as well as established writers whose books we love introducing to a new generation of readers.

We won Trade Publisher of the Year at the Independent Publishing Awards in 2023 and Best Publisher Award in 2024 at the People's Book Prize. We have been shortlisted for Independent Publisher of the Year at the British Book Awards for the last five years, and were shortlisted for the Diversity and Inclusivity Award at the 2022 Independent Publishing Awards. In 2023 we were shortlisted for Publisher of the Year at the RNA Industry Awards, and in 2024 we were shortlisted at the CWA Daggers for the Best Crime and Mystery Publisher.

We built this company with your help, and we love to hear from you, so please email us about absolutely anything bookish at feedback@joffebooks.com.

If you want to receive free books every Friday and hear about all our new releases, join our mailing list here: www.joffebooks.com/freebooks.

And when you tell your friends about us, just remember: it's pronounced Joffe as in coffee or toffee!

www.ingramcontent.com/pod-product-compliance
Lightning Source LLC
Chambersburg PA
CBHW011314170925
32734CB00025B/2145